CONTACT NOT FOUND

by

Jared Austin

Huntsville, Alabama

This is a work of fiction. All of the characters, organizations, and events portrayed in this novel are either products of the author's imagination or are used fictitiously.

CONTACT NOT FOUND

Table of Contents

Dedication

To Mom
You taught me a love of reading from an early age
Thanks for making me read so many stories to you!

Acknowledgments

Book four is complete. Wow! And so many people to thank for helping me get here. My wife, Dana Austin, for her encouragement. Lisa J. Prince, Shirley Garrett, Lee Judge, Kenny Emmanuel, Heather Montgomery, Nellie Maulsby, Jamie Dodson, Amy Herring, Debbie Yutko, Lin Cochran, and Jim Anderson, thank you for the careful critiques and discussions of each of these stories, which helped me grow my world first created in *Space City,* and expanded in *Escape* and *Space City Outbreak.* Thank you to my Southside Scribes and the North Alabama Science Fiction and Cake Appreciation Society (NASFCAS) writing groups, which listened to me read through these stories, sometimes multiple times, and offered insightful critiques.

I'd also like to thank 100covers for my fantastic cover designs for my series.

And thank you readers for taking the time out of your busy lives to spend it with me and the world of *Space City.* I hope you enjoy yourself and consider it time well spent!

Fearless

Chapter 1 — Trini

Trini ran through the canyon, an ant traveling along a superhighway lined by Everest-sized sloping walls. She chased herself over rocks and debris from massive landslides, as well as ash from a nearby chain of volcanoes.

She'd pursued a hologram of her personal record for approaching an hour now through an offshoot of the Mariner Valley; the Martian canyon being the largest in the Solar System. Nico had added code to the Mariner Valley sim that created a digital version of her past runs, so she could compete against herself each time she trained. Competing with her past self provided more motivation than a timer in her explorer suit helmet, telling her if she was ahead or behind pace.

Each week she picked a new location in the Mariner Valley for a change of scenery, and on her first day in that location she'd run alone. The rest of the week, she raced against the hologram of her personal record for the sim in that area. As she became familiar with that week's path, she would notice ways to shave off a second here or there. And with each trip through, she gained strength and endurance.

Her PR hologram leapt high to hurdle over a wide fissure, mere seconds before she did. Thanks to the reduced gravity on Mars, her PR floated in the air for a second, the way a gazelle does while bounding through the wilderness.

A camelback rested on Trini's shoulders for hydration. A drinking tube extending from the pack had a spout that remained in place to the left of her mouth for easy access. And to counter the reduced gravity on Mars, she'd attached weights to the pack.

Up ahead, an impact crater the size of a football field marred her path. She charged into it and down the slope, maintaining pace on her

PR's heels. At the same time, she focused on not overextending her legs on the downhill, which might lead to injury. Heading into her final year at the Academy, she wanted to ensure she was in top shape for the Games season. Not only was she hoping Ursa would finally take home the Sun Trophy as league champions, but a strong senior season should ensure a professional Space City Games team drafted her next year. She had spent most of the past three years training to go pro, and she wouldn't let up now.

Trini cruised through the middle of the crater, then pushed herself to pick up the pace as she hit the upward slope. That little extra effort propelled her past her PR hologram.

Her muscles ached, her skin slick with sweat, but she controlled her breathing. Her energy remained good. She could keep this up for at least another four or five K. And today would become her new PR. Even one second faster was improvement.

As she crested the crater, someone in a silver explorer suit and helmet to match her own stood up ahead, waving. An ID popped into the air beside the person, projected by the contacts in Trini's eyes. Cho Tamura.

When had the girl entered the sim?

Trini gritted her teeth, hating the interruption. Rather than stop, she motioned for the younger girl to join her.

Despite being three years her junior, Cho had a few inches on her, and fell in beside her effortlessly. But Trini had been training for an hour, while Cho had fresh and longer legs. Of course, she could keep up over a short distance.

For several minutes Cho ran beside her, saying nothing. But her presence had ruined Trini's good mood. It wasn't that she disliked the younger girl, just that the intrusion divided her focus and prevented her from giving her best.

Her breathing grew labored, causing pain in her chest. Surprised by the dip in energy, she realized she'd been clenching her teeth since Cho had joined her. She had lost focus on her breathing and the rhythm in her stride.

Another half K would get her to the cooled lava flows. Arms pumping, she fought to smooth out her stride.

Her PR hologram appeared at her side.

Trini's legs were turning to lead, and her chest felt like it was deflating. She groaned as she struggled to maintain her pace.

Her PR surged ahead, running flawlessly as it pulled away. Trini wanted to quit, to stop right there, but she refused to suffer that humiliation. She would at least finish.

The last two hundred and fifty meters sucked. There was no other word to describe it. Her PR reached the lava flows and vanished, the simulation complete. Seconds later, Trini reached them and doubled over, hands on her knees as she gasped for air.

"Why don't you run with someone instead of a sim of yourself?" Cho asked, sounding only a little winded.

Trini forced herself upright. "What did you need?" She placed her hands on the back of her helmet and walked toward the nearby canyon rim while taking deep, calming breaths to slow her heart rate.

"Have you heard of the quinniq?" the other girl asked, an enthusiastic smile lighting up her face.

Trini shook her head.

"A small creature on the planet Nereus. Like a fox with no legs. At least in the winter."

"No legs in the winter?" Trini asked. Was Cho making the creature up?

Cho nodded. "That's what the Nuukimak say. It grows short legs in the summer to move around, but sheds them in the winter to slither through the snow as it hunts unsuspecting prey."

Trini snorted. This had to be fake. Some of her fellow students, disbelieving that she'd encountered the thought-to-be-mythical creature Satu the previous summer, and envious that the Space City historical database listed her as discoverer, had begun making up fake creatures, thinking she'd go searching on rumor alone.

But Cho's smile appeared genuine, not smug like those thinking they could pull one over on her.

"What do you think?" Cho asked. "Want to travel with me to Nereus to look for one?"

Trini bent over again, this time to stretch her legs. "I don't know. I'm training hard right now, getting ready for the Games this fall. It's my last year and I need to be in top shape."

Besides, she hadn't gone to Letos last year to hunt for Satu. Her aunt had forced her to go help with an outbreak among the Ukka.

She'd only learned about the creature after Otso, a local child, had shown her its tracks.

Cho's shoulders slumped, the smile dropping off her face.

Not a make-believe creature then. At least not in her mind, Trini thought. *She genuinely wants to search for this… what did she call it?*

"Aren't you supposed to be working out, too?" Trini asked as she resumed walking. "I thought you wanted to try out for the Games this year?"

"I have been. A lot," Cho assured her. "Jiro's given me some exercises. I work on them almost every day." Cho and Jiro were cousins—his mother and her father.

There was a "but" coming, Trini knew. She could see it in the younger girl's expression.

"I just… I haven't been off ship yet." Cho ducked her head, as if embarrassed by the omission.

Trini had taken Cho on a couple of tours of alien worlds within the sims, and was sure the girl had gone on others, but as realistic as the sims looked, they couldn't match the real thing.

"When I heard about the quinniq, I thought it might interest you to confirm their existence. Our database still lists them as unconfirmed. Plus, mom and your aunt said I could travel to Nereus if it was with you."

Trini stifled a groan. Her aunt would volunteer her to go with Cho. Aunt Teresa always helped others, or voluntold Trini for duty. And Naomi Tamura, Cho's mother, worked with her aunt in the university infirmary. It was the main reason Cho and Trini had developed a friendship, albeit more on Cho's side than her own.

"I saw Nuukimak drawings of the quinniq," Cho added. "They're cute. Plus, if you confirmed their existence, you'd be in the database as the discoverer."

Trini stifled a smile. It had been cool to learn her name was listed as the discoverer of Satu for as long as Space City existed. Though she'd had them co-list Otso with her, since he and his grandfather had been the real discoverers.

They neared the canyon rim, revealing enormous volcanoes in the distance around the Tharsis region.

"Oh, wow! Are those volcanoes?" Cho asked, eyes widening. "They're huge!"

"Yes, the Tharsis Montes volcanoes," Trini answered. "The smallest is twenty kilometers high, more than double the largest on Earth. Mt. Everest is only a little under nine kilometers for comparison."

The sheer size underscored the foreignness of the area, one reason Trini loved to train here. Loved visiting alien worlds, whether in person or in sims.

"Okay, why not," Trini said. She'd worked hard all summer, and it wasn't like traveling to Nereus and searching for a rare species would involve sitting on her butt being lazy.

Cho squealed, her face brightening into a broad smile once more. "Thank you!"

"But I have to be back in a week," Trini warned. "I promised Otso we'd visit Letos before summer ended. He hasn't been back since he came to live with us. He wants to visit his village."

"A week is more than enough time," Cho replied, bouncing on the balls of her feet. "You'll see."

Trini typed on her wrist-comp, preparing to end the sim. "Now, if you'll excuse me, I'd like to shower before breakfast."

"Of course," Cho agreed. "I'll go pack. Nereus is in the middle of an ice age, so you'll need all your best winter gear."

Trini hoped the smile plastered to her face didn't appear as fake as it felt. An ice age? Really? Aunt Teresa owed her big for this one.

Chapter 2—Cho

Cho's stomach fluttered as she waited on Trini to activate the thorneway. Her mother stood beside her, fidgeting with her nurse's scrubs, having come over on her break to see Cho off. Cho had told her mother she didn't have to come. After all, Dr. Flores wasn't here to see Trini off. But her mother's response had been that Trini was older. Nor was this her first trip off-ship.

Mom doesn't trust me.

A black substance filled the nearest sim cage, making Cho think of a black ocean. She shrank back, having second thoughts about traveling through a thorneway. She longed to visit her first alien world. Had wanted to since the day she learned of Space City's existence and that aliens were in fact real. Despite knowing thorneways were a common means of instantaneous travel—and completely safe—seeing one active for the first time was unsettling.

The thorneway reflected nothing. Quite the opposite, the facility seemed darker, like standing outside during an eclipse.

Cho imagined that black liquid sucking her in and drowning her. Or squashing her, compressing her to the size of a grain of sand.

"Are you all right?" her mother asked, either seeing something on her face or sensing her sudden discomfort.

"Fine." Cho forced a smile, redirecting her eyes from the thorneway to her mother. "Just nervous."

"You could still go to Sundara instead."

Her mother had advocated visiting Tanarille and the welcoming Azzaro. Many people chose Sundara as their first alien world to visit. Or Niveum.

But Nereus was sparsely populated, with minimal Space City visitation to date. Cho could explore like Mamiya Rinzo or Yoshiharu Sekino, the latter of whom's entire bibliography she'd stolen from her sister Riko and read through twice. She could be the first human to observe and document new species of flora and fauna on Nereus. With her contacts, she could record what ended up in the Space City database; take pics and note the locations of any new species she found. Once her fall semester resumed, she could plan a follow-up trip with proper equipment to better document her findings, and perhaps collect specimens.

"No, I want to travel to Nereus," Cho said, straightening. "Find the quinniq. Be the first to document their existence."

"Just don't bring one back as a pet," her mother warned.

This elicited giggles from Cho. Her mother joined in. While growing up in Nagano, Cho had often come home with wounded woodpeckers, squirrels, and even once a young macaque, intent on nursing them back to health and keeping them as pets. Each time, her mother had helped her research how to tend the animal's wounds, feed it, and create a temporary outdoor shelter; never in her bedroom like she'd begged.

Once each animal was on the mend, they'd learn how to reintroduce it to the wild so it could be free. Her mother had used the reminder of freedom, and of the animals returning to their families, to persuade her to let them go.

Her mother opened her arms for a hug. Cho complied, and her mother whispered in her ear. "Be careful. Listen to Trini. She's done this before." Cho rolled her eyes and tried to pull away, but her mother held on. "And have fun. Your father and I want to hear all about your adventures when you return."

This made Cho smile. She gave her mom one squeeze before pulling away. "I'll have many stories to share."

"Ready?" Trini asked.

Cho nodded. Despite her trepidation about the thorneway, she was ready to go. Ready to visit a snow-filled landscape for the first time since home.

"I'll go first. Follow me," Trini instructed, pointing at the thorneway.

"Okay." Cho could do that. She tried to squash the sudden relief washing through her at not going first, ignoring the thoughts that she shouldn't go at all, that she'd chosen too ambitious a plan for her first time.

Trini marched into the thorneway with all the confidence and determination that she displayed in her Games matches. No hesitation. She had a mission. She'd face it head on.

Cho shuffled toward the thorneway, her fists clenched. Her heart hammered in her chest. She drew in a deep breath, trying to push away her fear.

"Don't forget to raise your helmet," her mother said at the last moment.

Cho wondered if her mother had ever done this to Riko before her trips, as she raised it. Even with it up, she held her breath as she stepped into the thorneway. The black liquid pulled her in, then threw her. She gasped in surprise, instinct telling her to fall back, before she emerged in a furious snowstorm.

Chapter 3—Cho

The jarring change in the environment immobilized Cho. Her senses reeled. They stood in a dark landscape with a pale yellow sky. Heavy snow showered them, whipped about by powerful gusts of wind.

A small village existed about four kilometers away, but with the storm she couldn't make out anything beyond three meters, even though it was near midday on Nereus. All she could see were ugly gray snow drifts.

A loud pop behind Cho caused her to spin around. The thorneway frame stood empty.

"We have to go back." Trini, wide-eyed, pushed past Cho toward the thorneway controls on one side of the large metallic frame.

"It's just a snowstorm." Cho guessed Trini had never been in one before. In Nagano, storms like this weren't uncommon.

"That's not snow. It's ash," Trini replied as she fumbled with the controls.

Cho frowned and surveyed the landscape again, blinking to activate her contacts. A stream of bright red text flooded her vision.

Danger! Danger! Massive volcanic eruption in effect. Seek immediate shelter. Danger! Danger!

Volcanic eruption? Where? Had they gone to the right place?

"Come on!" Trini yelled, slamming both fists against the thorneway frame.

"What's wrong?" Cho asked.

"The thorneway's dead." Trini pressed both hands against her helmet, her expression shocked.

"What?" Cho joined Trini at the controls. "How do we get it going again?"

A few minutes ago, she'd been reluctant to take her first trip through a thorneway. Now she was desperate to take her second.

"We can't."

"Can't? We have to. We can't stay here with a volcano." An edge of hysteria entered her voice as she tried to figure out what activated the thorneway.

Trini pointed at the space where the thorneway should be. "It's got no power. I think it short-circuited. Maybe because of all the ash."

Cho didn't accept this. None of the buttons had clear labels, so she hit one after the other. Nothing happened. When she'd gone through all the buttons, she tried a second time. One of them had to work. They just needed the right combo.

"That won't do any good," Trini said, surveying the landscape once more. "We're stuck. We need to find shelter."

Danger. Danger. The warning repeated on Cho's contacts as she tried the control panel again.

Trini slapped a hand over the controls, smacking Cho's fingers. "Stop! We have to go. Now!" Fear replaced the shock on her face, but also determination.

Cho tried to steel herself, but her fear burst through it like a flood through a dam made of straw. She hadn't bargained on a volcanic eruption when she signed up for Nereus. "Go where?"

Trini pointed east. "The Nuukimak village. From there, we figure out how to contact Space City."

"What if they're not there? What if they left because of the eruption?" Or worse? It wouldn't be the first place wiped out by a volcano.

"It's our best option."

"Wouldn't our best option be staying here? When we don't check in, someone from Space City will come looking for us and this will be the first place they'll check."

"It could be days or a week before anyone realizes we should've returned. Or at least checked in. We need shelter now. The Nuukimak village is the closest place."

"Could we fix the thorneway? I've got supplies for my 3D printer. We could make tools." Cho wished she'd listened to her mother and gone to Tanarille.

Trini shook her head. "No way. The engineers who work on thorneways have years of experience. No way we figure it out in a couple of hours. We should get to the village, then figure out what's next."

Without waiting for her reply, Trini trudged into the storm. Cho hurried after her, not wanting to lose her, which could happen in seconds in these conditions. There were no roads or trails to follow. No signs pointing the way to the village. What if they missed it? That would be all too easy in this storm. They could pass within a few meters and not see it.

"Where's the village?" she asked. "Are you sure you can find it?"

Trini pointed ahead without hesitation. "That way."

"How can you be sure? It's easy to get turned around in this." She glanced behind her and could no longer see the thorneway, which made her skin crawl. She took a step closer to Trini, not wanting to get split up by accident.

"I downloaded an AR guide to my contacts."

"AR guide?" Cho wondered why she'd never heard of such a thing.

"Augmented reality guide. Right now, an AR tour guide is leading me to the village. It provides information about the village and scenery, but I have the audio turned off. I'm not in the mood for fun facts."

"Can you share it?" If she wasn't so spooked, Cho would've found this revelation thrilling. Instead, she wanted the reassurance that it led them somewhere safe.

"Sure."

Trini turned to her and blinked once. A tall droid, similar to the ones that tended the garden outside the spaceport, appeared a couple of meters ahead of Cho. It wore a silver explorer suit, but without a helmet.

"Greetings," it said with a Latin accent, which was strange coming from a droid. "Where are you headed?"

"To the Nuukimak village."

"Would you like a guide?"

"Yes."

As the droid turned and headed east, it rattled off details about the place. "The Nuukimak live in small tribes. They are semi-nomadic, traveling based upon fish migrations at different times of the year."

The droid's legs glided through the ash-covered snow without disturbance, leaving no footsteps or parted snow in its wake. For a half second Cho puzzled over this, before remembering the droid was an image projected by her contacts. It wasn't moving through the snow. How lucky for it. Her legs steadily tired from pushing through thigh-high, dirty gray snow drifts. This wasn't the beautiful white landscape she'd hoped to explore.

"During the summer months, the Nuukimak move north to catch Patua from the rivers," the droid said. "The Patua are larger whitefish with blue-gray scales. They serve as the primary food source in the Nuukimak diet.

"In the winter, they head south toward the poles. There they subsist off Aqak, a smaller silver fish they catch through the ice."

Cho switched the commentary off, agreeing with Trini's assessment. The guide comforted her; gave her confidence they'd find the village. But the info dump... not helpful. Not in these circumstances.

Instead, she pressed forward, trying to see past all the heavily falling ash. She remembered her contacts had a magnification feature.

Zoom in, she thought.

The ash rushed past her for a moment before resuming its normal fall. But the change made no difference. Still no sign of the village or anything else of interest.

"How much farther?" Cho asked.

The droid glanced back, but said nothing. Right, she'd turned its audio off.

She didn't need the answer, anyway. She followed it, her legs complaining with each slogging step. Trini also hunched forward, fighting her way through the snow. Cho took solace that at least she wasn't here alone. It kept her matching the older girl step for step. If Trini could do it, she would, too.

How cold was it out here?

Again, the droid turned back to her, but she ignored it. Instead, she thought about the thermostat function in her contacts. The temperature appeared off to the side of her vision.

13° F / -10.56° C.

Well within their explorer suits' temperature range, though the helmet never kept her head as warm as the suit did her body. Her ears stung a bit from the chill.

The AR droid stopped and turned to her, waiting.

"What is it?" she asked, turning back on its audio.

"We have arrived at the Nuukimak village," the droid said.

"No, we haven't," Cho said. "There's no sign of a village. Was it possible the AR droid had taken them to the wrong location?

"Cho," Trini said, taking slow, careful steps forward. "Look."

More dirty piles of snow filled the area, but broken tools, abandoned sleds, and large, caved in mounds that could've been homes littered the place. Once more, her panic rose.

"This is the village?" she asked.

"What's left of it," Trini answered.

Tears welled up in Cho's eyes. Where were they supposed to go now? Was there another village somewhere? Was it destroyed as well? Icy fingers crawled up her spine. They were alone, cut off, the two of them amid a disaster with no obvious path to safety.

"What do we do now?"

Trini pulled something small from her pockets. "I've got some scouts. I'll send them out a couple and see if we can find signs of the Nuukimak."

The scouts leapt into the air and flew off, disappearing from view. Trini raised her wrist-comp and Cho joined her. On the screen, a grid appeared. For several tense minutes, nothing happened. Would the scouts find nothing? Were they alone?

Then a massive red circle appeared on the grid to the northwest, too large to be an individual.

"What is that?" Cho asked.

"Fire, if I had to guess," Trini answered. "I set the scouts to detect heat signatures. If we head there, I'm betting we'll find the Nuukimak."

Trini set the AR droid to lead them to the coordinates from the grid. They soon came across light filtering out from a single mound dug down into the ground. Voices and laughter drifted up from inside, cut short a moment later by warning barks. A dozen dogs surged out of the hole, bounding straight for them.

Cho tensed, unsure what to do as the growling dogs surrounded them. Large men in thick furs followed, shouting at the dogs. The entire pack dropped to their bellies, but continued to whine.

"Who are you?" one man asked, a harpoon in hand. The other three men also carried harpoons.

Trini raised both hands, palms open. "We got caught in the storm and need shelter. Please."

"From where?" the man asked, face wary.

Trini tapped her chest. "I'm Trini Flores." She motioned to Cho. "My friend is Cho Tamura. We come from Space City."

The man studied them, his expression giving away nothing about their unexpected arrival.

"We didn't know there was a volcanic eruption before we arrived. We got cut off," Trini said, arms still outstretched. "Please help us."

"Inksuuk, they are girls. Let them in." An elderly woman stepped forward, past the man.

The man who'd spoken, Inksuuk, pursed his lips, but made no move to contradict the old woman.

"Please, come inside," the woman said, gesturing to the caves. She had long, gray hair split into a pair of braids. "Would you like some tea?"

Chapter 4—Trini

The entire Nuukimak village, thirty people, including children, had crammed into what Trini could best describe as a root cellar. They huddled on the ground, split up by mounds of supplies. Lamps from Space City lit the place.

All eyes locked on Trini and Cho, the Nuukimak murmuring amongst themselves as the dozen dogs found places to lie down.

"Offer tea to our guests," the old woman snapped, as she waded between people and a stack of salted fish.

Not wanting to climb over anyone, Trini settled for a spot against the wall inside the door. She lowered her helmet. An overpowering scent of smoke from the ash outside hit her. She wrinkled her nose, wishing to raise her helmet back. Would raising it offend the Nuukimak?

Cho sidled next to her, bumping her shoulder. *I wonder who's more nervous, Cho or the Nuukimak?*

A young girl balanced clay mugs of steaming tea as she waded through the crowded cellar to Trini and Cho. Trini thanked the girl, who nodded and retreated before taking a small sip. The tea was bitter, but the warmth welcome.

Despite the number of people in the cellar, a damp cold pervaded. Still, it was shelter.

"You come from Space City?" Inksuuk asked, pointing at the ceiling as he reasserted himself after the old woman's interruption.

Trini nodded and sipped her tea once more. "Yes. We didn't know about the volcano eruption. It stranded us."

"Can your elders help?" Inksuuk asked. He had black bags beneath his eyes. He wasn't the only one among the Nuukimak.

The old woman hissed at Inksuuk and he waved her off.

"If you didn't notice on your way in, Cupuen's anger destroyed our village. If your elders can help…"

"Inksuuk. They're little more than girls. And alone," the old woman scolded. "We should offer our help, not lay our burdens on their shoulders."

"Space City can help if we contact them," Trini cut in, annoyed that the woman had dismissed them as too young. Not that either she or Cho could offer much help at the moment. "At present, we can't reach them."

Several Nuukimak murmured sympathies to the girls as Inksuuk frowned.

Undeterred and wanting to show they could help, Trini asked, "How long has this been going on?"

"Since dusk, three nights past," Inksuuk answered. "Fire filled the sky from Cupuen. It burned straight through the night, darkening the skies. The sun disappeared."

Several villagers muttered about this.

"Ash has fallen like aput from the sky, chasing away game and souring the water. So far the patua are still plentiful." Inksuuk pointed at a fish being cleaned by a boy in a corner. "—but if the ash doesn't dissipate soon and the sun return, we'll have to depart for the winter grounds."

"We need a sacrifice," an old man blurted from Trini's left. "The gods are displeased."

Again the old woman hissed, this time at the old man.

"I speak truth, Ahnai." The old man raised his nose.

"Speak not of gods in Atak's land," Ahnai replied. "The Goddess alone holds sway and has forbidden sacrifices."

Many shouted approval, but a few grumbled, brows darkening.

Inksuuk waved them all to silence.

"I don't know the cause for Cupuen belching fire, but we must leave soon or starve. Already the dogs fight from hunger. We've little food for the touvak, yet we'll need them to pull our sleds."

"We head south to the winter grounds as planned," a man spoke up. He was almost as large as Inksuuk and his black hair hung to his shoulders. He had a long scar on his neck below the jaw.

"We don't have reserves, Tigua," Inksuuk said. "It'll be a hard winter if we go now."

"Better a hard winter that we prepare for than to head east into unknown lands," Tigua shot back.

Several others around Tigua voiced agreement. He smiled at their support.

"Taamaruq has traveled East." Inksuuk pointed to a girl who leaned against a wall next to the food and tea supplies. "Taamaruq found a sea with pammtuuk aplenty on the ice shelves."

Taamaruq was taller than Cho, and slender, but strong. As Inksuuk spoke of her, Taamaruq stood taller, eyes beaming, though the rest of her face remained flat.

"We risk our families on the word of your daughter?" Tigua asked. "Be reasonable."

A few others around Tigua repeated, "Be reasonable."

"Not risking your families, no," Inksuuk replied. "Saving them from starvation. And there are caverns in the ice flows we can live in."

"Sure, if we fight off the namouns for them," Tigua said.

Taamaruq leaned back against the wall, giving no sign that Tigua's words bothered her. Trini wanted to hit Tigua for her, though the girl didn't need her help.

"Taamaruq saw minimal signs of namouns," Inksuuk said, crossing his arms as he leveled his gaze at Tigua.

"And we're to trust the tracking skills of your daughter?" Tigua asked.

Once more several of the people around Tigua added, "Be reasonable."

"I am," Inksuuk replied. Despite the attacks on his daughter, he showed no emotion nor gave further rebuttal. He trusted her and felt no need to defend her.

That was all it took to put Trini in his corner, despite her initial impression of him upon their arrival.

At that moment Trini received an update from the scouts with surface measurements. On every planet where Space City placed thorneways, they also launched satellites into orbit for visiting personnel. When she'd launched the scouts to find the Nuukimak, she'd also tapped into the satellite to obtain measurements of the volcanic activity.

The news wasn't good.

According to the data, the fallout from the Cupuen volcano covered most of the continent. No matter which direction the Nuukimak chose, they'd find no shelter.

Trini hated that Taamaruq's efforts wouldn't save her people.

******

Cho lifted the teacup to her lips, only to remember she'd finished it. A couple of women and several children all huddled around a tea kettle along one side of the cave. The children played quietly with small dolls. The women listened to the exchange and sipped their tea.

She eased over toward them, doing her best not to step on or disturb anyone else in her path. They each eyed her and pulled back to let her pass. She apologized to several for the inconvenience, but none responded.

When she reached the women at the tea kettle, the closest regarded her but said nothing.

"Sorry to disturb you." Cho held up her teacup. "Could I trouble you for a little more?"

"It is a frigid day," the woman said, retrieving the tea kettle from its stand over a hot coal stone oven. She poured some into Cho's cup.

"It is," Cho agreed. "Thank you."

The woman nodded. A little girl on the floor beside her played with a small toy.

Cho smiled at the girl. "What are you playing with?"

The girl, couldn't be more than four, smiled with head bowed and inched toward the woman.

"Elsapi, will you answer her?" the woman asked, cajoling.

"It's a very nice toy," Cho said.

The girl smiled again and hid her face behind her mother.

Cho checked to see if she'd missed anything important in the discussion. When she glanced back, Elsapi studied her. The little girl ducked back behind her mother, then peeked one eye out at Cho, a grin on her face. Cho winked at the girl, who ducked again, before peeking out once more. Then Elsapi blinked both eyes at her.

Cho smiled wider and waved discreetly at the girl. After a second's pause, Elsapi mimicked her, before hiding her face once more.

Unsettled murmurs passed through the room, and Cho turned back to find out what she'd missed. Most eyes were on Trini, including Inksuuk and Tigua, both with mouths agape as if unsure how to respond. What had Trini said?

"It's a little more than a day's travel north to the second thorneway," Trini said.

What? A second thorneway? Trini hadn't mentioned there was another on the planet. Had the scouts identified it? Cho didn't believe the scouts had that kind of range.

"You would have us travel straight toward Cupuen." Tigua glanced at those around him with an expression like he couldn't believe what he was hearing and wanted others to confirm. "Doing so is lunacy."

"I know it seems that way, but it's your only chance at survival," Trini said. "Cupuen's destruction is too widespread. There's nowhere safe you can reach. You must come with us to Space City."

More unsettled murmurs passed through the Nuukimak.

Cho blinked. She'd known things weren't great, but they must be dire for Trini to suggest the entire village come with them. The prospect of traveling a day toward a volcano sent a shiver through her.

"And how do we know your way of thorns works?" Tigua asked. "Cupuen has destroyed much. The closer to it, the greater the destruction."

"We have satellites in space that give me updates," Trini answered, pointing upward. "The Thorneway is shielded and safe."

"And your…" Inksuuk paused for a moment, then pointed upward, "says everywhere to the east and south is like here?" He glanced toward Ahnai.

"You must trust me," Trini said. "The thorneway is our only choice."

"We are to take the word of an outsider?" Tigua again appealed to those around him. "Abandon our safe places and entrust the lives of our families to a young girl?"

Trini strode over in front of Tigua, arms crossed in front of her, hands clenched in fists, eyes narrowed. "I know what I'm talking about."

Tigua's eyes widened at her approach, before he controlled himself, his expression returning to neutral. However, his posture remained rigid.

She then turned to face the others, eyes flashing. "If you want to live beyond the next week, you must come with us."

Everyone in the place stood silent, frozen. Trini hadn't raised her voice, yet Cho heard every word, as had everyone else. And now an oppressive tension filled the room, thick as honey in a beehive.

Inksuuk was the first to break the silence. "We have three choices before us. Head east based upon Taamaruq's scouting. Travel south to the winter grounds and hope we can stock up on enough supplies before the seasons change. Or abandon our homes and travel to Space City."

"There's only one choice that ensures you survive," Trini shot back.

Inksuuk smiled without mirth, eyes dropping to the dirt-packed floor.

"I must agree with Tigua," a third man said, rising to his feet almost at Inksuuk's shoulder. He resembled Inksuuk, if a little shorter and thinner. "We cannot abandon everything we know based upon the word of an…." He gestured at Trini. "Outsider."

Trini scowled at this new challenger, but this time said nothing.

"But I trust the scouting of my niece," the man said. "If Taamaruq says there is shelter and food to the east, I believe her. I will travel east or south, whatever the families decide. But to head north, toward the volcano." He shook his head. "It's too great a risk."

"Yoskalo speaks sense," Tigua said.

Again, Inksuuk turned to Ahnai. "What say you, mother?"

The old woman rose and crossed the room to Trini. She sat on the ground, crossing her legs, and motioned for Trini to join her.

Cho wondered what the old woman was doing.

When Trini sat, her knees were so close to the old woman's they almost touched.

"You have things in the sky that watch our world?" Ahnai asked, speaking as though they were the only two people in the room.

"We have satellites, yes," Trini answered.

"And these sat—ell—ites," Ahnai stumbled over the word, "it sees all the land? The fire and ash from Cupuen rains down upon it all?"

Trini leaned forward, expression earnest. "In every direction. As far as there is land and beyond. You'll not find the shelter you seek here."

"Except for this place you speak of?"

"Thorneway. Yes."

"And how will it protect us?"

"It's how we travel from our home to here," Trini answered. "You must've seen the one we arrived in. It's not far. Perhaps you've even seen others from Space City arrive through it?"

"Why don't we escape through it?"

Trini grimaced. "It was destroyed by the elements shortly our arrival. But if you come through the other thorneway with us, you will be on Space City, far away from here. You will all be safe."

Cho expected people to gasp or talk among themselves or something. Instead, they all remained frozen, attention trained upon Ahnai and Trini.

Unmoving, Ahnai continued to look into Trini's eyes. "We will trust you, daughter. I hear truth in your words."

"Thank you," Trini replied, not breaking eye contact.

Ahnai nodded, then stood and turned to Inksuuk. "We will load the sleds in the morning and head north."

Inksuuk nodded. No one protested.

The old woman turned to Taamaruq. "Granddaughter, I do not wish for you or your brother to be the last Nuukimak generation."

Taamaruq nodded as her father had, accepting her grandmother's words without visible disappointment.

"It is decided," Inksuuk said. "We must prepare to head out tomorrow."

Cho rose and rejoined Trini, wondering if they could find a quiet spot to talk alone. Cho had so many questions.

Chapter 5—Cho

The next morning, Cho awoke with a headache. She'd tossed and turned in her sleeping bag all night. It had kept her warm, but with so many people crammed into the small root cellar, they had all slept shoulder to shoulder. She'd worried she might roll onto Trini or the woman on her other side during sleep. And the nausea triggered by the reek of volcanic ash wasn't helping any.

Around four, she'd woken up needing to use the restroom, thanks to the tea she'd drunk. It had taken her some time to wade through everyone and back.

In a tired stupor, she ate fish cooked with berries that Kierama, Inksuuk's wife, offered her and Trini for breakfast. Cho accepted a small portion, not sure her stomach could handle much. Nor did she want to consume the Nuukimak's limited resources. She and Trini had both brought plenty of travel rations. The thought of the energy bars worsened her nausea, so she packed the food away.

Trini devoured hers, the stench not affecting her appetite. Cho wanted to hit her.

After eating, Trini left, heading north to check out their route and send out a few of the scouts.

The Nuukimak packed up as much of the cellars' contents as they could store on their long sleds. Cho offered to help Ahnai, Kierama, and Taamaruq, so Ahnai set her to packing garments in duffle bags and backpacks from Space City. As they worked, she also recognized travel rations among the Nuukimak supplies. She wished Space City had left behind the PSA field shelters that self-assembled.

"What is this place you're taking us?" Ahnai asked her as she folded fur blankets.

"The thorneway?" Cho asked.

"Space City."

Cho pondered this for a minute, wondering how to explain it to the old woman. They walked and rode sleds as their principal forms of transportation. Had they seen any of Space City's ships during their first visits to the planet?

"It is enormous. Many of our buildings are taller than dozens of your homes stacked on top of each other. And you won't believe the number of people who live there."

Ahnai nodded simply, but Kierama's eyes widened and she paused in the middle of stuffing wooden dishes into packs. Cho wondered if she should tell them they needn't bother bringing all this stuff. It would only slow them down. Space City could provide all they needed, but something told her that might offend them.

"If you have so many, will your leaders accept us?" Ahnai asked. "You must take care of your own."

"We have all that we need and more," Cho replied. "And plenty of room for you. All of you."

She grimaced at hearing her words. Instead of generous, she felt guilty, as if she was at fault for having so much when the Nuukimak were losing everything.

"And we can return when this is over?"

Cho blinked, not having thought that far. The volcano's eruption darkening the skies was no small thing. How long would it last? Days? Weeks? Longer?

And because of the volcanic spew raining down on them, how many plants would wither and die from lack of sunlight? How many animals would freeze or starve to death? It might take years or decades before the Nuukimak could hope to have a normal life here again. She didn't know how to voice these concerns, but the old woman had stopped to study her, waiting for a response.

"Space City will bring you back whenever you are ready," Cho said.

This seemed to satisfy Ahnai. At least she returned to packing without further questions. But Cho couldn't stop dwelling on it. What if this was a major extinction event, like the meteor strike that had wiped out Earth's dinosaurs? What if the Nuukimak could never return? She knew that Space City would help them find a new home, but what would that look like? Space City had the space to provide permanent homes to the Nuukimak. But it was so different from the simple lives they now lived. Would they find a new planet?

What was it like to wake one day to find your whole world devastated by a natural disaster? Yet the Nuukimak bore it without complaint. Very matter-of-factly. Perhaps they didn't comprehend the impact to their lives yet? Except, how could they not when perpetual darkness had replaced the daylight? If it weren't for the second thorneway, Cho would've curled up in a ball on the ground in despair.

"Grandmother, come quick. Tigua is leaving." A boy hustled into the cellar and straight up to Ahnai. He wore a leather facemask over his mouth to block the inhalation of ash outside.

"Leaving where, Panuik?" Ahnai asked her grandson.

The boy, almost painfully thin, shrugged bony shoulders. "Inksuuk told me to get you."

"Atak, save us," Ahnai muttered as she bustled outside, slipping on her own mask.

Curious, Cho raised her suit helmet and grabbed a pair of full duffle bags. She carried them outside and loaded them on top of a bin on a sled. Pale blue and purple feathers adorned the heads of the sleds. The colors contrasted nicely from the dismal gray ash covering everything.

Thin dogs with ribs showing yapped around the sleds, bristling with energy. They fought over the little scraps tossed to them. At least they weren't snarling at her today.

"What is this about, Inksuuk?" Ahnai approached her son and Tigua, who led large, caribou-like creatures into place to pull a full sled.

A quick scan of the creatures with her contacts told Cho they were touvak. They served the Nuukimak like horses on Earth. The touvak had gray and brown coats of fur, and most possessed grand racks of antlers.

"Tigua plans to take his family to the winter grounds," Inksuuk answered through his facemask. Every Nuukimak outside wore them.

Beside them stood the woman who had served tea to Cho the previous night. She held a crying Elsapi in her arms.

"Tigua, this is unwise." Ahnai unhooked a touvak from the sled.

"It is the rest of you who are unwise." Tigua finished hooking a touvak into place in front of the sled, then strode over to Ahnai. But rather than cross her for the other touvak, he put his hands on his hips. "Heading to the winter grounds, away from Cupuen, is the safest decision. Yet you want to go neither away from it, nor to the side, but directly toward it."

"Our winter grounds won't be any safer," Ahnai said.

The touvak behind her brayed and attempted to retake its place with the other. Ahnai snapped her fingers, halting it.

"The winter grounds aren't far enough away. Nowhere we can reach is safe from Cupuen."

"So those girls say, but I won't risk the lives of my wife and child based on the outsiders' claims." Tigua was rigid, hands in fists at his sides, but he spoke calmly, even politely, to Ahnai.

"I won't give you my blessing to split from us," Ahnai said.

This caused Tigua to grimace, but he replied, "Save your blessing for your family. They'll need it."

This seemed to take Ahnai aback. She stepped aside, letting Tigua retrieve his touvak and return it to its place in the sled line.

"Tigua," Inksuuk began. He paused, waiting on Tigua to finish and turn to face him. Tigua crossed his arms, lips tight in a thin line.

"Once we find the passage to Space City, I'll come to the winter grounds. Make sure you're safe."

"May the gods keep your family safe," Tigua said.

"May the goddess protect your path," Inksuuk answered, moving away from the sled.

Tigua motioned to his wife, who moved to a rail on the back of the sled with the still crying Elsapi. She set the girl down upon their belongings and wrapped her in a great blanket of dark orange fur.

"Please, wait," Cho called to Tigua and the mother. "Don't do this. Come with us for your daughter's sake."

Cho thought she detected a little worry on the mother's features—drooped mouth, distressed eyes—but she didn't respond. Neither did Tigua. He moved alongside the touvak and whistled as though she'd said nothing. The pair of touvak hauled the sled forward while Tigua jogged beside them. Two dogs bounded around him.

Tears to match Elsapi's own blurred Cho's vision. Tigua's stubbornness might cost the little girl her life, unless Trini's projections were wrong. But Trini seemed confident that heading to the thorneway was their only real choice.

Why couldn't she be stronger like Trini? She should demand they listen to her. She should take the little girl from them, do whatever it took to save her life. Instead, all she did was watch as they left.

Cho raised a hand to wipe the tears from her eyes, only to have it bump against her helmet. She hoped Inksuuk would have the opportunity to find them after they'd reached the thorneway. Hoped things wouldn't have already gotten too bad to find them.

Chapter 6—Trini

Trini trudged to the top of the high rise to get her own view of the area she'd seen in the scouts' footage. Her breath misted off the inside of her helmet.

With the winds settled, the falling ash resembled large, gray heads of cauliflower that pulsed like jellyfish. She switched her contacts to night vision. Flat-topped mountains filled the way forward. Ordinarily, they might've been a beautiful sight. As it was, they were a gray mess of snow and ash. She was thankful that her air filtration system removed the smoky stench that saturated the air, allowing her to breathe. How long before the filtration system became clogged with contaminants?

The area to the northeast had wide, gentle slopes that allowed for smooth, quick travel, especially with the sleds. Whereas the slopes to the northwest were steeper, with windy, narrow passages that wouldn't forgive mistakes. Guiding the sleds that way would slow them down a great deal.

She checked the latest volcanic eruption data she'd received from the satellites. The current dense-rock equivalent from Cupuen stood around 2,900 cubic kilometers, with much of it ash that smothered everything.

The eruption had caused a three degrees Celsius drop in surface temperatures, as if it hadn't been cold enough. Worse, a major storm was brewing. In two days, it would dump a ton of snow upon them, along with driving ash and poison gas from the volcano. With the storm would come more freezing temperatures. They needed to reach the second thorneway ahead of the storm to avoid severe travel conditions.

The ground shook, accompanied by what sounded like thunder all around her. Her hammering heart was the only part of her that moved during the five-second tremor. She half expected the ground to break open and magma to flow up out of the ground. But that was stupid. She was too far away for volcanic fissures from Cupuen to reach her.

After a minute had passed without follow-up tremors, another worry surged to the forefront. She checked her wrist-comp, pinging the second thorneway.

Please, don't let it have damaged the thorneway.

Holding her breath, she waited for the return response from the thorneway. It was online. No reported malfunctions.

She exhaled as she headed back to the village, thankful they'd caught a break. *And for these snowshoes Ahnai gave me.* After slogging through snow yesterday, these worked much better than her boots.

As she neared the village, the pack of dogs charged, barking ferociously until Inksuuk and others called them off. She counted sixteen packed sleds, all covered with large, dark orange fur blankets. Reins tied a team of four touvak to each sled. The creatures pawed the ground and playfully knocked antlers against each other, ready to run. The Nuukimak milled about their sleds, checking tie-downs.

Cho hurried over to her, backpack on her shoulders and also sporting snowshoes. "What's the latest from the satellites?"

Trini bit her lower lip and looked around to see who might be listening, but no one paid them any mind. "Projections indicate things are getting worse. A major storm is coming and with it freezing temperatures, plus more eruptions on the way."

Cho's shoulders drooped and she studied the ground. Trini knew how she felt. But these things were beyond their control. *Like it or not, it's the reality we have to contend with if we want to reach the second thorneway.*

"Looks like everyone is ready?" Trini asked.

"Except Tigua and his family." Cho's eyes dropped to the ground as if she'd done something wrong. "They're gone."

"Where?" Trini asked, annoyance surging through her. They didn't have time for delays. "When are they due back?"

Cho grimaced and shook her head. "They're not returning. He's taking his family to the winter grounds."

Idiot! Trini couldn't believe the man's stubbornness, falling back on his own experience and the illusory sense of safety it provided. His actions were going to get his family killed.

Inksuuk stood beside a sled checking tie downs. Trini stormed over to him.

"How could you let Tigua leave?" Trini jabbed a finger south in the direction Tigua would've gone.

Inksuuk bristled. "I cannot stop Tigua from leaving. He may decide what is best for him and his family."

"That right shouldn't extend to putting his child's life in danger!"

"Calm yourself, girl," Ahnai said, appearing at Inksuuk's side. Her arms crossed her chest, her brow darkened. "What right do you, my son and I, or anyone else have to tell Tigua what is best for his family? You say what he's doing is a danger to his family, but you are leading us straight toward Cupuen."

Trini gaped at the old woman, unsure how to respond.

"I believe you possess great knowledge about what's happening at your disposal, but make no mistake, you are an advisor not our leader. We accept commands from Atak and no one else. Definitely not from an outsider."

Heat rushed to Trini's cheeks. She wanted to shout back that if they didn't want to listen, then she and Cho would head on alone. But it wasn't them, it was Tigua who wasn't listening. Still, their defense of his actions infuriated her. Why should anyone have the right to put their family's life in danger? Why should a little girl suffer because of her father's pride?

With a cough, Yoskalo interrupted them. "Everyone is ready to depart."

Inksuuk nodded to his younger brother, before turning back to Trini. "How do we get to your thorneway?"

She exhaled, trying to accept that she couldn't stop Tigua and his family. She needed to turn her focus to what she could control. "The most direct route is through the mountains to the northeast." She pulled up aerial footage on her wrist-comp and projected it into the air to give them a visual.

Both Inksuuk and Ahnai tensed up at the projection, but said nothing.

Trini wove a path with her finger across the landscape, leaving a red line across the projection for her planned route.

Inksuuk's face darkened. "We can't go that way. It's ighi."

It was the most emotion Trini had seen from him or any of the Nuukimak.

"I don't understand. What's wrong with it?"

"It's not safe," Inksuuk answered. "Too dangerous. We must go here." He traced an area to the northwest, leaving behind a second red line.

Trini shook her head. "I scouted both areas. That way is treacherous. It'll slow us down, which we can't afford." She pointed back at her red line. "This way is much easier."

"Not easier," Inksuuk disagreed, pointing at her path. "We cannot go that way. Too dangerous."

"Dangerous how?" Trini asked.

"Quinniq," Ahnai said. She shivered.

"That's where the quinniq are?" Cho asked, brightening despite the Nuukimak's obvious alarm.

"That way is their territory," Ahnai said. "We enter, they'll attack."

"Aren't the quinniq small?" Trini asked.

Inksuuk nodded. "Yes, but very dangerous. They work in packs. Hide in the snow to avoid detection. We could walk right over one and never know it."

"We have weapons," Trini said, pointing to herself and Cho. "We can fight them off."

Ahnai shook her head. "No. We won't risk the lives of our children through the quinniq's domain." Her eyes stared off into the distance. Trini saw something haunted in them. Some past story that Ahnai would not or could not share.

Deciding it was best not to push the old woman in this, Trini relented. "As long as you realize this will slow us down. We have precious little time as it is. Things are only going to get worse, thanks to Cupuen's continued eruptions."

"It's decided," Inksuuk said, turning to head back toward his sled. He raised his voice for all to hear. "Let's move out."

Chapter 7—Cho

Cho enjoyed the morning sled ride. The touvak's swift pace, combined with the darkness, created a measure of speed and danger that exhilarated her. Early on, the drivers let the touvak push themselves, burning pent-up energy. Their brays reverberated across the mountains. The sixteen sleds—half carrying people, the rest stocked full of belongings—covered the ground swiftly. The dogs ran alongside the touvaks and sleds, yapping and nipping at each other.

By the afternoon, Cho understood why Trini had wanted to travel northeast. All morning they'd climbed into the mountains. The further they'd gotten, the narrower the paths. For the last hour they'd navigated paths not much wider than the sleds, edged by precipitous slopes.

The paths curved back and forth. Every time Cho's side rode closest to the edge, she focused on her lap. Or the touvak. Even the upward slope to distract herself. But she couldn't completely block out the awareness that she was less than a meter from the edge. Her stomach churned, and all she could do was endure it.

Ahnai, perhaps sensing her discomfort, started rambling about past excursions into the mountains. The old woman had developed her love of the mountains from her father. When she was a little girl, he'd brought her up here to trap small animals and gather herbs for medical concoctions. Cho gathered that Ahnai's healing ability made her and Inksuuk the closest thing to leaders the Nuukimak had.

A man's shout jolted Cho. The sled in front of them had tipped over the edge and careened down the slope, dragging two bellowing touvak with it. The sled ricocheted off a tree and started tumbling sideways.

"Atak shield us," Ahnai cried.

Cho buried her face in her hands, but she couldn't silence the sickening sounds below. Had Yoskalo gone over with the sled? The thought made bile rise in her throat.

She sensed Ahnai standing beside her and opened her eyes to see the old woman climbing out of the sled. Cho watched as Ahnai and Yuta, their driver, moved to settle the spooked touvak. Trini leapt out as well. Cho followed her, not wanting to remain alone in the sled.

Her heart hammered in her chest as she dropped to a sitting position against the upward slope. Her hands shook, and she took deep breaths to try to calm her racing heart. Unbidden memories arose of Riko lying in the hospital after her rock-climbing accident. Both her arms broken. A black eye and a missing tooth. Her back—

Cho shoved down the memory and her brain's attempt to put her own face on her sister's battered body. The chill up her spine remained.

The touvak had settled. Inksuuk approached Yoskalo. "Yoskalo, what happened?"

Cho was relieved to realize he was alright.

"We rounded the curve." Yoskalo clenched an arm to his side, favoring his ribs as he stared down the slope. "The back end kicked sideways. I leapt free just before the sled went over the edge."

He crouched and retrieved a machete from the ground, which he raised in the air. "I hacked through the reins for these touvak or we'd have lost them as well."

Cho marveled at the man's dexterity to pull off such swift actions.

"You okay?" Trini asked her, extending a water bottle.

Cho shook her head, afraid she'd throw up any water she drank, along with her lunch.

"Let's see what we can salvage," Inksuuk said to his brother. Yoskalo nodded and the pair headed down the path.

"We don't have time," Trini interjected. "We need to press on."

"It's but a short trek." Inksuuk walked past Trini with barely a glance.

"Toxic smoke and dust are poisoning the air. What's more important, your lives or your stuff?" Trini called after the men.

"Trini." That simple word from Ahnai gave Cho uncomfortable flashbacks from childhood when she'd angered her mother.

The old woman crossed her arms beneath her chest and studied Trini for a moment. Trini didn't return her gaze. When it was clear she wouldn't argue, Ahnai turned and headed to check on the other sleds, leaving Trini and Cho alone.

Trini settled beside her, toeing the slush that would turn to ice overnight.

How much farther must we travel on these narrow paths? Cho wondered. No matter how careful the drivers, any of them could go over the edge at any moment. Her stomach plummeted at the thought. She'd rather walk the rest of the way. But she said nothing for fear that Trini would think her a coward.

And why wouldn't Trini? They were in a race to the thorneway to save their own lives and others. And she wanted to walk, slowing them down so she wouldn't feel scared. If Trini knew what she was thinking, she'd be disgusted. Cho was disgusted with herself. But that didn't dissolve her relief at sitting here on the ground. And she couldn't help but hope it took Inksuuk and Yoskalo longer than planned to return from the fallen sled.

A half hour later they returned, shoulders loaded with packs. Much too short for Cho's liking, though long enough that Trini paced in exasperation. She looked ready to chew them out, but one stern glance from Ahnai made her avert her gaze. Without a word Trini retook her seat in the sled.

Cho waited as long as she dared to join Trini and Ahnai. Once Inksuuk and Yoskalo finished tying the extra belongings to another sled, she reseated herself. Her hands resumed shaking. She had to clench her teeth to stop from screaming as Yuta urged the touvak forward. But he kept the pace slow and controlled as they rounded the curve.

Ahnai placed a hand on Cho's own. "Not far now. We're almost to the caves where we'll stop for the night."

Cho gave her a grateful smile, but Trini sat forward, tensing.

"What do you mean, we're stopping?" Trini asked. "It's midafternoon."

Not that time of day matters at the moment, Cho thought. It was always dark.

"A few more hours will put us on pace to reach the thorneway late tomorrow afternoon," Trini said. "We don't want to be out in the storm tomorrow night."

"It's been a hard day today," Ahnai said. "We need rest. So do the touvak. And the caves on this path present the only good location for shelter nearby."

"But complicates our chances of reaching the thorneway ahead of the storm. And if we suffer any setbacks tomorrow…" Trini shook her head.

Cho wanted to stay in the caves, but she couldn't argue with Trini's logic. What good was their comfort tonight if it endangered them tomorrow?

Ahnai glanced at the sleds ahead. "I know my people. They need rest."

"And if that rest costs them their lives?" Trini asked, scowling.

"Trini." Ahnai's tone was calm, but firm.

Cho had heard the same tone from her mother many times. It meant an end to the discussion. Trini knew it too, because instead of arguing, she folded her arms and stared off into the valley.

The Nuukimak in the sleds ahead all sat huddled in on themselves. No one talked. They appeared exhausted. Cho guessed it wasn't solely from the day's travel, but from the emotional toll of having their homes destroyed and leaving behind the belongings they couldn't carry, as well as not knowing what awaited them ahead.

Ahnai recognized the strain. Trini didn't. Cho knew she couldn't either. *We're returning home. It makes sense to hurry back to that safety net. For the Nuukimak, the safety net's gone. The caves provide some semblance of one.*

An hour later they reached the caves at a point where the mountain leveled out to a wide ridge. Cho breathed easier, hands relaxing.

The three caves were deep. Almost immediately, Ahnai's grandsons, Panuik and his cousin Siqiq, set off to explore them, a couple of dogs in tow.

Ahnai, Kierama, and the other women set about creating beds and putting together meals. Cho offered to help and was politely sent out in search of firewood. She doubted she'd find anything dry enough to burn. Nor was she excited about a fire after enduring the smell of ash all day. Yet the women seemed to want privacy.

Exiting the cave, she sighed as she raised her helmet.

"We should've left earlier this morning," Trini said, joining her. "With a little luck we might've reached the thorneway late tonight. We're cutting it very close."

"They've lost a lot," Cho replied. "They're doing the best they can."

"But all the stuff." Trini bent and grabbed a stone. She bounced it off a nearby tree. "Is that worth their lives? Is it worth ours?"

"It *is* their lives," Cho answered. "All of it. To them, saving it is saving themselves."

Trini shook her head and stared at the ground, saying nothing.

They walked on in silence. Cho understood Trini's point. Almost nothing the Nuukimak had brought with them was vital. Space City could replace everything and more, and make their lives a lot easier.

But, the Nuukimak might never be able to return. They want—no, need... need to preserve what they can. Control something in the face of such great personal turmoil.

It was the same reason Tigua had taken his family south to their winter home. He was trying to maintain some measure of control over his life. Preserve some of it. But he hadn't accepted how much they'd lost. He'd embraced denial. And his family would suffer for it. Little Elsapi would lose her life without the opportunity to choose for herself.

Tears filled Cho's eyes. She blinked them away.

"I see something promising." Trini pointed to their right, then took off in a sprint.

The ground sloped down to a fourth cave. Halfway inside the cave lay a fallen tree. It must have rolled or slid down the hill into the cave.

Trini pulled her 3D printer from her pack, along with some aluminum and plastic inks. She printed a hatchet, and they set about breaking off a supply of firewood for the night.

Chapter 8—Cho

Cho woke, her eyes flying open from a sense of something hovering over her. She gasped at two faces above her own.

Panuik and Siqiq burst into laughter and jumped to their feet. They dashed outside.

She sat upright, chest heaving. She was now alone. Sunlight drifted in through the cave entrance. After a second, it hit her. Sunlight? What was going on? Had things not been as bad as Trini projected?

She scrambled to her feet and headed for the cave's mouth. Outside, the Nuukimak all pointed at the dim sun in a gray sky that reminded Cho of smog. The boys ran circles around everyone, chasing each other, while dogs nipped playfully at their heels.

"Is it over?" Taamaruq asked, watching Trini. "Is Cupuen done? Can we return home?"

Trini studied diagrams on her wrist-comp. She shook her head. "No. It's a calm in the storm. A temporary break before things get worse. Much, much worse."

"Are you sure?" Inksuuk asked. Cho couldn't see his mouth for the leather facemask, but his eyes displayed skepticism.

Trini nodded, her nose wrinkled. "The storm will hit before sunset. Traditional sunset. We need to reach the thorneway before then."

Yoskalo mumbled under his breath, but Ahnai ushered everyone back into the caves. "Thank Atak for the light, but don't waste it."

Cho stared at the sun a moment longer. It offered no warmth. She rubbed her arms as she headed back in.

Her stomach grumbled as she returned to her sleeping bag. She fished out dried fruit and a peanut butter and honey power bar from her pack. The power bar was bland, like stale crackers.

The Nuukimak babbled with excitement and energy.

"Do you think we'll have sun the whole day?" Kierama asked.

"It's the first sun in a week!" Umiak said.

"Tend to the packing," Ahnai scolded.

Kierama fetched some dried patua and offered portions to Panuik and Siqiq with orders to pass them out. The dogs begged the boys for shares, circling them until Taamaruq chased them out of the caves.

Siqiq, grinning, brought some to Cho. Not wanting to offend Kierama, Cho accepted a small portion to avoid depleting what little they had. But as she took a bite, she regretted not taking more. It was delicious. She saved the last two bites for after her power bar and fruit, savoring them.

They didn't make it far down the mountain before the sleds got bogged down in the snow and ash. The touvak strained to budge the sleds.

"We'll have to walk," Inksuuk decided. "Spread the supplies across all the sleds to lighten the loads."

Trini huffed and stormed off. The Nuukimak eyed her before adjusting the sleds and resuming the trek. Panuik and Siqiq darted around everyone. Before long, the pair started sneaking up on a touvak, slapping it on the rump, then running away, squealing in glee at the creature's brays of irritation.

When the boys tired of the game, they explored the mountain range, pushing farther out from the group, dogs in tow. Kierama and Umiak regularly scolded them to stay close.

During one foray, something in the trees moved close to the boys. Small but quick. At first Cho thought it was a dog, but realized they were all nearby. The boys had gone alone.

"Boys, get back here," Kierama shouted.

Inksuuk and Yoskalo handed over the reins to two sleds to Taamaruq and Kierama. They moved alertly into the trees.

"What is it?" Cho asked Ahnai.

The old woman shook her head. "A vaitchak or itkan looking for scraps most likely. Inksuuk and Yoskalo are handling it."

Despite her words, Ahnai looked unsettled.

Trini activated half a dozen scouts, which swirled around her head. The boys ran up, eyes wide.

"What are those?" Panuik asked.

"Scouts," Trini replied. "They search the area and tell me what is nearby. They fly fast."

She sent them after the men. Both boys' heads whipped around, following the scouts' flight.

"Kuvrakuk! Kuvrakuk!" Panuik exclaimed, jumping up and down as he watched the scouts depart. The words translated to 'very joyful.'

A short time later, Inksuuk and Yoskalo returned empty-handed, their shoulders slumped.

"What was it?" Kierama asked.

Inksuuk shook his head. "Couldn't find anything."

"What about tracks?" Taamaruq asked.

"No tracks," Yoskalo answered.

The Nuukimak shared uncomfortable glances.

What has them so worried? Cho wondered.

From that point on, whenever the boys got more than a few meters from the sleds, someone was quick to call them back. And the men formed a perimeter around everyone, even keeping the dogs close.

"What's out there?" Cho asked Ahnai.

The old woman stared at the forest, silent for a moment before replying. "The quinniq."

"That's what we came for, to find the quinniq."

Taamaruq frowned at her. "The quinniq are dangerous."

"But they're small creatures."

"Small but mean," Taamaruq answered. "Vicious."

"They hunt in packs," Ahnai added. "Attack vulnerable prey. They'll never attack an adult, but the children or other small creatures…"

Cho eyed the boys and shivered. "What if they rode on the sleds? They wouldn't add much weight. Couldn't the touvak handle them?"

Ahnai agreed, and the boys were loaded onto the sleds amid their protests. But as they resumed their trek, Cho kept watch for the quinniq.

"Catch any footage with the scouts?" she asked Trini.

"Nothing so far."

"Quinniq are sneaky," Taamaruq said. "They hide in snow. Hard to spot. Hard to catch."

"They could be close, but hidden," Inksuuk said. "In the snow, underfoot even."

"We're far from their domain," Kierama said. "They shouldn't be around."

"They're getting hungry. Desperate," Inksuuk said. "Cupuen has destroyed their prey."

******

They stopped for lunch in the early afternoon, despite the darkening skies.

"We've got four to five hours left before the storm hits," Trini warned.

Cho leaned against a sled, chewing on a power bar. They couldn't afford to sit long, though Cho wished they could stay for an hour. Her feet were blistering. The prospect of another five plus hours hiking made her groan.

They were all tired. Even the touvak panted.

On a sled, Panuik whispered to Siqiq. The younger boy grinned and nodded. Suddenly, Siqiq fled from the sleds as fast as his little legs could carry him. Shouts of alarm rose from the Nuukimak, along with yells for him to return, a couple with colorful language.

Before anyone could take more than a step after the boy, something small and white, no taller than his knees, sped across the ground toward him.

When it closed on Siqiq, it jerked him to the ground. He screamed in surprise and fear, and it dragged him into the forest.

Inksuuk, Yoskalo, and Taamaruq gave chase, hollering at the dogs to pursue. Cho lunged to her feet and ran after them, Trini at her side. The dogs surged past them, kicking up snow and ash in their wake.

"Was that a Quinniq?" Cho asked.

"I don't know," Trini replied.

They followed Siqiq's cries through the forest. Other yelps rose from the dogs in different directions.

They halted and spun around. A cry came from the left, another from the right.

"Where's it coming from?" Yoskalo shouted.

"It's echoing off the mountain rocks," Inksuuk said.

"Where is he?" Yoskalo shouted, looking half mad.

More cries drew Inksuuk and Yoskalo forward, but another from behind caused Cho to hesitate. She closed her eyes, listening, trying to calm her racing heart. Dogs barked and yelped. She tried to tune it out.

He was so little.

Another cry. This time she was sure it came from behind them. They'd overrun the creature and the boy.

She sprinted through the trees to rocky hills. It would be hard for the quinniq to drag him up those. She searched the nooks and crannies that she passed, but there were no signs of him. What if she'd gone the wrong way after all? What if the quinniq got away with him?

A shriek from off to her left drew her focus. Something struggled in the trees. Cho thought she recognized Siqiq.

She bolted toward him. Something white and furry bit at his legs. Cho aimed at the creature, but hesitated to shoot lest she hit the boy. Instead, she shot a tree, sending shards of wood and bark on the creature and boy. They froze in surprise, then the quinniq began dragging the boy by the ankle toward a small hole in the rocks.

A shout from behind startled Cho. Something raced past her. Trini, arms wide, charging toward the quinniq and screaming. Again, the quinniq froze, watching her, before this time abandoning the boy. It darted down its hole.

Within seconds Trini reached Siqiq and pulled him into her arms. Blood covered his arms and ankles. He bawled, burying his head in Trini's shoulder.

Cho glanced at the hole, but there was no sign of the creature.

"Is he okay?" she asked.

"I think so," Trini answered as she carried him back down the rocks.

Cho sighed in relief.

Moments later, Inksuuk and Yoskalo arrived, the latter taking his son from Trini.

"Thank you." Yoskalo held his son tight. "Thank you for saving my boy."

Trini nodded as they all headed back for camp.

"You are Arnakfaalap."

Despite his injuries, Siqiq insisted he walk on his own once they were away from the quinniq hole. But he stayed close to his father, almost close enough to hold hands. Cho wished Yoskalo would've carried the boy all the way back to the sleds to be safe.

Why did I freeze up? If not for Trini and her screams, the quinniq would've gotten Siqiq down its hole. Would we have ever gotten him out alive?

I shouldn't have come. I should've stayed home or gone to Tanarille like mother wanted.

Chapter 9—Trini

Siqiq's mother scooped him up when they reached the sleds, inspecting his arms and legs and fussing over him.

"Put me down. Put me down." Siqiq squirmed in her arms. His eyes darted to Panuik.

Trini covered a smile with her hands. A wild animal had attacked the boy and tried to haul him off to its den. His wrists and lower legs bled, though from shallow wounds, but his greatest concern was being treated like a baby in front of his cousin.

He would be all right.

The same couldn't be said for the dogs who limped, bloodied, back to the sleds. Three were missing.

"Bring him back to the sleds so I can tend to him," Ahnai ordered.

"I can walk. I'm fine." Siqiq struggled to get down, but Umiak carried him back to the sleds and set him on one. He slid to the ground, glaring at his mother, daring her to put him back up.

"Hueq. Hueq, boy," Ahnai scolded.

Siqiq shut up, chin dropping as he crossed his arms over his chest and glared at his feet.

Ahnai rummaged through a pack on the sled and pulled out a water pouch and a cloth. She whetted the cloth and set about wiping the blood from his arms and legs, leaving behind angry red bite marks. Ahnai set aside the bloodied cloth and retrieved a salve from her pouch. She applied it liberally over the wounds.

He hissed once, but his eyes darted to Panuik once more. He gritted his teeth to silence any further complaints.

While she worked, Trini searched her own backpack for her first-aid kit. She always carried it whenever she went off-world; Aunt Teresa had put it together for her years ago.

She found the antibiotic from her aunt that had been modified for the Nuukimak. Whenever Trini visited a new planet, Aunt Teresa always sent her with some basic medicines developed for the natives for emergency use. The antibiotic would reduce the chance of infection and eliminate contaminants in the bloodstream.

"Here, this is medicine." Trini offered the small pill to Ahnai. "Make him take this with water."

The old woman studied it for a moment, before nodding. "Give it to him."

Trini offered it to Siqiq, but the boy side-eyed the pill, clamping his mouth shut.

"Siqiq," Ahnai scolded.

Grimacing, he reached for the pill. He put it in his mouth and washed it down with water.

While Ahnai bandaged his cuts, Trini checked the latest projections for the storm. It was growing in force. Sixty mile per hour winds, hurling volcanic spewage and poison gases. At its current rate, the storm would hit in less than three hours. A full thirty minutes before they had any hope of reaching the thorneway.

She found Inksuuk and Yoskalo tending to the dogs' wounds.

"We need to get moving," she said. "We have little time before the storm hits."

Inksuuk didn't respond as he wrapped one of the dog's legs.

"Did you hear me?" Trini asked, a little louder this time.

Without looking up, Inksuuk said, "We stay until Ahnai is ready. She is the healer. When she is satisfied with Siqiq's care, we leave."

"They can ride in a sled. The touvak can handle those two," Trini said. Why couldn't she make them understand they had no time to waste?

"Not until Ahnai says we go," Inksuuk said. There was ice in his voice.

Huffing and throwing her arms in the air, Trini returned to Ahnai. "Would it be acceptable for you and Siqiq to ride in the sleds while you tend to his injuries? Things will be very hard for everyone once the storm hits."

Panuik snorted, eyes gleaming maliciously. The edges of Siqiq's mouth turned down. She'd embarrassed him, but she didn't care. Things were getting too crazy to worry about what embarrassed a child.

When Ahnai didn't respond, Trini raised her voice so everyone could hear.

"I don't want to interfere with Siqiq's treatment, but if we fail to reach the thorneway, he'll lose his life."

Ahnai stiffened and turned to her. A heat pulsed in her eyes for a second before they calmed again.

"It is in his best interest for me to examine each wound to avoid infection."

"That's why I gave you the medicine!" Trini exclaimed. "He'll be fine. But none of you will be if we don't get going."

Ahnai glanced once to Inksuuk. He stepped forward in front of Trini, forcing her to step back.

"Perhaps it's best we find other shelter instead," Inksuuk said.

"What?" Trini asked. "There's nowhere safe. Your only hope is to get off this planet with us."

Inksuuk shook his head. "Our path has carried us too far east. Too close to the quinniq's domain. We almost lost a child because of it."

Trini placed her hands on her temples, trying to take calming breaths. "This storm will bring so much dirt and debris you won't be able to breathe, even with the masks. Not to mention the poison gases.

"Even if you find temporary shelter, like the place Taamaruq scouted, it won't take long for your food supply to run out. If you don't die from the lack of breathable air, all the animals will. Plants, too. You'll starve." She was shouting now. "Is that what you want for Panuik? Siqiq? Taamaruq? Your wives and families?"

Inksuuk crossed his arms and opened his mouth to reply. Before he could, Cho stepped forward and grabbed Trini's arm, pulling her way.

"Pardon her, please," Cho said to the Nuukimak. "Let me talk to her."

When Trini tried to pull free, Cho gripped her arm tighter, almost dragging her off to the side.

"What are you doing?" Trini demanded.

"Trust me," Cho said through gritted teeth.

"We don't have time to waste. Do you want to die here? I am trying to get us safely to the thorneway."

"I know," Cho answered. "But your anger is upsetting them. You're driving them away."

Trini felt her mouth drop open in surprise. "What?"

"Haven't you noticed the Nuukimak restrain their emotions? They don't show anger. They're calm. They keep themselves under control."

"What does that have to do with anything?" Trini demanded.

"Right now, they see you as Wolf Spider. Your anger seems a bigger threat than the storm."

"That's crazy!"

Cho shrugged. "It's their culture. Anger is the inability to control one's self. It makes you unpredictable. Dangerous."

Trini wanted to snap that they didn't have time for this foolishness. She debated suggesting that if the Nuukimak were so worried about her anger, then they should go on alone. Let the Nuukimak find shelter while they continued to the thorneway and got help from Space City.

"Let me try to talk to them?" Cho asked.

Trini didn't want to leave them behind no matter how frustrated she was, so she nodded. Normally she prided herself over the Wolf Spider moniker. Was it truly a problem now?

Cho walked back towards the Nuukimak, Trini following. The first thing Cho did was check on Siqiq. She bent down in front of the boy, a big smile on her face.

"How're you feeling?" she asked. "The quinniq attack must've been scary."

Trini bit down on a growl of impatience.

The boy held up his arms and pointed at his bandages as if showing off old war wounds. "It tried to get me, but I got away. But I got hurt."

"I saw. I'm glad you're safe," Cho replied.

Siqiq bent over and peeled back the bandage above his right ankle, pointing out a nasty cut. "This one's huge."

"You're very brave and strong. Your father must be very proud."

The boy puffed his chest out at the compliment. Cho ruffled his hair and stood, turning to Ahnai.

"Will he be okay?" she asked.

Ahnai nodded. "With Atak's blessing. He needs rest, but should be fine as long as we keep his wounds clean."

"That's great," Cho said. "I'm glad Trini scared off the quinniq. I was afraid for him."

Inksuuk and Yoskalo gave Trini uncertain looks.

"It was Trini who saved Siqiq?" Umiak asked.

Cho nodded.

When Umiak's eyes shifted to her, Trini confirmed, "I wasn't about to let him get hurt."

Again, Yoskalo said, "Arnakfaalap. She who inspires fear in the heart of hunters."

It struck Trini, the similarity between the name Yoskalo had given her and her own nickname. Yoskalo said it with respect, but the words didn't feel like an honor.

Cho bent down to Siqiq again. "Are you ready to resume our march?"

"Yes!" the boy's eyes lit up. "I'm ready. I can do this."

"Trini is passionate because she wants to keep you all safe," Cho said to the boy, though loud enough for everyone to hear. "As she said, we're running out of time. Even at a fast pace, we may not make it in time. We may get lost in the storm and never find our way. She's trying to do what's best for everyone."

Ahnai nodded. "As are we all."

"Of course," Cho agreed.

"I care about all of you," Trini added.

Ahnai gave her a quick glance then turned to Inksuuk. "The conditions seem more favorable now." She gestured to the sleds. "Can we all ride again?"

Trini felt her heart beating faster at the possibility.

"Conditions are favorable," Inksuuk answered.

Ahnai nodded. "Then that is what we should do."

Inksuuk gave orders for everyone to shuffle what supplies they could without untying too much.

Chapter 10—Cho

Underway on the sleds once more, Cho and Trini rode alone, except for Yuta driving. Ahnai moved to a sled with Siqiq and his mother to monitor the boy.

The passing landscape—tree and rock after endless tree and rock and mountains—felt eerily calm, belying the danger from the approaching storm and the quinniq. There were no signs of the creatures, but Cho couldn't shake the unease that they were following.

"What's wrong?" Trini asked.

She eyed Cho's hands, one of which gripped the rail of the sled so tightly it hurt. Cho relaxed her grip. Her other hand rested across her arm, fingers splayed, ready to fire her suit weapon.

"What if the quinniq attack again?" Cho asked.

"The scouts are running a perimeter. They'll alert us if the quinniq or anything else breaks it."

Cho shook her head. "The quinniq can hide under the snow. What if the scouts miss them?"

Trini smiled. "The scouts gather visual data on multiple wavelengths—scan for heat signatures, decipher audio at high and low levels, and even detect scents. They'll know if the quinniq get too close."

"That's good," Cho said. "We're not depending on me to spot them."

Trini cocked her head, brow wrinkling. "Why would you worry about that?"

Cho studied her hands, finding it hard to answer. "I didn't… I was afraid… Siqiq almost died because of me."

"What are you talking about? We saved him."

"No." Cho shook her head. "You did. You scared the quinniq off."

"Because you found him."

"And if I'd been there alone?" She saw herself frozen back in the forest, the quinniq dragging Siqiq toward the hole in the rocks.

"You would have saved him," Trini said.

Cho shook her head again. "When the Quinniq had him, I tried to shoot. Wanted to, but I was afraid. And when I did I missed."

Trini laid a hand on Cho's arm, squeezing. "It was chaos. Siqiq's cries echoed off the rocks all around. I had no idea from where. Inksuuk and Yoskalo ran the wrong way. I'd have followed them if not for you. We saved him thanks to you."

Cho wanted to believe that, but she hadn't known. She'd guessed and gotten lucky. That wasn't heroic.

"It was a mistake for me to come," Cho said. "I thought I could be like Riko."

"Who?"

"My older sister."

"I didn't know you had a sister. I've never met her."

"She's fearless." Cho sighed. "But before we came to Space City she was in an accident. She'd gone rock climbing with friends. During her ascent something startled her. She fell. The drop fractured her spine. Left her paralyzed from the waist down." Tears filled her eyes at the memory of her sister lying in a hospital bed, unable to do anything for herself.

Trini opened her mouth to say something, then closed it.

"I came to have adventures like her," Cho rushed on. "For her. But I'm not brave. I've been afraid since we arrived. Afraid we're trapped here. I was afraid riding the sleds up the mountain where one wrong move might send us to our deaths. I was even afraid of the quinniq. I missed my shot because I was too afraid to get closer. I'm a coward."

The word hung in the air between them, a hidden brand exposed.

"You're not a coward. Or if you are, then I am as well, because I've been terrified this whole time."

Cho blinked. "Terrified? You took charge the moment we arrived. And looked calm doing it."

"Calm? We just discussed my lack of calm unnerving the Nuukimak."

Cho chuckled. "You know what I mean. You've been leading us all."

Trini nodded. "Because I focused on one problem at a time and used that as a lifeline to get me through my fears. I'd wager Riko would be afraid in our shoes, too."

Cho doubted her sister feared anything.

"Bravery isn't only shown through physical feats," Trini said. "What about the bravery to pull me aside and tell me I was screwing things up with the Nuukimak? Or the bravery to make them feel safe again?"

A confused jumble of emotions roiled inside Cho.

"Your sister would be proud of what you've accomplished. You were ready for this. And you'll be better—"

Alarms on Trini's wrist-comp echoed across the landscape.

Cho flinched. "What is it?"

Trini tapped on the screen. "The quinniq are following us again."

Cho spun in her seat. She searched the path behind them. "Where?"

"One K back, but approaching slowly," Trini replied as she studied her wrist-comp. "Probably watching for a weak target."

A second alarm sounded. Trini swiped a finger across the screen, before biting her lower lip.

"What is it?" Cho asked, her gut knotted. The quinniq were bad enough without something else to contend with.

After a few moments, Trini said, "That was the new forecast from the satellite. We've got two hours till the storm hits. And projections have worsened. Eighty mile per hour winds hurling ash and dirt in our faces, blinding us. It will be difficult for the touvak to pull the sleds through it."

"How far are we from the thorneway?" Cho asked, hoping they'd shaved off enough time.

"Still about four hours away."

"But we're making better time riding," Cho protested. How could they have lost time?

"The storm is moving faster than projected."

"We need to alert the Nuukimak." Cho whistled and waved her arms.

Inksuuk signaled the others to stop.

Cho barreled out of the sled before it had come to a complete stop, jogging over to Ahnai's sled. Inksuuk and Yoskalo joined them.

"How is Siqiq?" Cho asked.

"He's well," Ahnai answered warily. "No sign of infection. But you didn't stop us to check on him."

It was Trini who spoke as she arrived. "The storm will be here faster than expected. And it's worse than I feared."

"It gets worse," Cho added, casting a glance behind her. "The quinniq are following us."

Inksuuk grimaced. "We're pushing the touvak as hard as we can. In this landscape, it's dangerous to push harder."

"We have no choice," Trini said, a little heat coming into her voice again. She flushed and Cho saw the struggle to calm herself.

"We should find shelter until the storm passes," Yoskalo suggested.

"There's no time," Trini replied.

"We're more vulnerable to the quinniq while traveling," Insuuk said.

Cho sensed the exasperation building in Trini again. The older girl glanced over at Cho, an appeal for help in her eyes.

"Pushing the touvak any harder won't help," Cho said, focusing her plea on Ahnai. "But the last storm lasted for days. This one will last for weeks. Now might be our one chance to reach the thorneway and save your families."

And what about Elsapi and her family? Would they get caught out in the storm? But she could do nothing for the girl right now, so she forced those fears aside.

"Please," Cho said to Ahnai. "Stay with us a little longer."

Ahnai nodded before turning to Inksuuk. "We haven't come this far to lose our children now."

Inksuuk nodded once. "We can push the touvak a little harder."

Cho exhaled. "We can be the rear sled. The scouts will monitor the quinniq. If they get too close, we'll be the first line of defense."

"Thank you," Ahnai said. "Let's not waste any more time."

Chapter 11—Trini

The storm descended on them, first as rising winds howling through the mountains. It whipped up ash mixed with dirt and debris, and hurled it against them. The skies darkened further, slowing their pace and crowding them together. Trini tracked the thorneway's exact coordinates to the current mountain's base on her wrist-comp.

Once more they zigzagged along narrow paths, this time in descent. Trini moved to the front sled with Inksuuk to guide the way.

"Easy. Easy," Inksuuk said, tugging on the touvaks' reins to slow them as they approached a curve in the trailhead.

The touvak gasped and choked, their lungs filling with detritus from the storm. She hated their suffering, but had no way to help them. And they couldn't stop.

Startled shouts from behind was followed by the brays of the touvak and a familiar, terrible rumble. Trini spun around, heart racing. Had another sled gone over the edge? Something small swept past, growing as it rolled down the hill and out of sight.

Inksuuk jerked their sled to a stop. Behind them, one sled had toppled onto its side, dumping its contents over the side of the narrow trail. But the sled hadn't gone off the path. Somehow.

Four touvak strained against the reins of the overturned sled. Yuta rushed to calm them.

Trini activated a flashlight in her wrist-comp to illuminate a short distance down the mountain. The sled's contents had caused a small avalanche, eroding the middle of the path. They were lucky the sled had only carried supplies.

"We need to check the damage," Yoskalo said, joining her. "This may block our way."

Trini wished he hadn't said that last part, an irrational part of her brain thinking if they hadn't voiced it out loud it wouldn't be true. Maybe if she didn't acknowledge it, they'd be fine.

They also didn't have time for another delay. As they started down the trail, Cho caught up with them.

"I can't believe this happened again," Cho said over their suit comms.

"At least we didn't lose anyone," Trini said, relief muted by a new fear. "I hope we didn't lose the thorneway."

"You think the avalanche could've buried it?"

"No," Trini said, though 'yes' pinged in her head. "We'll find a way to it."

The avalanche had left behind a steep grade of loose snow and sediment.

Trini groaned. "The sleds are out." Even travel on foot would be challenging. "What about the touvak?"

Yoskalo shook his head, his hands balling into fists as they came to grips with their new situation.

Trini felt for him. For all the Nuukimak. They'd already lost their homes. Now they would have to abandon everything they'd brought with them, that they'd fought so hard to keep.

Upon their return, they found Inksuuk ordering the others to cut the touvak loose from the sleds and transfer what supplies they could carry to the packs. He'd apparently already guessed the situation. A few Nuukimak protested, but he raised his voice to be heard over the storm.

"We can abandon the sleds here or die with them."

"What if we transfer supplies to the touvak?" one Nuukimak suggested. "Let them carry as much as they can."

"We don't have the time," Trini interjected, hoping they'd see reason.

Inksuuk, after a moment's hesitation, nodded agreement. "Take only what you can carry."

To her surprise, no one offered further complaints. The Nuukimak got to work.

Trini opened her own pack, wanting to shed some weight for the treacherous descent. She tossed her sleeping bag first. She no longer needed it. They wouldn't spend another night here unless the thorneway was buried. If it was, she'd have other concerns than sleeping. She also removed her spare clothes, but kept her few remaining travel rations and the 3D printer and inks.

With that done, she grabbed the reins of a touvak, wanting to help. Nor did she want to abandon the poor beast.

What could they do with the touvak when they reached the thorneway?

Space City didn't have a great place for the creatures. The dogs yes, but the touvak wouldn't be comfortable anywhere. Perhaps Instructor Tereshkova might have ideas.

Inksuuk led them forward once more, setting the pace. Cho, Trini, and Taamaruq followed him. Panuik and Siqiq marched in the middle with their mothers and Ahnai. After the rest of the Nuukimak, Yoskalo brought up the rear. The dogs mixed in among them.

They had to go slow, testing out each step. The howling wind continued to pelt them with debris.

A blinking red light on Trini's wrist-comp alerted her to further warnings from the scouts; she'd turned off the siren to avoid causing another avalanche.

The quinniq.

Trini gritted her teeth. That was all they needed. She sent the warning to Cho, who checked her wrist-comp, before glancing back. Trini couldn't discern her expression, but when Cho turned forward, her shoulders slumped a little more.

The storm and quinniq made Trini want to hurry, even as the poor footing and steep slope forced restraint. With each step, gravel gave way beneath her foot. Her heart beat in terror that one false step, from herself or the touvak, from any of them, might be their last.

They wound their way past one turn then another. As they crossed the center of the path for the fifth time, a small rockslide showered Trini from above. Her head shot up.

Another avalanche?

She braced herself, willing herself to be heavy. "Please don't let the ground give way beneath my feet," she whispered.

Instead, something leapt out of the ground, all teeth and claws. It collided with her leg, biting and slashing at her suit.

Shock gave way to anger at the quinniq's attack. She smacked at it with her fist, knocking it to the ground. She shot it, and the thing went limp, sliding on past her.

Chest heaving, she couldn't believe she remained standing. But her wrist-comp's warning indicated that three more quinniq closed in on her.

You've got to be kidding!

Hoping to catch up with Cho and the more stable path along the edges before the quinniq attacked, Trini pressed forward. A few steps more. Almost there.

Her touvak reared up, kicking its legs. Braying in fear and pain, it charged forward. The reins jerked Trini as the ground gave way beneath her feet. She fell hard, the impact stunning her. Downhill she slid, everything a blur. She flailed arms and legs, desperate for purchase to stop her fall. Rough edges bludgeoned her torso and arms in a dozen places.

Something gripped her arm and yanked her up into the air. She clung to it, terrified she'd lose her grip and get swept away once more.

"I've got you." Inksuuk held her tight. He'd rescued her.

Heart pounding in her ears, all she managed was a nod as she hung on, still not quite believing she was safe. After a moment he set her down. Her whole body tensed, bracing for another fall.

"Trini! Trini, are you okay?" Cho rushed to her, eyes wide, face pale.

"I... I...?" Trini wasn't sure of anything at that moment except that she wanted off that mountain.

She examined herself. Gray and brown stains marred her explorer suit from the ash and dirt she'd slid through, but no holes. Or blood. Her chest and arms ached.

"I'll be fine."

"What happened?" Cho asked. "I heard your touvak cry out in alarm, and when I looked for you, you were falling downhill."

"The quinniq. My touvak!" She searched below for some sign of the poor creature.

Cho pointed back up the path behind them. "Taamaruq settled it down. It's fine."

A short distance up the mountain, Taamaruq held onto two cal touvak.

"Where are the quinniq?" Trini asked, searching for them. There was no sign of them, not even on her wrist-comp sensors.

"Carried away by the avalanche when your touvak bolted," Inksuuk said.

Trini grabbed one of his hands in both of hers. "Thank you. Thank you for catching me. You saved my life."

"We have not reached your way of thorns yet. I had to make sure you got us there." His eyes gleamed, and she felt sure he had a big smile beneath his mask.

"Still, thank you." Trini exhaled, part of her on a high that she'd survived, and the other half eager to get to the bottom. "We should get going."

Inksuuk and Cho nodded.

Trini returned to Taamaruq to retrieve her touvak.

"You're well?" Taamaruq asked, holding reins in both hands.

"I'll manage." Trini stuck out her hand for the reins to her touvak. "Can't afford to stay here any longer."

"I'm glad you are safe." Taamaruq said and they resumed their march.

They reached the mountain's base half an hour later to nothing. There was no visual sign of the thorneway anywhere.

"Where is this way of thorns?" Inksuuk asked, scanning the area.

"I don't know," Trini said, trying to figure out its location based on her wrist-comp.

"Did we come all this way for nothing?" Yoskalo asked.

"Was the place destroyed by the avalanche?" Ahnai asked.

Apprehensive questions passed through the Nuukimak.

"It's here," Trini assured them. Based on the coordinates on her wrist-comp, the thorneway lay buried inside the mountain. "The avalanche sealed the entrance."

"What do we do?" Cho asked, her voice jittery.

There were no signs of the entrance, but with her wrist-comp, Trini could estimate its location. "We need something to dig through to it."

How much debris blocked the way?

"Like shovels?" Cho asked.

"No." Trini shook her head. "That's like emptying a pool with a syringe."

"What about a light grenade?" Cho suggested. "Blast our way through."

Trini pursed her lips, musing. She had enough printing ink for a couple of grenades, but printing one in this storm with all the dust and debris swirling around… even a small amount of contamination could have disastrous consequences.

"What is a grenade?" Taamaruq asked.

"A weapon that creates a big explosion," Trini replied. "It'll get rid of a lot of the debris blocking passage to the thorneway."

Cho studied the mountain above. "But would it cause another avalanche?"

"Probably, but what else can we do?"

Cho said nothing.

"We'll need to cover the grenade during printing to prevent contamination." Trini removed her pack from her shoulders. "I got rid of my sleeping bag thinking I wouldn't need it. And my extra clothes."

"Me, too," Cho said.

"I'll be right back!" Taamaruq rushed toward her touvak.

Trini opened her pack to find a jumbled mess of food, her 3d printer, and a cracked inks case. All her inks had mixed at the bottom of her pack. Her stomach turning at the loss, she turned frantically to Cho. "Tell me you have some inks."

"Yeah." Cho frowned. "What happened?"

Trini raised her broken, empty inks case.

Cho's mouth formed an O, and she removed her own pack and opened it. A moment later she sighed, raising her own still full case.

"That's a relief," Trini said. They'd only get one shot at this.

Taamaruq returned with an old, worn out hide blanket. "This big enough?"

"Where did you get that?" Cho asked, blinking in surprise.

"My touvak. We all have them."

"Brilliant! I should've done that," Trini said, wondering how she'd missed the Nuukimak adding the blankets. She sat on the ground, motioning for Cho to join her. Cold seeped through her suit, chilling her underside. She gestured to the hide blanket. "Can you cover us?"

Taamaruq draped it over the both of them. "How is that?"

The weight of the blanket was a little oppressive.

"Can you raise the center a bit so we can see what we're doing?" Trini asked.

The blanket lifted off her head and shoulders. It smelled musty.

Trini held up her wrist-comp with flashlight on where Cho could see the ingredient ratios for the grenade. Cho measured and poured, taking her time. Wind whipped at the blanket, nearly knocking the 3D printer from Cho's hand.

"Lower the blanket," Trini told Taamaruq, "—as much as you can, but keep it taut."

The blanket rested on her head once more, but with less weight.

Trini dug away the snow and debris from between Cho's legs and laid her print mat on the bare ground. When Cho had finished the mixture, she activated her printer. It rose into the air about belly height. A red light scanned the surrounding space to set the print area, then went to work adding layer upon layer of the grenade. Trini studied it, terrified some contaminant might get mixed in.

It took ten minutes to print, with Taamaruq asking about halfway through if it was working. Trini believed so, but they wouldn't know for sure until they tried to use it.

When the print job had finished, the grenade lying on the print mat looked normal. Trini picked it up gingerly anyway, wrapping it in the mat to keep it covered until they could place it.

Cho removed the touvak blanket from their heads.

"Is it ready?" Taamaruq asked. Inksuuk and Yoskalo cast them questioning glances.

Trini nodded. "Let's hope it works."

"And if it doesn't?" Taamaruq asked, eyeing the blanket-wrapped grenade.

"Then we're in trouble." Trini carried the grenade to the mound of debris blocking the entrance and dug a good-sized hole to stick it down.

Turning back to the Nuukimak, she waved for them to retreat. "We need to away from the immediate area."

She urged them back until they stood a good forty meters from the blast site. She had to use the wrist-comp to measure the distance. Between the darkness and the winds hurling dirt, debris, and volcanic gases at them, she couldn't see the mound blocking the cave entrance.

"Ready?" Her finger hovered over the trigger button on her wrist-comp.

"Go," Cho said, clutching her 3D printer.

Trini took three deep breaths. "Let this work," she whispered. She pressed 'detonate' on her wrist-comp.

Nothing happened.

She glanced at her device. Had she not pressed it properly? More likely the printing process hadn't worked, despite their efforts to protect the print area from contamination.

An explosion erupted. Trini flinched, eyes searching for signs of the explosion. The Nuukimak shouted in surprise. Touvak brayed and bucked. Dogs whined.

"Let's go." Trini ran to the base of the mountain. Had they made things better or worse? The explosion had cleared a lot from the cave entrance, but it remained sealed.

"No!" Trini dove onto the mound. She shoveled away snow with her hands. A branch poked out. She ripped it free and tossed it. She'd failed. After all she'd done to lead them here. Pushing and prodding. After everything they'd endured, this was supposed to be their path to safety, not their end.

Taamaruq put a hand on her shoulder. "Stop. I may have another way."

"What?" Trini asked over her shoulder as she continued to dig even as she knew it would never be enough.

"Your blast exposed a lot of broken trees and rocks."

Trini paused. Taamaruq was right. But how did that help them?

"We've got plenty more blankets. If we tear them into strips and tie the branches to the touvak, they can haul the debris away."

Trini grabbed the nearest branch in both hands and tugged. It rocked back and forth, but wouldn't come free. Growling in frustration, she released it and backed away.

"Okay. Let's do it."

It didn't take the Nuukimak long to divide the blankets and tie the strips together to create longer chains which they secured between the touvak and the largest branches and trunks in the mound. With careful coaxing, the Nuukimak guided the touvak. Coughing from all the debris they inhaled with every breath, the beasts worked hard, straining to pull away the detritus that blocked the cave entrance.

Everyone helped, even as their coughing grew. Those not working with the touvak grabbed rocks or other small pieces and hauled them away. Before long, falling snow and gravel revealed a hole near the top of the cave.

Tears formed in Trini's eyes. They were no longer trapped. They would get through. The Nuukimak had succeeded where she had failed. After everything, it was they who had saved her, not the other way around.

They worked until they'd cleared enough space for the largest of them to fit through, including the dogs.

Inksuuk called a halt to their work. "For everyone's safety, we need to get inside."

"The touvak won't fit through that hole," Taamaruq protested.

"No, they will not," Inksuuk agreed, eyeing the panting beasts. "But I fear we haven't the time to clear enough for them. They've worked hard. Once we are safe, we'll return for them."

Trini hated to agree, especially after the Nuukimak had used the touvak to save them all. But listening to the hoarse coughing all around her, she knew they needed to get the Nuukimak to Space City for medical attention. Everyone looked ready to collapse on the ground.

No one argued further, just assembled according to Inksuuk's instructions. He sent the mothers and children through first. Trini and Cho followed, while the male Nuukimak led dogs inside.

"Where is this way of thorns?" Inksuuk asked, blinking as his eyes adjusted to the light from Trini and Cho's wrist-comps.

"A short distance back," Trini answered, enjoying the quiet inside the cave—the absence of pounding wind hurling volcanic spewage at them.

They found the thorneway twenty meters back from the entrance. Within seconds Trini pulled up the coordinates for Space City and activated the thorneway. She heaved a sigh of relief, her gut easing, as black liquid filled the thorneway.

They'd made it.

"What is this?" Inksuuk asked, frowning at the oily liquid.

"It's a special travel method," Trini said. "It'll take us home."

"Looks like filthy water," Inksuuk said, nonplussed. "And with a cave wall behind it. How can you take us anywhere?"

"I'll show you," Cho answered, stepping through the thorneway, much bolder than she'd been a few days ago. She'd changed a lot since then. And not at all.

After three seconds, when she didn't return, Inksuuk asked, "Did she make it?"

"Hold on," Trini said, holding a hand up.

A few more seconds passed before Cho emerged from the thorneway.

"I told the guards we had you coming with us," she explained, "and requested medical personnel."

"Good thinking." Trini turned to Inksuuk and Ahnai. "Follow Cho through one at a time."

Inksuuk followed first, then both boys, who bubbled with excitement to see where it led. Trini expected it would exceed their wildest expectations.

The other Nuukimak were less eager, but each stepped through the thorneway leading a dog. Trini came through last.

Emerging in the sims warehouse on campus, she took a deep breath and sat at the base of a sims cage, thankful to be home.

The Nuukimak stared, wide-mouthed, at the facility. Siqiq and Panuik darted through the cages, pointing and asking questions. The dogs growled at the guards, but Inksuuk and Yoskalo quieted them.

Seconds later, medical personnel in hazmat suits arrived. An anxious expression marred Aunt Teresa's face until Trini rose and they locked eyes. Then Trini rushed forward and threw her arms around her aunt, hazmat suit and all.

"You're safe!" Aunt Teresa clutched her. "I was worried. We got your notification of trouble from the satellite. We had a ship en route to Nereus. I feared the worst when Cho arrived and requested medical personnel."

Off to one side, Cho hugged her mom. Trini wondered if Cho regretted taking the trip.

"I'm fine," Trini said, "but the Nuukimak have been breathing in volcanic sediments for days, though they have worn facemasks."

Aunt Teresa nodded, taking in the refugees. "Glad you're okay." She gave Trini a once over glance again, then supervised the rest of her staff in leading the Nuukimak back to the University infirmary.

Chapter 12—Cho

Emergency crews needed two days to reach Nereus. Cho and Inksuuk had joined the ship via a thorneway, then Cho spent much of the remaining time worrying about Elsapi. Would they be too late to rescue her and her family?

The storm ravaged the continent, burying it under over three meters of ash in some places. By the time the ship landed at the winter grounds, there was no sign of anyone. They scoured the desolate landscape past the river where the Nuukimak fished during their winters.

Cho began to fear Elsapi and her family had never made it. Had the quinniq attacked them as well? Or had they suffered some other accident? Cho decided she'd hike all the way to back to the Nuukimak village if need be to find the girl.

Voices drifting up out of the ground drew Cho to a deep shaft.

"Anyone down there?" Cho asked, using the flashlight app on her wrist-comp to search for the bottom.

"Yes," a raspy male voice answered. "We're here. Help us!"

"I found someone!" She waved for help.

Everyone closed in around the hole.

"What is this?" Cho asked, hoping Elsapi was among those trapped below.

"A well," Inksuuk explained. "Taps into drinking water for the winter once the river freezes over."

Emergency personnel lowered ropes into the hole and instructed those down there to hook themselves in with straps. After a moment's discussion, they pulled out a woman covered in dirt and grime. Elsapi's mother.

"Is Elsapi with you?" Cho asked. "Is she okay?"

The woman nodded, her eyes dazed and tired. She needed support to stand.

Cho exhaled in relief.

A medic led the mother away for treatment. A few minutes later, Elsapi emerged from the hole wrapped in Tigua's arms. The girl clung to her father and buried her head between his head and one shoulder.

"Do you or your child need medical attention?" another medic asked Tigua.

"Just tired and hungry," Tigua answered.

"If you'll follow me, we can provide food and do a precautionary health check."

Instead, holding his daughter to his chest, Tigua moved toward Inksuuk.

"You made it." Tigua smiled. "Where are the others?"

Inksuuk placed a hand on Tigua's free shoulder. "We made it to Space City. It's...." He hesitated a moment, seeming to search for words. "You'll never believe what it's like. But it's safe, much better than this. Come with us."

"We can't travel," Tigua said "The area's too treacherous. We never would've made it if not for that cleft we found as boys."

Inksuuk smiled. "Ahnai almost killed me for going down there."

"My father as well," Tigua responded.

"We aren't traveling by sled," Inksuuk said, gesturing to the ship. "They have other means of travel."

Noticing it for the first time, Tigua gaped, his eyes widening. "In that?"

"It flies," Inksuuk said.

"We should get inside," the medic interrupted. "Get you checked out and leave."

As they started for the ship, Tigua hesitated and turned back to Cho. "Thank you for coming back for my family. You saved us."

Cho nodded, accepting the thanks, before turning her attention to the little girl.

"Hi, Elsapi. It's me, Cho. Do you remember me?"

The little girl lowered her head to her father's chest where she could see them. Her hair was matted, her face smudged, and her lips a little blue, but she smiled.

“We came to rescue you,” Cho said. “I wanted to make sure you’re okay.”

Elsapid nodded before burying her face back in her father’s chest.

“She’ll be fine, thanks to you,” Tigua said.

Cho teared up. *Elsapi’s alive. She’ll be fine. She’ll have the chance to live her life and make her own choices, whatever those may be.*

Sims System

Chapter 1

Maliek raced across the bullet train's roof as it ascended the mountain slope. Trees whizzed by in a blur. Wind buffeted him, roaring in his ears.

Igata would not beat him this time.

A few paces ahead, the Bazij leapt from the end of one train car to the next. Her slick gray skin reminded him of a dolphin. With each jump, the tips of the three short orange horns on Igata's forehead caught the sunlight and shone like embers.

Maliek jumped after Igata, determined to catch up with her. As he landed on the next car, his right foot slipped. He fell to one knee. Pain vibrated through the tendons down his leg to his ankle. His magnetic gloves locked onto the bullet train's roof, holding him in place. He clenched his teeth and breathed through the pain before rebounding to his feet and resuming the race. Igata had extended her lead to more than a half car's length.

As the bullet train neared the mountain's peak, its roof began blinking red. Maliek skidded to a halt, his arms extended wide to maintain balance. Igata hurdled to the next car and froze before the blinking roof turned solid red.

"You won't beat me again," he shouted.

She half turned her head back toward him, though he couldn't be sure if she'd heard him, or was gauging her lead. Tiny indentations on the side of her head served as ears and she lacked any hair. A couple of hoop rings protruded from the right side of her lower lip.

The train crossed the peak, one of a half dozen mountains grouped together to form a roller-coaster chain. Two other bullet trains raced along other slopes.

Beyond the mountains, a dozen flying saucers fired laser beams at each other in a mock battle. Beside them, large log boats plunged down one kilometer water slides into ocean waters. There they transformed into submarines that took their riders on scenic tours of the deep. On a nearby low-gravity moon, guests rode bouncing dune buggies through craters. The shielded buggies collided with each other, knocking their riders in all sorts of directions.

The train started its descent. Its roof blinked green and red for a few seconds before going all green. Maliek charged ahead once more, intent on making up ground. It was a pleasure to run again, something he hadn't done since before the outbreak.

As he neared the front of his car, Igata dove off the side to a hover car that paced the train. She veered away.

Advancing to the next car, Maliek peeked over his right shoulder. Another hover car shot out of a tunnel and approached.

The bullet train jolted. Maliek froze again, crouching with arms wide. This time he didn't bang his knee for which he was grateful. The hover car reached the front of his train car and maintained pace alongside it.

Knowing it wouldn't stay for long, Maliek vaulted off the side into the hover car. Clamps rose from its floor and locked around his ankles, while a steering wheel emerged to waist height. He grabbed the wheel and steered the hover car sharply down a side pass into an eight-lane tunnel. It's walls, ceiling, and floors glowed with neon graffiti. Thousands of pictures and messages lit the way through the five-kilometer-long tunnel. Maliek accelerated to the hover car's max speed: one hundred fifty kilometers-per-hour.

He loved the Bazij sims—the energy and heightened alertness he felt whenever he entered them. Much better than the real world where, at the moment, he couldn't walk more than a quarter mile before he had to rest. His recovery from the Azymi fungus remained slow. His mother ensured he attended every physical therapy session and did more than his allotted daily exercises. She had already raised the possibility that he wouldn't be physically ready to participate in the Games this fall, at least the early part of the season.

But here in the Bazij sims where he could run and jump even faster and higher than before, he felt like himself again.

Better.

Ahead, the tunnel split into two, the left half rising while the right drilled deeper. Igata chose the latter.

Maliek chased after her. Through this part of the tunnel, sharp turns forced him to cut his speed to around seventy-five miles per hour.

Right turn. Another right. Left, down, right again, up—Maliek faced a dead-end wall a hundred meters ahead with no visible side passages, nor any sign of Igata.

His instincts screamed at him to stop. Rather than brake as he'd done his first time through this tunnel, nearly getting rear-ended, he accelerated. The hover car crept toward eighty then eighty-five. At the last minute, before he crashed into the tunnel wall, the floor dropped, sending him careening into a new, wide open tunnel slick with ice.

Skis emerged from the hover car as he landed. The back end of the car kicked out. Rather than fight the slide, he turned with it. The car straightened from its skid just as he reached a slalom course, Igata ahead.

He steered the car through the series of flags. Each pair he passed between gave him a temporary speed boost. Igata missed a flag pair, then a second, allowing him to close the gap. He neared her rear bumper as light filled the tunnel ahead.

Passing through the final flag pair gave him another short speed burst out of the tunnel. The reemergence into full sunlight forced him to shade his eyes and adjust the tinting on his eye contacts, but he thought he had enough speed to catch Igata over the final twenty-five meters. They could no longer speed up, having to use their momentum to coast to the finish.

About five meters out, as he pulled alongside Igata, she bumped him. His hover car swerved to the right. He jerked the steering wheel left, steadying, but the slue cost him his momentum. She coasted across the line in first place and slid up a steep embankment of snow until her hover car eased to a stop.

"You cheated!" Maliek jumped from his car as it stopped beside her. But his accusation was half-hearted. He loved racing her.

Igata shrugged. "You didn't try hard enough. I wanted it more."

Not for the first time, Maliek wondered if Igata looked like her avatar. He'd asked once, but she'd shrugged off the question. 'What did it matter when we live our full lives in the sims?' she'd asked.

They had long ago cocooned their bodies and left them to AI droids to tend.

As much as he loved the Bazij sims, with millions of worlds, all with amazing designs and unusual properties, he couldn't imagine giving up the real world and living inside one.

"What are you thinking about, Maliek Johnson?" she asked.

He dropped his eyes to the ground, grimacing as he realized he'd been staring at her. "Nothing."

She moved over, snow crunching underfoot, and bumped his shoulder with her own. "Come on," she challenged. "You were absent there for a minute."

He shook his head. "I just… I thought I had you there at the end."

She shot him a beatific smile. "You never had me."

They stood there in silence a moment, Maliek unable to think of a clever comeback. Their breaths puffed out in a milky cloud. The tips of his ears burned from the cold.

"How long until you need to head back?" she asked.

He checked his wrist-comp. His parents expected him home for dinner in an hour. He needed fifteen minutes to get from the sim's studio on Space City to his home.

"I'm good for another thirty minutes," he said.

"What's it like to walk between places?"

"What?"

"Out in the old world," Igata said.

He shrugged. "About like walking here. We can't instantly travel anywhere like you can within the sims."

He wished he could step out of the sims into his home. He'd have more time here with her.

"Is it the same?" she asked. "Moving about in your own body. Your home on Space City. The universe. Do the sims truly mirror it?"

Maliek shrugged. "Some things, yes. Others, no."

They walked to the top of the snow mound. Overhead, triangle-shaped boats floated through the air. Most held families with little children thrilled at the prospect of flying.

"There are no theme parks close to Miran-silya's size in the real world. They'd disappoint you."

"I'd kinda like to see them," she said. "Feel what the old world is like."

The statement surprised him. He didn't know how to respond. Most Bazij scorned those who still lived outside of sims. With their bodies tucked away in their cocoons, protected from disease, accidents, and pretty much any other bodily harm, they never worried about so much as breaking a bone. They spent their lives in perfect health doing whatever they wished. The Bazij couldn't comprehend how others could, in good conscience, expose themselves and others to harm in the old world. To them, it was pure arrogance and selfishness to do so.

"If I wanted to leave the sims to visit the old world, my world, would you visit me?" she asked.

He hesitated. He longed to say yes; wanted to see her, rather than her avatar. But Melathia, her home planet, was on the Space City banned travel list.

"Are you sure you want to leave the sims?" he asked. "Aren't you afraid of getting sick or hurting yourself?"

"Oh, I wouldn't leave for long," she said. "I just want to experience the old world one time. Understand why so many like you still live out there. Will you come visit me?"

"I'd like to," he said, his voice trailing off, which embarrassed him.

A coy smile broke across her face. "How about this? I want to see the old world and I want someone to share it with. I'd like it to be you, not some emotionless AI droids. So, if you want to see me again, then come to Melathia."

With that, she disappeared.

Chapter 2

Maliek signed off, waking in the sims rig at Space City Sims. He unstrapped the harness holding him suspended inside a near floor-to-ceiling rotating ring.

What was Melathia like? The Bazij had transitioned to living in the sims decades ago. Would nature have reclaimed most of it?

He'd likely never find out. With Melathia on the banned travel list, he had little chance of receiving an exception to visit. Would Igata hold that against him? She couldn't. Unless she was unreasonable like Kiera, who had broken up with him last year because he wouldn't skip Games practices to spend more time with her.

Sighing, he exited the private, soundproof sims rig room and returned to the studio entrance. Velos, the Kali proprietor, hovered over a series of monitors behind a counter. The two dozen monitors showed each of the individual sims rig rooms in the studio. He also received health and stress data on each user. If something went wrong, he could deactivate any sims rig.

"How's Igata doing?" Velos asked, his voice raspy. Like all Kali, Velos possessed a form that resembled black smoke. He could mold it to whatever shape he desired. For the comfort of his customers, he maintained a human male form in the studio.

Did he keep that when he wasn't at work?

"We visited Miran-silya today," Maliek replied. "Raced the bullet trains again."

"Ah, yes," Velos said. "Speed and danger. The preferred pastimes of youth. At least for those with physical bodies. Did you win?"

Maliek gave him a sheepish grin. "She rammed my hover car right before the finish line. I recovered, but not fast enough."

"Don't underestimate the value of the girl you like winning the games you play together," Velos said. A portion of the smoke on Velos's face darkened and curved upward into something resembling a pseudo smile.

Maeliek stared out the studio front window. The foot traffic wasn't bad. He shouldn't have much trouble making it home in time for dinner. "A lot of good it does when I can't visit her."

"A minor obstacle."

"Minor?" Maliek glanced back at the Kali, wondering if he was joking. "Melathia is on Space City's banned travel list."

Velos's smile widened into a large 'O' that reminded Maliek of a snake trying to inhale prey too large for it. "I visit Melathia twice a month."

Maliek blinked. "You do? How?"

The Kali gestured toward the rear of the shop. "I've got a private thorneway."

Maliek glanced down the hallway, despite knowing all he'd see were closed doors. He'd been down it enough times. "You can visit Melathia?"

He knew rich people, or those in certain positions, had their own private thorneways. Wouldn't Space City travel bans apply to them as well?

"I conduct business with the Bazij," Velos explained. "Most of it I do through the sims, but I sometimes need to visit in person."

"Why? I thought all Bazij lived in sims?"

Velos nodded. "Deliveries. When I visit, I speak to them through their AI droids."

Would it really be possible for him to visit Igata? "Why is Melathia on the banned travel list?"

"Because the Bazij are hyper-concerned about contamination from a virus or bacteria that is alien to their planet. Not only do they hide their bodies and live in sims, but they don't want visitors that might harm their planet, and by extension, them. Space City respects the Bazij's wishes. The ban prevents accidents."

"So how can you go?"

"I have a special exemption due to my business; Bazij-approved," Velos said.

"How does that help me?" Maliek asked.

"The Bazij have quarantine facilities on their planet for visitors. Rarely used, but they do exist."

"Wouldn't I need approval?" Maliek asked, his hopes rising.

"I could hire you. Send you on a business trip in my stead."

"Really?"

Velos's off-putting smile returned. "Sure, if you wouldn't mind working part time for me, at least for the rest of the summer."

"Doing what?"

Velos patted the monitors. "Keep an eye on the customers while they're in the sims. Clean the rigs at the end of the day. The occasional delivery."

"Sure," Maliek blurted. He didn't love the idea of cleaning the rigs, but he'd do it if it meant more time using the sims. "Would I still have to pay to use the sims?"

"No, but you can't do it while on the clock, and only when there's at least three open rigs."

That would limit him to evenings or early mornings, but he could deal with that. "When can I start?"

"Tomorrow if you want. I've already got a business trip scheduled. You can make the delivery in my stead, assuming I can get approvals ready in time."

"Wow, okay. Count me in."

"Of course, if Igata left the sims to visit you, she'd have to quarantine in the facility for two weeks after your visit. Perhaps even a month to ensure she didn't catch anything from you that would harm the rest of the Bazij."

"Oh." Maliek's excitement plummeted. "Could she enter the sims from within the quarantine facility?"

Velos seemed to cough. "They won't take any risks with the population, which includes through their sims."

Maliek's stomach roiled.

"It's a big sacrifice she'd be making," Velos said, seeming to read the guilt on his face. "For young love, perhaps it's one worth making. That is her choice?"

"I don't know," Maliek said, unsure he wanted to admit to Igata that he could visit her. Not when she'd pay such an enormous price for it.

He checked his wrist-comp. Ten till seven. He'd have to rush home or be late for dinner.

"I'll think about it," he told Velos as he hurried from the studio.

As he rode the moving walkway through the city, he thought out a message to Igata. Thanks to a neural modification to the tradutor, the language-translation device, he could dictate messages to his wrist-comp by thought.

Not sure if visiting Melathia's a good idea. How can I ask you to risk your safety by leaving the sims for a month to see me? What if I unknowingly carried something that got you sick?

He waited for a response as he hurried along the moving walkway through the city. He wished he could jog, but he still lacked endurance.

I want to see you, Igata wrote back. *Nothing bad will happen. I want to see for myself what the old world is like, and I don't want to do it alone.*

Should he argue further or agree? He wanted to go. Wanted to see her.

Velos had suggested that he let her decide if she wanted to risk seeing him. But the potential danger and sacrifice for her was great.

Another message came through from Igata.

Don't you want to see me?

Chapter 3

The next morning Maliek told his parents he was returning to the Academy for the next week. As he'd lain in bed the previous night, struggling for a plausible excuse for his absence, he'd made up a special summer engineering program. This morning, his mother had gushed over his smarts for getting into the program, his initiative in taking a class over his summer break, and what it meant for his future.

Afraid she'd start showering him with questions, he'd scarfed down his breakfast and rushed off, insisting he didn't want to be late, though he didn't escape without receiving a hug and final praise on his way out the door.

Guilt tugged at him as he headed toward Space City Sims, but it paled compared to his growing excitement, and nervousness, at the prospect of seeing Igata in person.

Inside the studio, he found a line of people for the sims. He took a seat in the corner, hands jittery. Was he actually doing this? Visiting a planet on the banned list? He half expected Velos to retract the offer of employment and travel, relegating him to a week alone at the Academy to keep up the lie to his parents.

Velos ushered the last person to their sim room and returned. Maliek stood, clenching and unclenching his fists.

"You ready to travel?" Velos asked.

"You're sure it's okay?" Maliek wanted the Kali to take him to Melathia, yet a part of him wanted Velos to backtrack on his offer.

"Got the approval for you to travel in my stead first thing this morning. A simple delivery, then you're free to spend a few days with Igata," Velos answered. "When you get back, we'll figure out a work schedule for you."

Maliek hoped everything went that well. "What am I delivering?"

"First, I need you to do a health scan," Velos said. "The Bazij want confirmation that you're healthy."

"Sure." Maliek pulled up the health scanner app on his wrist-comp and conducted a scan of his body. After several uncomfortable minutes where he stressed that the wrist-comp would tell him he was coming down with something that he didn't' have symptoms for yet, the device chimed with his results.

"All clear!"

The Kali drifted behind his counter and retrieved another wrist-comp. "I need your wrist-comp."

"What for?" Maliek instinctively covered his device with his free hand.

"You can't take yours with you." Velos held out the new device. "You'll take this company one instead."

Maliek eyed it, but didn't reach for it. He hadn't handed over his wrist-comp to anyone in years, not even his parents. Space City rules dictated everyone kept their wrist-comps on them at all times, especially when visiting alien worlds. It allowed for quick location in an emergency.

"For travel to Melathia it's necessary," Velos said, guessing his thoughts. "We don't want a Bazij hacking into your wrist-comp while you're there."

"But why…?" Maliek began, wondering who would want to hack into his.

"The Bazij government employs excellent hackers. They consider it normal procedure to steal data from foreign governments. If you take your wrist-comp, someone will break into it, steal whatever information they can find, and exploit it."

"But I don't work for our government." Maliek couldn't believe anyone would bother with him. He had nothing of interest.

"To the Bazij, every individual is a part of their respective government. They don't see a distinction. It's safer for you and anyone you know if you travel with a clean wrist-comp. No personal information is stored on it, except my contact number so you can reach me when you're ready to return."

Was he making a mistake? Bazij hackers trying to steal his personal data gave him pause. *Is there more to Melathia being on the banned travel list than Velos is letting on?*

"You can use this one same as yours. It has all your standard features. Just be careful what you access or who you contact while on Melathia. Don't log into anything personal and you'll be fine. It's the price of doing business with the Bazij."

Maliek hadn't planned on messaging anyone. Certainly not his parents, where he'd risk conversations that required more lying. Still, giving up his wrist-comp… that felt like getting dropped in the ocean without a boat, lifejacket, or lifeline.

"Don't worry. Lock your wrist-comp and I'll store it in the safe while you're gone."

"All right." Maliek relented, removing his device and handing it over.

Velos traded him the new one, which Maliek strapped in place. Then the Kali secured his device in a safe behind the counter.

"It'll be right here when you return," Velos promised.

Still uneasy about the exchange, but eager to see Igata, Maliek followed the Kali down the hall and into a back room. A cart parked next to a thorneway frame held a hefty metal crate.

"What am I delivering?" Maliek asked.

"New connection ports for our sims rigs. The Bazij use them to update their interfaces to our systems." Velos activated the thorneway. "Ready?"

Maliek took a deep breath, wanting to step forward and retreat at the same time. But seeing Igata in person meant taking a chance. With a simple nod, he strode forward.

"Let me know when you're ready to return," Velos said. "Hope to hear some scandalous stories."

Maliek's eyes widened, his face burning, as he pushed the cart through the thorneway.

******

The thorneway deposited Maliek and the cart in a windowless room, with only the thorneway frame behind him and a single arched exit. Had Velos sent him to the wrong place?

The moment the thorneway deactivated, the far door opened. In marched a bronze droid with three short, dark gray horns on its forehead. That wasn't what Igata had meant by seeing him in the real world, was it?

"Igata?"

"Bazij attendant at your service." The droid stopped before the cart. Vein-like cables covered its arms and legs.

Maliek grimaced. He'd hoped she'd be the one here to greet him, but it made sense that one of the facility droids would pick up the delivery. Maliek pushed the cart handles toward it.

"Can you verify your identity first?" the droid asked.

Maliek blinked. Without his wrist-comp, he didn't have his ID.

"I… um… give me a second."

He activated the company wrist-comp to contact Velos, and noticed a redacted version of his ID. Relieved, he offered it to the droid. A light from its eyes slid across the wrist-comp's screen.

"ID verified." It took control over the cart and wheeled it toward the door. "Follow me."

The droid led him through the facility, down windowless hallways and closed doors. Numerous cables, similar in design to the ones on the droid, covered the walls and crisscrossed the halls above doorways in haphazard fashion. The place was devoid of dust or debris, but stale air filled the hallways.

Other than the two of them, the facility appeared deserted. Nor did the droid seem programmed for hospitality. It set a swift pace and said nothing.

At last they entered a room with glass walls on three sides, revealing that the facility rested atop a remote mountain. Clouds hugged snowcapped peaks all around them, making him feel he was alone on the entire planet. That might be true, unless he counted the droid. At least until Igata arrived.

"Where's Igata?" Maliek asked, wondering if they'd spend his entire visit here in quarantine. It would be a shame not to hike some of those mountains.

"I apologize," the droid said. "Igata's original estimated arrival time coincided with yours. My data indicates she encountered a delay. She plans to join you soon."

It retreated with the cart to the door.

"Wait!" Maliek reached for the droid even though it was out of arm's length. "You're leaving me here alone?"

"I must handle this delivery. Refreshments will arrive soon," the droid replied. "Igata is in transit. Enjoy the view."

At that, it exited.

This trip was not starting off as he'd hoped. He reminded himself this was her first visit in the real world. Unexpected delays shouldn't come as a surprise. They'd likely encounter other issues as she got accustomed to her body and, more significantly, the limitations of physics.

He grabbed his wrist-comp as he sat on a single bench facing outside. He entered the messages app and added in Igata's contact information. Then he dictated a quick note to her.

"Arrived. Can't wait to see you. This week will be great!"

Chapter 4

After an hour in the glass room with only the mountain ranges for company, the door opened. Maliek jumped to his feet, ready to greet Igata, but her name died on his lips. Instead of her, the AI droid had returned.

"Where's Igata?"

Something had gone wrong. Had she changed her mind? Had her family prevented her from leaving the sims?

"Small plans change," the droid said. "I will escort you to Igata now."

"Great," Maliek said, relieved that he'd still be seeing her.

"If you'll follow me," the droid said.

It returned him through the cable-covered hallways to a platform resembling an elevator. The back wall rose to waist height, revealing a massive room on the other side. Countless artificial spheres, about three meters in height, filled the place. Myriad cables surrounded and connected with the bronze orbs.

"What are those?" Maliek asked.

"Covums. For the Bazij," the droid replied.

"Are all the Bazij kept here?"

"No. There are eight hundred sixty-three facilities on Melathia."

"How many Bazij are here?"

"Ten million three hundred ninety-eight thousand, six hundred and twenty-seven," the droid replied.

"All in this one room?" Maliek asked, reeling at how large this cavern must be to hold them all.

"Other storage rooms exist within this facility," the droid replied.

The platform descended, carrying them past hundreds of covums. This was where the Bazij kept their bodies while living out their lives in the sims. Had he met any of the Bazij stored here?

Then he realized of course he had. Igata—

"Are you taking me to Igata's covum?" He hadn't expected to see her removed from the sims. Would she come out naked? The droid wasn't carrying anything. "Do we need to get clothes for her?"

The lift stopped at a narrow floor, covums attached to the wall all along the perimeter. They exited to a floor which provided little walking space between the covums and the low wall looking out over the vast cavern—a sight at once daunting in its enormity, yet also vulnerable. A giant nest. If a predator got in, he wouldn't want to put his faith in this droid to save them.

The droid stopped before a covum. It pressed one finger into a hole in the side, and the covum hissed as it opened.

Was this it? He glanced into the opening, then diverted his eyes, unsure what to do. This wasn't how he expected to meet Igata in person.

But it was empty.

"Get in to see Igata," the droid commanded.

Maliek took a step backwards. "What? No. Igata's visiting me here."

"Get in the covum to see Igata," the droid repeated.

"No way!" Maliek's stomach churned. "This isn't what we agreed to."

His eyes shifted from the droid to the empty covum and back. He retreated toward the lift. What was going on?

"Insertion assistance protocol activated," the droid said. Two other droids appeared, seeming to materialize out of nowhere. They seized his arms.

"Stop!"

He struggled to break free as they dragged him toward the open covum. He recalled Velos's warning about hackers. He didn't have his wrist-comp with personal information. Had someone devised another plan to exploit him?

"I don't want to go in the covums. You can't force me."

Except they could. None of his efforts to fight free worked. He reached for his wrist-comp, but the droid holding his left arm jerked it behind his back. A jolt of pain shot through his arm.

"Send message to Velos," Maliek shouted.

A droid's hand clamped over his mouth, silencing him.

He planted his feet and push backward, fighting for leverage. The droids lifted him clear off the ground. Suspended in the air, unable to make a sound beyond a moan, he kicked futilely as they deposited him inside the covum.

They strapped his arms and legs in place, then covered his mouth as well. He screamed, panic flooding through him, as the covum closed, locking him in darkness. He fought against his restraints, which only made them tighter.

This couldn't be happening. They couldn't do this to him.

A white screen appeared before him asking if he'd like to initiate the sims insertion sequence. He struggled against his bonds. When that didn't work, he shouted, voice muffled by the gag. "No, I don't want to go in the sims. I want out."

The 'Yes' button blinked and a loading sign appeared.

"No! Stop. Let me out!"

A stinging scent filled his nostrils, making his eyes water. Too late, he tried to stop breathing. All sensation of himself, his body, his prison evaporated. He felt his consciousness pulled under.

The void lasted only a moment before he appeared on the outskirts of a giant city stretching one hundred meters or more into the sky. Bright lights pushed back dark skies. The covum and his restraints had vanished. A familiar rush of energy welled up inside him.

Igata approached, but she was different. Older. Expression flat. There was no warmth in her demeanor. Her gray skin seemed paler. Her three horns, always so bright orange before, had dimmed like light bulbs running low on power.

"What's going on?" Maliek asked. "Why did they put me in the sims? I thought we were meeting on Melathia?"

"I'd never enter the old world," Igata said, nose scrunching in disgust.

"Then why invite me here?"

"To save you. The covums are more suitable for permanent insertion."

The word 'permanent' sent a chill sliding down his back. "What are you talking about?"

"I brought you here to live in the sims, same as we do."

He stared at her in shock. "Is this a joke?"

Her face had a hardness about the eyes. No hint that this was a prank. Or misunderstanding.

She gestured into the city. "It's a wonderful place to live. So many opportunities."

Why was she doing this?

He backed away from her. "You can't keep me here. I'll contact Space City, let them know where I am and request help."

"This is our closed system," Igata said, unperturbed. "There is no means of contacting anyone from here."

He grabbed his wrist-comp, the avatar version of it, which worked inside the sims. He typed a message to Velos.

"Your message won't go anywhere. You're cut off."

He finished the message and sent it. "Velos knows I'm here. When I don't return, he'll know something's wrong."

Igata sighed, as if she was tired of the conversation. "Velos is a recruiter. He will inform no one."

He shook his head, mind scrambling. This had all been a trap. A plan to lure him here and imprison him. Had Velos betrayed him?

"Let me go. Please," he pleaded.

Rather than respond, she disappeared, leaving him alone on the edge of the city.

Chapter 5

Igata had lied about Velos betraying him.

Uncertainty nagged at him. She had invited him to Melathia, a banned planet, and Velos just happened to own a private thorneway in his studio. Space City sims did interface with the Bazij system though, so it made sense that he might need to conduct business with them in person. Except with whom, when all Bazij lived in the sims?

Velos had also convinced him to leave behind his wrist-comp against Space City rules. And his wrist-comp provided the primary means by which his parents or Space City leaders could identify or track him. His family would track his wrist-comp to Velos's studio and learn where he'd gone. All thorneways kept records of their traffic. And Velos *had* provided him another wrist-comp for emergencies.

But if Velos had tricked him, he might know how to deactivate the wrist-comp so no one could track it.

Maliek searched the messenger system for his parents. A 'Contact Not Found' notice popped into the air in front of him. He dictated a short message anyway, telling them that he was a prisoner and needed help.

Then he checked everyone he knew who used the Bazij sims. Each time he received a 'Contact Not Found' error, panic grew a little further, like a plant sprouting in his stomach and rising into his chest.

He sent messages regardless.

Was everything Igata said true? Was he in a closed system cut off from everyone he knew? And why had he trusted her? He should've known something was wrong about her invitation to visit. The Bazij all viewed living in the real world as dangerous. And having lived their whole lives in sims, they weren't accustomed to using their bodies. Igata couldn't have interacted with him in the real world in that short a time span. He should've known better.

When he started to receive 'undeliverable message' errors, he crumpled to the ground. After the undeliverable notice for his parents, his heart throbbed in his chest like a dam threatening to burst. He'd lied to them that morning. They thought he'd gone to the Academy. He might never see them again. And they'd never know where he'd gone. For the rest of their lives they'd wonder what happened to their son who vanished one day on his way to school.

He buried his face in his hands. For a time, he lost all sense of the world around him as his thoughts cycled through the day's events. Igata had no right to do this to him.

He'd never go to the Academy and see his friends again.

No! He'd find Igata and force her to let him go.

He'd never participate in the Games again or explore new worlds.

He shook his head, determined to destroy the sims system if he necessary in order to escape.

He'd never hug his mom again.

Mental exhaustion drove him to his feet. He wandered toward the city, thinking only to escape the darkness. And the bright city lights left no place for darkness, illuminating every bit of the soaring buildings.

Without the limits of physics, the city took on all kinds of unusual shapes. Buildings connected in ways and at angles that would be impossible in the real world. A giant, interconnected Jenga city with so many pieces removed or sticking out at odd angles that it should crumble.

A buzz filled it all. Bazij ate, drank, paraded, scaled the sides of buildings. Some leapt from ledge to ledge at impossible heights, before dropping to the ground with a superhero landing. In the sims, everyone had superpowers if they wanted them. Greasy and sugary aromas saturated the surrounding air.

Maliek approached an old Azzaro man resting in a chair at the entrance to a convenience store. Music with heavy bass blared inside.

"Excuse me, sir. I need some help." Maliek kept his voice hushed.

The Azzaro sized him up, then lifted a green bottle to his lips and took a deep swig.

"I've been kidnapped," Maliek said. "I'm from Space City."

The Azzaro diverted his gaze, pretending he hadn't heard.

"Please, can you help me contact my family?"

Scowling, the Azzaro waved him away with a dirty, wrinkled hand.

"At least point me to where I can get help."

Eyes still studying passersby, the Azzaro replied, "I'm sorry kid, I can't get involved. You're on your own."

Maliek gaped, unable to believe what he'd heard. The Azzaro shifted uncomfortably, as if Maliek's closeness unsettled him.

"Get out of here, before I call the authorities," the Azzaro warned.

Maliek hurried off. The last thing he wanted was for Igata to return. Or a droid.

Among the Bazij he passed, some had horns on their foreheads while others didn't. Among those with horns, the number ranged from one to three for most, though he spotted someone with six. The horns came in a wide variety of colors, some orange like Igata's, others purple, teal, or a darker gray than their skin. Was the variety natural? Something from the real world? Or did they just enjoy embellishing their avatars?

He didn't dare approach any of them for help. Whom could he trust? Igata hadn't been who she'd led him to believe.

Why had she lured him here? Why lock him in a covum and imprison him in this closed system? His parents weren't rich. Nor did they hold leadership positions within Space City. What could Igata want from him?

He wandered, avoiding everyone as much as he could. He kept his head lowered. If anyone paid him too much attention, he'd detour along the nearest side street. His caution likely meant very little if Igata wanted to find him. She'd locked him in a sim. If she or anyone else with control wanted him, it wouldn't take much to locate him and materialize at his side. He was a mouse that Igata had dropped in a maze to study. An endless maze without an exit. Or any cheese. And like a mouse, he had no clue about his captors' intentions.

Not long after sunrise—a simulated one (he'd likely never see a real one again)—he stumbled on a park deep in the city. In one corner, Bazij played all sorts of games, shoes thudding on the courts. Some games he recognized, like basketball and dodgeball, but many others he didn't.

Beyond the courts, people climbed through a complex column of bars. Younger kids ran squealing through a series of tunnels, while their parents talked off to the side. In an outdoor workshop, kids of all ages hammered and sawed on wood scraps, which seemed a little crazy. They lived in a sim where they never needed to build anything again. Add a little code to the sim, and they had anything they desired. Why did they need to learn to build anything?

As he reached the park's far corner, he found a crowd his own age lounging on benches. A Traga, two Bazij, an Azzaro, and a couple other species he couldn't identify, assuming their avatars weren't complete fabrications. After all, people could pretend to be anyone online. Until now he'd never quite accepted that. He had always believed the danger minimal, more likely to happen to someone on a questionable alien planet… like Melathia, on the banned Space City travel list.

How could I have been so stupid? I deserve this punishment.

Would it be permanent? His eyes burned, but he blinked to clear them. He wouldn't cry in front of these strangers. He almost ran from the park, but after so much walking his feet begged him to rest. He didn't feel hungry or thirsty despite having nothing to eat or drink in… how many hours had it been?

The covum. It fed and hydrated him. He'd never eat or drink anything ever again. Or go to the bathroom? How did that work? Unbidden images floated to mind.

"What's wrong with you?"

The Traga in the group had spoken to Maliek; they all stared at him now. He realized he'd been wrinkling his face in disgust.

"Nothing. Sorry. Nothing," he said, averting his eyes. He took a step to go.

"This one has the look of a new root," an Azzaro taunted. He had a green mohawk and three earrings in his left ear.

"Couple hours planted at most," a male Bazij agreed. The two horns on his brow shone neon yellow. A color-matching tattoo covered the left side of his neck down into his shirt.

"Root?" Maliek asked.

"Someone newly planted in a covum," the Azzaro with the mowhawk said.

A chill ran through Maliek. If they could tell, everyone else would, too. Right now was not the time to stand out.

"Definitely a root."

"Are there many?" Maliek asked, wondering how often this occurred.

"Every one of us," a Macab said. Instead of the traditional white fur, this one possessed neon blue.

"Even them?" Maliek asked, gesturing to the couple of Bazij.

"What do you mean, even us?" the Bazij with the yellow tattoo demanded. He flexed sinewy muscles.

"Calm, Rikus," a Bazij female said, slapping Tattoo Boy on the chest. She possessed green horns, four of them. "He's in shock." She offered Maliek a smile. "Everyone in this sim is a prisoner."

"Everyone?" Maliek asked. "Why would the Bazij imprison their own here?"

"Because we're sympathizers," Rikus said.

"We don't agree with capturing and forcing others to live here against their will," the Bazij female clarified. "Those of us here tried to do something about it. As punishment, they threw us in here, too."

"Why me?" Maliek tapped his chest. "I've done nothing."

"None of us have," the Macab said.

"For the same reason we Bazij live in the sims," the female Bazij explained. "Safety."

"Safety?" Maliek asked. "I'm not a danger to the Bazij."

"You live in the old world. To many Bazij, that presents a danger, to them and to yourselves. Imprisoning you here is viewed as a public good."

Maliek pictured the huge covum room with millions stored together. "Aren't they worried about putting us in the covums near you? Aren't contaminations possibly passed through them?"

Rikus snorted. "That facility is for outsiders only."

"You mean they kidnapped everyone in that facility?" Maliek rocked back on his heels.

"Some might have come on their own," the female Bazij said.

Maliek doubted many of them had chosen. Which meant that what had happened to him was a widespread problem. How did no one know?

"Is there any way out? Any way to get help?" Maliek asked.

No one met his gaze before the Azzaro spoke.

"If there were, none of us would be here."

Chapter 6

Maliek sank to a bench.

"Is the root going to cry?" Rikus sneered.

"Cut him a break," the Bazij female said. "Your first day inside, you curled up in a ball in the tot tunnels, bawling."

"I'm fine." Maliek gripped the bench seat in both hands. "I just need a minute. It's a lot to process."

"Sure, invertebrate," Rikus snapped.

Maliek wanted to tell him off, but before he could the Bazij female kicked Rikus in the back of the leg hard. Rikus howled, bouncing on one leg and shouting a stream of words the tradutor didn't translate.

"There's got to be a way out of here," Maliek said. "An emergency escape for those inserted by mistake."

"No one gets rooted by accident," the Azzaro said. "But you're welcome to try the local guards. See if they'll accommodate you."

Maliek's stomach churned at the mere thought of it. He shook his head. "No, but…"

"No one builds an escape route for a prison," the Azzaro added.

"There must be some way," Maliek said, feeling he grasped at straws.

"Rock-headed, this one," Rikus said, having calmed, but still not putting his full weight on his left leg.

"Quiet," the Bazij female hissed, raising a foot to kick him again.

"I will not." Rikus jumped out of her reach. "He's delusional. Even if the Bazij leadership hadn't intended to root him, they'll never let him go now. Not when he can tell his people about this place."

"So… what?" Maliek asked, surging to his feet. "I should hang here with all of you? Accept this as my life now?" He glared at Rikus. At the group.

No one met his gaze, except Rikus.

"You're on the horn," Rikus said, touching his right one. "No other choice."

"No chance." Maliek couldn't believe they'd suggest it.

"Many others like you have come through here," Rikus said. "Refusing to accept reality. They didn't last long."

"Meaning what?"

"They were captured," Rikus replied, with an expression indicating he didn't think Maliek was that bright. "Taken away. And I guarantee you not released."

"How do you know?" Maliek asked.

"Because we're all still here." Bitterness was thick in Rikus's reply.

"It doesn't matter." A flare of stubbornness shot through Maliek. He rubbed his eyes, drained. He'd lost track of time. How long had it been since he'd left home? A day? But none of it mattered. He couldn't join this group to hang out in a park sim and pretend this was a life.

"If there's not a way out of here, I'm going to make one."

"Count me in." The mohawked Azzaro offered his hand to shake. "I'm Jana."

"You're crazy, Jana." Rikus scowled. "Headed to zero. Is that what you want?"

Maliek hesitated a moment before shaking the Azzaro's hand. "Maliek. But why would you want to help if you think there's no way out?"

"What, you think I like this place any more than you do?" Jana shook his head.

"Then why are you hanging out here?"

The Azzaro dropped his gaze to the ground at his feet. "I had a friend a while back. We all did. She tried to escape. She got caught and zeroed. I stopped searching for a way out after that."

"And now?"

Jana shrugged. "I miss my family. My home. I've been waiting for a reason to try again."

"You've fallen off the maze bars too many times." Rikus turned his back on Jana, shaking his head.

Maliek didn't know how to respond. He needed the help. Discovering a way out on his own would be hazardous, and staying out of trouble in the process even more unlikely. But he inhabited a world where he couldn't verify anyone's identity. And he definitely couldn't be sure of their intentions.

"I better go with you, too," the female Bazij said.

"Fejan, no!" Rikus spun back. "You know what they'll do to you if you're caught."

"Same thing they'll do to these two if they do something stupid."

Maliek agreed with Rikus, but for different reasons. After Igata, he didn't relish trusting another Bazij with his life. Fejan claimed to be a sympathizer, but how could he be sure?

Jana stepped up to Fejan and placed a hand on her shoulder, squeezing. "We'd love to have you along. You're smarter than anyone else in this sorry group. If anyone can help, it'll be you."

Maliek groaned inwardly, but he couldn't contradict the Azzaro and risk having him change his mind. Besides, they were right. On his own, he was likely to do something stupid that got himself caught. But that didn't mean he'd trust Fejan. He'd watch her for anything suspicious.

"Anyone else?" Jana asked, his gaze roving over the others.

To Maliek's relief, the rest glanced away. The fewer he had to trust, the better.

"Not even you, Ganden?" Jana asked the Macab, who turned away.

"Better this than dead," Rikus said, glaring at Maliek.

Maliek wondered if Rikus blamed him for Fejan joining them.

"Accepting life in prison isn't better off," Maliek argued. While he didn't want anyone else's help, he also hated Rikus's comments.

"You'll change your mind," Rikus snarled. He pointed his arms out wide at the surrounding city. "This isn't your typical prison. You can do a lot of great things here. Live a fantastic life."

"Imprisonment is still imprisonment," Maliek shot back.

Rikus charged. Maliek flinched, raising his arms to defend himself. But the Bazij stopped so close Maliek could smell his bad breath. Rikus's arms, shoulders, and chest flexed.

"If you get Fejan hurt, you'll have to worry about me more than the guards." Rikus glared down at him, but didn't touch him. Maliek sensed the Bazij wanted to, though.

Fejan placed a hand on Rikus' arm. Maliek hadn't even noticed her close in.

"I'm doing this because I want to." Fejan tugged Rikus back. "I've wanted out for a long time. Come with us."

Pain flashed across Rikus's face, and he shook his head, backing away from her. "You'll get caught like Fluera. Don't do this. There's no difference between these sims and the open system."

Fejan shook her head. "It's not the same. It's never been the same."

Chapter 7

As Maliek, Jana, and Fejan left the park, they passed a long line of Bazij waiting to enter a building above which 'Subaqueous' flashed in neon lights.

"Looks popular," Maliek said, gesturing at the crowd.

"It is," Fejan agreed. "An underwater sim with extinct monsters from Melathia's prehistoric past, and a few from our myths."

"So, what? You swim with them?" Maliek asked, intrigued by the possibility. Or he would if he weren't searching for an escape from unjust imprisonment.

Fejan laughed, her green horns pulsing in rhythm. "Yeah, if you want your avatar eaten."

"Particpants pilot small ships," Jana explained.

"Some thrill seekers do hunt vicious creatures, though," Fejan said. "Either for fun or competitively."

Maliek frowned. "Where's the fun in that? They're not hunting real predators."

"You know how amazing our sims are," Fejan replied, sounding a little defensive. "We have complicated formulas that calculate the strength and speed of those creatures. It takes a lot of skill to hunt them."

"I suppose," Maliek said. "Though hunters in sims are at no risk. At worst, if someone fails while hunting, their avatar gets destroyed."

Fejan shook her head. "No, no, no. If you die hunting, not only do you not get a kill for the creature, you lose a previous kill from your record. If you've no previous kills for that creature, you're banned from hunting one for the next six weeks."

"Still not the same as dying," Maliek mumbled.

Fejan exhaled, and her horns pulsed quickly, a sign of irritation. "I'd also argue hunting fake creatures in a sim is less brutal than doing so in real life."

He wondered if Fejan hunted. Deciding a change in subject might be best, he pointed out a building surrounded by a bottomless pit. A rickety wooden bridge spanned the chasm from the road to the entrance. A larger crowd than the one outside Subaqueous stood in line.

"What about that one?"

"Cliff jumping." Jana's eyes brightened as he regarded the entrance. "A world filled with endless canyons."

"Okay, what's special about that? And why the difficult entrance?"

For an answer, Fejan held out her hand, curled into a fist. "Watch this."

Maliek placed his hand on top of hers and his vision shifted. He stood on a vast, wobbly bridge. Ahead, he could scarcely make out the end of the bridge as it connected to a canyon wall. Wind whipped around him, jostling the bridge. He reached for the rope, but his hand didn't move.

His eyes swung around, disorienting him. Not his eyes. He observed through Fejan's eyes. The process was called self-porting, a recording of her past.

Their eyes rested on the other end of the bridge behind them, attached to the other end of the canyon wall. He estimated they stood in the middle. Then their eyes dropped, studying clouds below.

The wind ruffled their clothes, chilling the skin, making it tighten like a flexed muscle.

"Fun, huh?" Fejan asked.

"Fun… or crazy." He wanted to let go and end the self-porting, but didn't want her to know the scene disconcerted him—not from a fear of heights, but because of the lack of control. To his senses he was there, but he had no ability to move.

"Where does the cliff jumping come in?" he asked, half-afraid he'd regret it.

Their vision changed. They now stood on a canyon floor, the walls stretching up one hundred meters into the air.

"Ready?" Fejan asked.

"For?" He tensed, but that had no effect on the body.

They backed up to one wall, before running forward. After building up speed, they leapt, and rocketed into the sky.

"What the—"

"There are special gravity rules here," Fejan explained.

They flew up and out of the canyon to soar over red-clay plains. Other canyons filled the landscape in all directions, as if the entire continent had dried out and cracked.

They reached the peak of their jump and descended.

Oh crap. Oh crap. Knowing this was a recording didn't stop his stomach from climbing into his chest. Or theirs? He couldn't tell if it was from the self-porting or his own personal response to it. Both?

They plummeted, arcing into another canyon. Way too fast, the ground rushed up at them. Unable to hang in any longer, Maliek let go of Fejan's hand.

He stood with her and Jana once more, on the city street outside the Cliff Jumping entrance.

"You didn't want to finish the jump?" Fejan asked, bouncing on her feet as if she wanted to do it again.

Heart hammering, Maliek tried to swallow his stomach back into place.

"If our plans don't work out, you should visit it with us." Jana clapped him on the shoulders. "There are a ton of cool jumps to do there."

Maliek had no intention of ever visiting.

"Do all the buildings lead to sims?" Visiting them might be fun under normal circumstances, but he wasn't sure any of them would help him escape.

"Most." Fejan spread both arms wide as she began walking. "Trendium is a central hub for all the sim worlds in the closed system."

Like Miran-silya on a grander scale, he thought as he and Jana followed her.

"None connect to sims in the open system?" he asked.

"This sim is only connected to the old world," she said.

"How did Bazij sympathizers discover your government kidnapped people and imprisoned them here?"

"This is our original sim system," Fejan explained. "For when we first rooted our bodies in the covums."

"Why did you leave?"

"As great as this system is, we grew tired of being isolated from the rest of the universe. We longed for contact with others.

"A new, more powerful open sims system was built, one designed to handle the trillions of individuals that log-on every day. The creators designed new safeguards that allowed outside access without compromising our security."

The smell of fried food caught Maliek's attention as a female Bazij passed carrying something large, round, and breaded. She ate gingerly from the food, as if it were hot.

"If everyone moved to the new sim, why is this one still around?" Maliek asked.

"The government saw no reason to dismantle it, so they kept it as a backup. But eventually they decided that lawbreakers, and those who could no longer be trusted in regular society, would be sent here. We don't banish them to the old world. That's considered too cruel."

"Okay, so how did you discover your government started capturing innocents and imprisoning us in the system?"

Fejan shifted and her expression seemed uncomfortable. "Some within the government didn't agree with the leadership that started the practice. They leaked it to the public hoping to pressure our leaders to end the practice and free those wrongfully imprisoned. While we prefer to live our lives in the sims, and encourage everyone else to join, it's not okay to take that choice away from you."

"And your government didn't care?" Maliek sidestepped a group of boys running past in the opposite direction.

Fejan's shoulders dipped. "Unfortunately, many Bazij approved of the government's actions. They believed anyone living in the old world presented an enormous risk to their own health and safety. In their minds, the government protected our people and anyone they rooted. The intel leakers became the first alien sympathizers thrown in here."

Maliek clenched his fists, furious, but with a greater sense of hopelessness. He'd hoped that Igata and those with her represented a minority. If a majority of Bazij knew and agreed with the government's actions, the obstacles to escape were greater than he feared.

"How long has this gone on?"

"The public's known for five years. I'd bet the government's been doing it for ten."

Maliek halted, unable to believe such kidnappings had remained hidden for a decade. How many others were stuck here against their will? How many families had lost sons and daughters, with no idea where they'd gone?

Then he had another thought. "You said the government leaks started five years back?"

"Yes," Fejan confirmed, grabbing both his and Jana's arms and pulling them forward once more.

"And those first sympathizers are here?"

Fejan nodded.

A glimmer of possibility welled up inside of him. "If we can find them…." Maliek picked up his pace. "As former government workers, maybe they know a way out."

Fejan pursed her lips. "I suppose. But the Government will control access."

"So how do we find one of these sympathizers?" Jana leaned in close, speaking in a hushed tone.

Maliek glanced at Fejan. "Any ideas?"

She didn't respond.

"Fejan?"

She waved him off, indicating silence. Her eyes shifted left and right as though reading.

"Nando," she said. "And also Zawella. There are others, but I don't know where they're located."

"Great, so how do we find Nando and Zawella?" Maliek asked, ready to head in any direction.

"I know what you're doing," a cold, gruff voice said.

The trio halted. A large Bazij, more than a head taller than Maliek, glared at them. He had bright orangish-red horns, which clashed with his maroon uniform.

As Maliek scrambled for a response, Fejan stepped forward to intercept the guard. "We're discussing the history of Trendium." She pointed back at Maliek. "My friend here is new today. I'm giving him a tour."

The Bazij officer shoved her out of the way. She fell backward on the road, grimacing in pain. Maliek leapt forward to help her up. As he reached for her, a fist crashed into the side of his head. He collapsed to the ground, the impact stunning him.

"You're trying to escape," the officer accused.

Maliek's vision swam. The back of his head, elbows, and tailbone ached from hitting the ground.

"We're not," Jana protested, moving to shield Maliek and Fejan before the officer struck again.

The Bazij officer punched Jana twice in the gut. Jana doubled over, and the officer popped him on his temple, which dropped him to the ground.

A few bystanders shouted in protest, but no one intervened.

The officer closed in. Maliek shielded his head with an arm, but the officer kicked him in the side. Pain shot through his ribs. Bile rose into his throat. His vision blurred.

The officer bent over him. Maliek cringed, trying to beg the man to stop, but he couldn't form the words.

Instead of further attacks, the officer whispered, "We don't tolerate escape attempts. I'm adding you to our watch list. All three of you. Next time we'll do a lot worse."

He straightened and walked away, whistling.

Chapter 8

Maliek opened his eyes and rolled to a sitting position. Jana and Fejan stood nearby, the Azzaro doubled over with his hands on his knees. Fejan stepped forward and offered her hand to Maliek. He shook his head, clearing it, before accepting. She pulled him to his feet.

As he took deep breaths, the pain in his ribs and face subsided; the guard had beaten his avatar, not his actual body. In the sims, he experienced pleasure, pain, the greasy goodness of burgers, but the sensory inputs soon dissipated.

"I should've expected they'd watch you," Fejan said, her horns pale.

Maliek had suspected they might watch him, but he'd let down his guard in Jana and Fejan's company. *I can't forget this place isn't safe again.*

The guard had disappeared into the crowd. Others patrolled in the area, though none were close. But guards might not be the only ones listening in.

"Why do the Bazij even have guards here?" he asked. "Who would want to be stuck here in the closed system?"

"Oh, they aren't from our government," Fejan said. "They're part of the government that formed here in the closed system."

"Why are they concerned with keeping us here? If they're all prisoners, wouldn't they want to escape?"

Fejan shook her head. "I doubt it. Why would they? Returning would mean changing their identities. Keeping a low profile. Here they're in charge. They're the gatekeepers controlling access to all the sim worlds in the system, and they want to maintain that power."

Maliek scrunched his nose. "Gatekeepers? Why would you need gatekeepers? Why would you need to control access to the sims? Everything is plentiful here. You can go wherever you want. Do whatever you want. Food is abundant. If you want more, code more into existence. It's a world with unlimited resources."

"It is," Fejan confirmed, "but that doesn't stop the most powerful from putting controls in place. They are the only ones with unlimited access. Access to all the worlds. To food, drink, and anything else they want. Meanwhile, even our home size is dictated. Based on our position, we're told what size home we live in and how many resources we're allotted."

"Everyone goes along with it?" Maliek asked, disbelieving. "No one tries to fight against it?"

"Most are too lazy to rebel." Fejan's horns pulsed dark green. "It's not like anyone's homeless or starving. Eating is a luxury. Their bodies are well tended in the covums in the old world. No one's forced to work. Everyone can do what they want within the limits assigned to them. They see no reason to fight against the restrictions."

"No one's cut off from visiting other sim worlds," Jana added. "Just limited in how often they can travel."

"Is there anyone who doesn't submit to government control?" Maliek asked, frustrated that everyone seemed okay with this existence. Particularly the non-Bazij held here for committing no crimes other than living.

Fejan hissed at him, her eyes darting, suspicious of everyone around them.

"Sorry," Maliek said, again chastising himself for his lack of awareness. He needed to calm down, before he angered himself into another beating. Or worse.

"This way." Fejan lead them along a side street to another block and into a skyscraper food court.

Overhead, hundreds of floors held countless restaurants, bakeries, and shops, with food from planets and races all over the universe. Such abundance could never exist in the real world. But here, without constraints, it was no wonder so many didn't struggle for freedom when the cost was so high.

"Let's hide out here for a bit. Get some food," Fejan suggested.

Wanting something familiar, Maliek chose a cheeseburger topped with chili and chili fries. Fejan grabbed fried nuggets with a yellow vegetable and soup. Jana selected a sandwich.

They found an empty table. The juicy smell of the hamburger with melted cheddar cheese topped with lettuce and tomato made Maliek's mouth water. His stomach grumbled. As he tore open ketchup and mayo packets and applied them liberally to the burger, he wondered if he was actually hungry or if the smell tricked his stomach. He hadn't eaten in more than a day, but then the covum must nourish his body to keep him alive.

Whatever the answer, he bit into his burger. His excitement soured at the bland, weird texture of the meat and the nutty taste of the cheese.

"What is this?" He scowled at the burger, noting the inside looked nothing like meat.

"Veggie burger," Fejan answered around a spoonful of soup. "Bazij are vegetarians."

Maliek groaned, dropping the burger on his plate. "Veggie burger? This is all simulation." He stabbed at the burger. "This is nothing more than lines of code. Couldn't they make it like the real thing instead of an imitation?"

"Could, yes, but we don't eat meat," Fejan replied, horns pulsing again.

"What about the rest of us?" Maliek picked at the chili fries. "Couldn't they change some programming for those of us who do like meat?"

"They do that a few floors higher."

"What? And you couldn't tell me that before I chose the fake burger?" As he said it, he realized the silliness of the last part of his question, which only annoyed him more.

Fejan popped a fried nugget in her mouth, ignoring him.

With a huff, Maliek turned his attention to the fries. At least they tasted like warm, crispy potatoes. And the chili covering them, though meatless, was well done.

"You know, I've been wondering," Maliek said around a mouthful of fries. "What made the Bazij decide to live in the sims? I know you're concerned about safety, but there had to have been something that first drove you into the sims."

Fejan stirred her soup with a spoon, watching the steam rise off it. "No choice. We'd ruined Melathia. Our ancestors had the choice to live in the sims or die."

Maliek pushed away his plate, appetite curbed by the disappointing food. "Ruined how?"

Fejan sipped her soup before answering. "Overpopulation drained Melathia's natural resources. We'd destroyed our forests and turned much of the land into dust bowls. Pollution killed off three fourths of the marine life in our oceans. If our world governments hadn't put a stop the endless wars over the precious few remaining resources and created the covum facilities and sims, we would've wiped ourselves out two hundred years ago."

"Why go into the sims? Why not leave the planet?" Maliek asked.

Fejan's horns dimmed to a pale green. "And ruin another planet the way we had Melathia?"

Maliek didn't have an argument for that.

"Besides, we hadn't the technology to travel to another viable planet. We'd made contact with the Azzaro but they didn't trust us enough to help us. So into the sims we went, a place we couldn't destroy."

Fejan focused on her food, and for several minutes she and Jana ate in silence. Since he had little interest in his own, Maliek observed those around them. A young Bazij girl bounced in her seat at a nearby table while eating Razia, a light pink fruit no larger than a berry. Juice dribbled down her chin. As she bounced, her head rocked from side to side as if to music only she heard.

How had she ended up in this sim? She was too young to be a sympathizer. Had she been born here? The start of a new society among the condemned. He couldn't imagine that her parents, sitting on either side of her, liked that she had to live here, cut off from the outside world.

Leaning over to Fejan and Jana, Maliek whispered. "How do we find those two sympathizers you mentioned earlier? Or anyone else who might help us?"

"The Oomael," Jana suggested, keeping his eyes trained on his food.

"What?" Maliek asked.

"The two you're talking about live among the Oomael," Fejan replied, before sipping soup from a spoon.

"And they are?"

"The Oomael are Bazij who didn't go with us to the open system," Fejan said. "While most of us wanted the new system and to interact with others in the universe, some stayed behind. They viewed the open system as too risky. They liked the security of the closed system."

"If they like this place, why would they help?" Maliek asked.

"They wanted the system to themselves," Fejan said. "Once the government started rooting prisoners here, the Oomael retreated to a restricted corner of the system."

"How do we find them?" Maliek asked, sitting straighter.

"I'd be wary of asking for their help," Fejan said. "They keep to themselves. They don't welcome outsiders."

"Still, it's worth a shot, right?" Maliek asked. "At least to find our two leads."

"Maybe."

At the entrance to the food court, a half dozen Bazij guards entered, all armed. Maliek thought he recognized the guard who had attacked them earlier. The guards appeared to be looking for someone.

"Uh, guys…" Maliek broke out in a sweat.

Fejan looked at him before spinning to look behind her. "Time to go. Follow me."

Leaving her food and tray, she led them at a steady pace deeper into the food court.

Chapter 9

They stood at the entrance to a pitch-black tunnel. After escaping out a rear entrance to the food court, Maliek had convinced Fejan that finding the Oomael was their only choice. Though reluctant for reasons she wouldn't discuss, she'd agreed to take them.

One meter into the tunnel, the darkness swallowed the walls and floor, as if everything ceased to exist, including light.

"Can we get something to carry us through?" Maliek asked, uneasy at the prospect of entering the tunnel. "Or better yet warp to the other side?"

Fejan shook her head. "Transport never makes it."

"Never makes it?" Maliek glanced at Jana, hoping Fejan was messing with him. Neither gave him any sign she was joking.

"The tunnel's programming prevents their use," Fejan said. "On foot's the only way to get there."

"Flashlights coming up." Jana extended his hand and three small gray ones appeared in his palm.

Maliek added Space City contacts with a thought and activated the night vision feature.

Fejan refused the flashlight Jana offered her. "Those won't do us any good. Nor torches, night vision goggles, or anything else. Use them and you'll immediately get lost."

Maliek tried to scan the interior of the tunnel anyway, but the now green-shaded walls and floor abruptly ended at the wall of darkness, the same as without the night vision enhancement.

"Wandering through the pitch black is what's going to get us lost," Maliek protested. "Is there another way to the Oomael?"

"No." In Fejan's hand appeared a Kevlar rope. She handed one end to Jana. "We'll tie ourselves together. I know the way."

"You do?" Maliek asked as Jana slipped the Kevlar rope through a ring on his belt and handed over the end.

"Yes," Fejan replied, tying herself to the front of the rope.

"Is the tunnel straight through?" Jana turned on a flashlight and pointed it into the tunnel. "Or are you leading us into a maze we might never escape from?"

No corresponding beam touched the darkness. It disappeared, as if into a black hole.

Fejan rolled her eyes. "You're being dramatic. If you try to cheat, you might get lost inside a long time. But if you'll trust me, I can get us through."

Maliek didn't like that he'd ended up last in line. In horror movies, the person at the rear was always the first one taken.

"Ready?" Fejan asked, tugging at the rope.

"Lead the way, Mielele." Jana gestured to Fejan while getting rid of the flashlights.

Maliek tensed as Fejan entered the tunnel and disappeared. For a moment the Kevlar rope hung suspended in midair, and then Jana vanished, too.

Maliek instinctively shifted his upper body backward even as he stepped forward into the darkness. He inhaled, then held his breath. He raised his hand in front of his face, but couldn't make out even the outline. Glancing back, he could no longer see outside the tunnel. His instincts screamed for him to retreat.

"Relax," Fejan said somewhere ahead. "I can feel the way."

"Feel it?" The rope tugged at Maliek's waist, pulling him forward. He took a deep breath.

"Subtle, but it's there," Fejan answered. "Like a force drawing me forward."

Maliek tried to sense what she meant.

"I don't feel anything," Jana said. "Is it something for Bazij only?"

"I'm not sure."

Maliek felt nothing, and as much as he wanted to trust Fejan, walking without sight was terrifying. He reached out in front of him, half afraid he'd collide with something. When he touched nothing for a couple of steps, he reached sideways for the walls, needing support, but they seemed to have vanished as well. Only the floor beneath his feet and the rope at his waist offered physical contact.

Desperate for something to take his mind off his unease, Maliek asked, "Fejan, how did you end up here?" His voice echoed several times, as if they passed through a giant cavern. He flinched at the changes in acoustics.

Wait, if they were in a cavern, could they be walking near a pit and not know it?

"My father," Fejan replied, though her voice didn't reverberate.

What was going on? Were they in a tunnel? A cavern? A digital void? The possibilities on top of his inability to see caused his chest to constrict, straining his breathing. To calm himself, he tried to focus on Fejan and her story, while hoping she knew where she was leading them.

"My mother passed away when I was a child. For a long time, my father and I lived alone. But a few years ago his horns leapt for a Macab. Fleura. She fit right in with us, and I wondered if they'd unify."

A sadness as strong as an undertow filled her voice.

"One day Fleura skipped a trip we'd planned to Miran-silya. I tried to find out what happened. She never responded. I asked my father and he said she was gone. At first, I figured they'd had a fight, but he wouldn't tell me anything more.

"Then her family contacted me, asking after her. She'd disappeared and they wanted help to reach her. I asked my father about her again. He reiterated that she'd left, but wouldn't look me in the eye. I realized then what he'd done."

With growing horror, Maliek understood as well.

"He'd sent her here," Fejan said. Her sadness hardened. "He wanted her safe in the sims, so he had her kidnapped and inserted in the covums. But that meant rooting her here instead of in the open system."

Maliek opened his mouth, but he couldn't speak. Couldn't snap the spell of her words.

"Once I knew what he'd done, I was so angry with him and so heartbroken for Fleura. I didn't want her to be alone, so I joined a protest. I made threats I knew would get me sent here."

Maliek wondered if he'd have the courage to do the same, for his parents or anyone else.

"Did you find her?" Maliek asked. Again, his words echoed. "Do you hear that?"

"The echo?" Jana asked. His words sounded muffled, as though passing through water.

"It's a trick," Fejan replied.

"A trick?" Maliek asked.

"I sound weird." Jana said.

"The sounds you're hearing, they're meant to disorient you," Fejan said. "Keep you from finding your way through."

"Why does your voice sound normal?" Maliek asked.

"I've visited the Oomael before. They don't like visitors, and this is another means of trying to keep anyone from finding them. I'm allowed, so it doesn't affect me."

A hand clasped Maliek's arm. He gasped, yanking free.

"We have to turn around," Fejan said, voice right in front of him. The hand grabbed his arm again and tugged back the way they'd come.

"What? Why?" Maliek followed her lead, but he glanced over his shoulder for some obstacle. It could be anything and he wouldn't see it.

"What's wrong?" Jana asked.

"It's the way forward," Fejan explained. "I know it makes no sense, but we have to double back. It's how the tunnel works."

They backtracked a short distance. Of a sudden, pale light shone upon them through a glass ceiling. Stars filled the sky. Glass windows formed a new tunnel. Maliek halted. The tunnel led them through outer space to a massive space station.

"The Oomael live in space?" Maliek asked, taking it all in.

"A sim of space," Fejan corrected.

Hundreds of ships flew around the station, docking at various points. Satellites orbited it.

Maliek longed to grab a ship and make a run for it even though he knew that he couldn't escape a sim by flying from it. That didn't mute his desire to try.

The place seemed a fortress. It could serve as a haven for them while they sought escape.

Maliek removed the rope and handed it Jana, who unhooked himself before handing the whole thing to Fejan. They proceeded along the tunnel to the entrance to the space station. A half dozen Oomael guarded it, each armed with heavy guns. Despite knowing that guns couldn't harm him in a sim, they still intimidated Maliek. He wondered if that was their real purpose.

"Who are you?" one Oomael asked. He had a pair of neon horns connected by a scar.

Fejan took the lead. "Commander, we're prisoners seeking refuge."

"That's obvious or you wouldn't have come," the commander said.

"My friends didn't commit any crimes. Our people kidnapped them and rooted them here."

"You haven't answered my questions." The commander fingered his gun, though he kept it aimed at the ground.

"I'm Fejan." She tapped a horn with her hand in what resembled a salute. "I travel with Maliek and Jana. We're hoping you might have information on how to escape the sims."

The commander about-faced and walked away. He spoke over comms, though Maliek couldn't hear what he said. The remaining guards closed ranks and glared at them.

It was not the welcome Maliek had hoped for. Would the commander let them enter the station after consulting with his superiors?

"What do we do?" he whispered to Fejan, afraid to move anywhere.

"Wait," she replied.

A few minutes later, the commander returned. "Take them into custody."

"No, I'm Fejan." Her horns pulsed in rapid fire. "I've permission to visit."

The guards aimed their guns and fired. In shock, Maliek dove for cover. A net landed on him, pinning him to the ground. He tried to lift himself, but the thick-corded net seemed to adhere to the ground like a magnet. Similar nets covered Fejan and Jana who lay beside him, trapping them all.

Moments later, Igata arrived with her droids.

Chapter 10

Igata's droids approached and snapped gray ankle bracelets around their legs before removing the nets and hauling them to their feet.

"Couldn't stay out of trouble, could you?" Igata asked Maliek as if he was a wayward child. "And drew others into it."

Fejan bristled between two droids and glared at Igata. "He didn't have to convince us to join him. I was happy to help. What you're doing is wrong."

Jana turned his pleas back to the Oomael commander. "We have done nothing wrong. We just want our freedom. Don't let them take us."

"I have no choice." The commander didn't meet their eyes. "We can't risk a war with the BJC."

Frustrated that they'd made it this far, only to be betrayed, Maliek eyed Fejan. "Are you the only good Bazij?"

She lowered her eyes to the ground, not answering.

"I tried to take it easy on you, Maliek, but you've forced my hand." Igata shook her head.

The spaceport dissolved. They now stood in a huge covum room. It looked a lot like the one Maliek had been imprisoned in, with bronze, egg-like covums large enough to hold a full-grown adult filling every level as high and low as he could see.

Igata led them to an elevator. They traveled upward several levels past hundreds of covums, before exiting and making their way around to a single one. Along the way, a new droid joined them at Igata's side.

"Initiate erasure protocol," Igata said.

The new droid raised one of its fingers from which a long needle emerged. As it stepped over to the covum, the lid turned clear, revealing Jana's unconscious body inside.

Were they back in the real world? Except they couldn't be. Otherwise, Jana would be in his body, not staring at it inside the covum. So, they were somehow viewing the real world.

"What are you doing to me?" Jana struggled to free himself, his voice rising in pitch. He fought and kicked, but the two droids controlled him.

Maliek wanted to look away, but he couldn't. His stomach turned acidic and cold as the new droid inserted the needle into Jana's covum. A murky white liquid filled the area around Jana's body.

"What are they doing to him?" Maliek shouted at Igata. He struggled to free himself, desperate to get to Jana's covum and break it open to free the Azzaro. The droids tightened their grips on his arms until it hurt and he relented.

Within seconds Jana stopped struggling. He doubled over, moaning.

"Leave him alone." Fejan's horns had paled to almost no color. "How could you do this?"

"Please," Jana begged one time before disappearing.

Maliek reached a hand for where his friend had been a moment before. Only Jana's comatose body inside the covum remained. Was Jana dead?

"We have no choice," Igata said in a tone of sympathy.

"Yes, you do!" Maliek screamed at her because it was the only thing he could do. "Just because we live outside the sims doesn't mean we pose a threat to your safety. You have no right to imprison us."

Igata shook her head. "It's not about that."

"What is it then?" Fejan asked, eyes still locked on the spot where Jana disappeared.

"We are dying out," Igata said. "We're trying to save our people."

Chapter 11

As Maliek tried to process this new bit of information, and what it had to do with him, the facility disappeared. They emerged in a new facility, this time with silver covums.

"I don't understand," Fejan said to Igata.

"An anomaly appeared in our DNA, making it impossible for the Bazij to have new children." Igata led them past covum after covum. "Scientists struggled for years to identify the problem. The lone solution they've devised is to mix our DNA with other races. We recruit new people—"

"This is not recruiting," Maliek said through gritted teeth. That's what this was about? They were stealing his DNA to allow their species to reproduce? His, Jana's, and everyone else they'd locked into the sims.

Igata shrugged. "Call it what you want, we're ensuring the survival of our people."

Maliek stared at her, dumbstruck by the callous disregard for what they were doing to him and others. Stealing his DNA. Using him to procreate against his will. It was something he'd never considered possible before, and it left him with a powerless dread clamping down on his chest.

They stopped before a covum.

"Initiate erasure protocol," Igata commanded.

The needle-fingered droid stepped forward once more. The covum became transparent, revealing Fejan's body inside.

"No," she gasped. She slumped forward, only the droids keeping her from falling in a heap on the ground.

Maliek kicked the droid holding his right arm to dislodge it. He got in only the one ineffectual kick before his ankle bracelet sealed his feet to the floor. He struggled to free himself, but the droids' grips on his arms tightened until he cried out in pain, relenting.

Rikus materialized beside Fejan. He held a device in one hand and with it stabbed a droid holding Fejan. The droid seized up and toppled backward to the ground, immobilized. Rikus stabbed the second droid, dropping it as well and freeing Fejan. She fell into his arms.

"I've got you," Rikus said, cradling her.

"All you've done is seal your own fate with hers," Igata snarled at Rikus.

"Rikus, get the needle droid," Maliek shouted.

Rikus' head shot up, focusing on the droid bent over Fejan's covum. He dropped Fejan and lunged at the droid. He passed right through it, as if the droid was only a hologram. Or rather, Rikus was—an avatar witnessing the real world. They all were. Only the one droid was in the real world.

It inserted its needle in Fejan's covum, which filled with the white liquid as Rikus tried in vain to attack the droid. With another moan, Fejan vanished. Rikus howled in anguish, running for her too late. He dropped to his knees screaming. Seconds later, he too faded away.

Maliek stared in shock at the spot. They were gone… just like that.

"This is what your resistance has led to." Igata glared at him as though he'd orchestrated a major crime.

The facility blacked out, and they reappeared in another one.

Was this all his fault? If he hadn't agreed to Jana and Fejan joining him, would they have lived their lives in peace? Rikus, too? Fejan had said otherwise in the park, but would she have made the same decision if not for his arrival?

The droids dragged him to a bronze covum. The cover turned transparent, revealing his unconscious body inside. Seeing himself like this left him with a weird sense of unreality, as if he'd gone to another dimension. Igata smiled as the needle droid approached the covum.

Terror filled his entire body. He was helpless to stop it. He would die. And watch it happen as an observer. Would he feel anything?

On his left arm, his wrist-comp remained. The Bazij hadn't bothered to remove it from his body when they rooted him. An idea formed in his head.

The droid injected the white fluid into the covum. A fogginess enveloped his brain, as if he was being drugged. He had to act fast.

Message Devonta and Katherine Johnson, he thought, staring at the wrist-comp. Would it still accept his thought commands even if his consciousness wasn't exactly in his body? It was his only option.

Help! The Bazij kidnapped me. I'm locked in a secret closed sim on Melathia.

His surroundings blurred. Sleep tugged at him, but he fought it.

Investigate Velos at Space City Sims. Please hurry!

With the last of his strength, he thought to send the message to his parents.

Chapter 12

Laaj sprints across the roof of the bullet train, chasing after Igata. A hover car flies up adjacent to the train. Igata leaps into it before steering the car into a side tunnel.

A second hover car arrives for Laaj, but he hesitates. Not out of fear. If he misses the car, he won't get hurt; he's in a sim.

No, he doesn't want to jump. He doesn't want to pursue Igata. The chase fills him with anger. He resents it. Her. He doesn't care if he wins or even finishes.

Instead, he walks to the left side of the train and jumps off. He free falls toward the base below. As he plummets, he imagines flying a spacecraft; one materializes around him. He grabs the cockpit controls and steers the ship skyward. He dodges flying saucers in a dogfight and continues higher until he reaches orbit. Then he switches to autopilot, and the ship hovers.

The stars call to him. He longs to fly out among them. But he knows those stars aren't real, just a part of the Bazij simulation.

There's nowhere to go.

Thousands of Bazij sim worlds to explore, but he hates them all. He wants some place he can sense, but not define. As if he lost something. But what?

A bright light blinds him. He shields his eyes, but the light overwhelms him. Hands seize his arms. He struggles against them. How did someone get inside his ship?

Let me go, he attempts to say, but his tongue doesn't respond.

"Maliek, it's okay. Don't worry."

He tries to correct the person. Maliek isn't his name. It's… except the name *feels* right.

He's lifted from his ship and laid on a soft cot or stretcher.

What's happening to me?

"Relax," the male voice says.

It's familiar. In his mind, he can almost visualize a face. He tries to open his eyes, but the light hurts. He clenches them shut again.

"You're going to be fine. I'm taking you home. Your mother's worried about you."

A face with wrinkles lining the mouth pops into perfect view in his mind. Military style haircut with gray flecks on top. Tough eyes that demand responsibility, but also glow with warmth.

His father.

Laaj falls off of him like a bad dream.

He's Maliek. Maliek Johnson.

He's confused why he thought he was Laaj. Or how he ended up rooted in the Bazij sims, but before he goes, he needs to find two friends. A… Bazij female and… an Azzaro guy.

Fejan.

Jana.

They aren't the only ones.

Rikus.

There are others. Many more.

He tries to tell his father about them, but only "others" comes out.

His father grips his shoulder and squeezes.

"Don't worry about anything. We're shutting the whole thing down. Everyone imprisoned here will be freed. Rest."

Reassured, he slumps back. A flood of memories surfaces, exhausting him. As he drifts to a peaceful slumber, he thinks, *The message worked.*

Evanesco

Chapter 1

Devika's twin brother appeared like an apparition in the middle of her dorm room, his hologram displayed by a small projector on the ceiling. He leaned on a cane.

"Are you taking your walks every day, Anand?" she asked him.

"Yeees," Anand drew out the word with annoyance. "Maellyn, Vahu, and I walk for a half hour each morning before breakfast. Then Instructor Fintan joins us for an hour after dinner. We're starting to remember our way around Pindair."

"You're taking the meds the Alfar give you?" she asked.

Anand still had patches of discolored skin from the explosion on Orestes, but the bruises had mostly faded. Soon no one would know how close he'd come to death.

"Yes, yes." He waved dismissively with his free hand. "I'm a model patient."

He'd never been a model anything in his life, but she let it go.

"I couldn't be lazy if I wanted to," he added. "Maellyn and Vahu won't let me."

"I'll send them a thank-you card," Devika said, giving him an impish grin.

It was strange to hear Anand talk about spending time with Vahu, a Dahaka and friend of Neil Ericson. *Why did Neil visit and make contacts on Siavash? How?*

Whatever the answers, she owed her life to Neil for it, as did many people on Space City and the Alfar on Ourania. He'd obtained the Emperor's Ruby flower on Siavash, the Dahaka homeworld. With it, Alfar scientists had devised a cure for the Azymi fungus. They'd stopped the outbreak that had infected so many, including her.

But delivering that flower to the Alfar had nearly killed Anand, Maellyn, and Vahu. Devika's breath caught in her throat at contemplating how close she'd come to losing him.

"What about you?" Anand asked. "When's the last time you got out?"

She diverted her eyes to the window. "I hit up the mess hall for a light breakfast. I still don't have much energy."

Even that short trek had left her sapped. No matter how much she slept, it never seemed enough.

"What does Dr. Flores say?" Anand hobbled a couple of steps. She guessed he'd moved closer to her hologram. Here, his hologram stepped in place.

"That my energy will return in time."

"Are you walking every day to build up your strength?"

"Yes," she replied, annoyed he'd directed her question back. "Every morning and night, same as you." She didn't mention that five minutes was her limit. On a typical night out to the Sims facility and back, wishing she had a way to Ourania. It was unacceptable that a hologram of Anand might serve as the only way she'd see her twin ever again. That they might never share another meal. Or explore alien worlds together as they'd endlessly discussed during their first year at the Academy.

In the fall, she would return to the Academy without him.

She didn't know how to explain it. The loss crushing her chest—the grief—as if he *had* died. Even talking with him right now wasn't the same, as if he was no longer her brother, but a mere shadow of him.

A knock at the door interrupted her thoughts. She ignored it.

The knocking repeated. Scowling, Devika glanced over her shoulder.

"What is it?" Anand asked.

"Nothing," she answered.

A third knock.

"I'm busy," she said, raising her voice. "Can you come back later?"

"It's me. Nico. Do you have a minute?"

"I'm talking with my brother."

Nico? Why would he visit? Outside of working together on Instructor Fintan's team last year, they'd never spent much time together. And after she'd woken up from the coma, they'd only spoken on one awkward occasion, the time when he'd checked up on her in the hospital and dropped off some white chocolate-covered blueberries and raspberries from Colombo Caramella.

"Who is it?" Anand asked.

"Nico."

"We can talk later," Anand said.

"No! I told him I'm busy." She refused to cut short her time with her brother. The hologram link had been spotty of late, and she missed their talks. For the first week after she'd woken up, they'd had zero communication. His wrist-comp had been destroyed on Orestes. Anand and Maellyn now lived among the Alfar. Their mother had sent him a replacement, along with a few other items, in a care package that included a sandalwood carving of Krishna, the sometimes prankster Hindu god.

"At least see what he wants," Anand cajoled.

Devika sighed. "Coming."

She rose from her chair and walked around her brother's hologram. Human instincts were deeply ingrained.

She opened the door to a bag of candy in Nico's outstretched hand.

"Hi, Devika. How are you?" he asked. "I didn't mean to interrupt."

"It's fine," she said, even though it wasn't. She accepted the candy, faking a smile.

"Nico, you better not be ruining my scouts!" Anand yelled.

Nico peered around her. "They're not your scouts. *I* designed them."

"They *are* mine," Anand argued. "I built them."

It was a familiar argument, but with most of the animosity now absent.

She frowned. Anand shouldn't have heard Nico's response. Unless… her brother had looped Nico into their conversation.

She gritted her teeth, wanting to snap at both boys. But she could do nothing without being rude.

"Please come in." She forced a smile.

Nico hesitated. "I can come back later."

"Nonsense," Anand replied. "Did you need Devika for something? Perhaps to get her out of her dorm room?"

That explained Nico's unexpected appearance. Anand had pushed him into it to get her out. Hiding her annoyance, she motioned him to enter.

"What's new?" she asked as she strolled back to her bed.

"I created a sim of Rome." He looked at the spare bed before choosing to lean against the closet door. "Hoped you might explore it with me?"

"No," she said, at the same time Anand said, "Yes."

After an awkward pause, Anand said, "Go, Devika. It sounds fun. Nico makes great sims."

"No," she repeated. It took all her willpower not to lash out at Anand for conspiring with Nico.

She had no interest in exploring a sim right now; especially not one of Nico's creations. Neil had accompanied Nico into the Venice sim the previous summer. It hadn't gone well. Getting trapped in a sim with invisible monsters that could kill her lacked any appeal, especially in her current condition.

Nico scowled, eyes dropping to her feet.

Devika realized she'd been too harsh. She softened her tone. "A Rome sim sounds amazing. I've always wanted to visit Rome. I'm just not ready for it yet. Maybe closer to the start of the new year."

"Of course." He turned to leave, looking like a boy who'd been told his puppy was ugly.

"Nico, wait," Anand said.

Devika had risen to follow Nico to the door. She clamped her mouth shut to stifle her exasperation.

"What about the Evanesco?" Anand asked. "You were telling me about it the other day."

Devika wondered. *Have Anand and Nico developed a friendship, or is this all about me?* If Anand had made her a charity case, she'd kill him. Somehow.

Nico's eyes widened. He shifted back to her. "Evanesco! You'd love it. It's amazing!"

"Hear him out," Anand added.

Devika stared at the floor. She had no interest, but Anand wouldn't let this go. Not unless she listened to Nico's pitch.

"What is it?" She tried her best to sound polite.

"Evanesco. The vanished." Nico beamed. "A lost alien civilization on the planet Havendesh. They disappeared some time ago without a trace."

"Interesting." She pursed her lips.

Nico nodded, face shining. "They left behind a trial, a puzzle of sorts in a temple in a jungle on Havendesh. Visitors have flocked to the temple for years, attempting to solve its riddles. None have come close. The belief is that whoever solves the trial will learn where the Evanesco have gone."

Despite her weariness, the familiar stirrings of intrigue tugged at her. An unsolved puzzle; one that people hadn't figured out after years of effort.

Puzzles, riddles, logic questions had always fascinated her. She loved mysteries. While she doubted she was ready to attempt this trial in her present shape, what would it hurt to check it out? If it appeared as interesting as it sounded, she could return later.

"Okay." She hoped she wouldn't regret it. "I'll go."

Anand and Nico shared a satisfied glance that made her want to back out.

Almost.

Chapter 2

Devika and Nico emerged from the thorneway into the middle of a jungle on Havendesh. Hot, humid air blasted them. After only a few seconds, Devika fingered her silver explorer suit, expecting it to be soaked. It was still dry to the touch.

A path wound through towering, vine-covered trees. Shifting statues—holograms or videos—lined the path, evenly spaced every half-dozen meters. The statues of creatures resembling a shark, a snail, snakes, a fox, and a bear acted out real life actions atop pedestals. Meanwhile a pyramid, a cube, and other geometric-shaped statues rotated on their bases. What powered them?

"Think there's AC in the temple?" Nico asked, brow already covered with sweat.

"I don't know, but I'd like to find out." She had grown up in this kind of heat and humidity in Kolkata, India. But seven years living with regulated temperatures onboard Space City had dulled her tolerance.

She wished Anand were there, so she could bring up the little house in Kolkata where they'd run around playing Chhupam Chhupai or Gilli Danda. Anand had always filled whatever they played with little pranks. Mischievousness had come naturally to him, while it had been a learned skill for her, thanks to his antics.

The memories threatened to make her cry, so she concentrated on the people studying the statues: A family of five with young children taking pictures around a bear statue; a handful of teens her own age joshing around a fish; a group of Azzaro and Macab taking notes as they examined a complex, multi-sided geometric shape; and a group

Devika guessed were veterans preparing for another stab at the Evanesco with plenty of gear in tow.

Mosquitoes buzzed all around their heads, drawn by the sweat of everyone out here. Good thing she'd gotten an anti-malaria shot before coming.

Other than the mosquitoes, birdsong in the canopy overhead offered the only other sign of life in the jungle, though that was to be expected with so much traffic on the path.

They passed around a bend in the path to discover an enormous pyramid made from greenish stone poking up above the canopy. Devika halted, breath catching in her throat as she took it in. Blinking once to activate her eye contacts, she did a quick check of the Space City database. Black text appeared in the air, providing general information about the pyramid, including that it stood one hundred and fifty meters tall. It also housed the Evanesco trial.

She marveled at not only its size but its perfect sloping lines. She had no doubt the pyramid's geometric structure was precisely aligned.

"I should build one of those in a sim," Nico commented. "The perfect place for a trial."

"Why do you need a sim trial when you have a real one right here?" she asked.

He grimaced as he focused on the pyramid.

She groaned to herself, wondering why she hadn't thought that comment through before speaking. They proceeded for a few minutes in an uncomfortable silence.

Over fifty people milled about outside the pyramid's entrance studying pillars covered with the language of the Evanesco, the vanished. She accessed the Space City database and looked up the Evanesco on her wrist-comp. *That is so strange. The database has their complete alphabet but doesn't include their name.*

"Oh man!" Nico exclaimed. "My candy melted." He held a couple of candy constellation wrappers in one hand, chocolate oozing out of them. Peeling a wrapper open, he dumped the goo into his mouth, then he offered her a bag of rainbow licorice, also covered with melted chocolate. She declined.

"Well, let's get inside before the rest gets ruined," he suggested.

"I think it's already ruined."

He sighed. "Yeah, you're probably right. I can't sell any of it to anyone here. I'll just have to eat it. Can't let it go to waste."

To the left of the entrance, a mini replica of the pyramid rested on a gray-green pedestal. Six people surrounded it. The data from her eye contacts indicated that the replica displayed the first riddle—two lines in an alien language finely cut into the stone.

Devika scanned them with her wrist-comp, before backing out of the way while her wrist-comp translated the text.

"What does it say?" Nico asked, popping another chocolate constellation into his mouth.

The translated riddle appeared on her wrist-comp.

What belongs to you but is used by everyone else?

"My candy before I sell it," Nico ventured.

"I'm betting these aliens didn't design a trial based upon your candy business," Devika deadpanned.

A logical answer didn't immediately come to mind.

"What belongs to me, but everyone else uses?" she mumbled. She glanced at her gray t-shirt, purple shorts, and tennis shoes. Nothing on or about herself would be used by others. She supposed she could share them, but that didn't seem right.

Something that belonged to her, but others used it. If Anand were here, he'd fire off ideas. Toss out all kinds of random options just for fun, or to distract people. Eliminating all his wild ideas made it easier for her to hone in on a correct answer. Or else she'd just learned to focus through his chaos. Either way, she missed it.

She tried to imitate his rapid fire guesswork. Her dorm room held her bed, the clothes in her closet, a dresser, pictures; these things belonged to her, but she used them. What would she own for the purpose of others? More specifically, what would she have in common with this lost alien civilization?

"If you think about it from the perspective of the Evanesco, this pyramid belonged to them, but they left it behind for us to use," Nico said.

Devika shook her head. It was a literal answer, but didn't fit in her mind. Too easy.

Again, it struck her as odd to have a pyramid with a trial, statues, and tools from a lost alien civilization, but not have their identities.

"Oh!" Devika grabbed Nico's arms, her eyes widening. "Name."

"What?" Nico asked, cocking his head a little.

"Name!" Devika repeated. "The riddle asked what belongs to you, but everyone else uses it. The answer is your name."

"Oh. Yeah," Nico agreed.

"Congratulations on solving the first riddle," a bald man with eyeglasses said, giving them both a smile. He gestured to three pedestals off to the side. "You'll find your reward for solving it over there."

Devika and Nico hustled over to the pedestals. One word adorned a simple, handled box on each one. Devika scanned the words with her wrist-comp.

The first one translated as 'Pyramid.'

"I told you it was a plausible answer," Nico said.

Devika rolled her eyes. "Still the wrong one." She scanned the middle word, which translated as 'Air.'

What was life like for these aliens that air was one of three possible answers?

But that was a question she couldn't answer, so she turned to the third word, which her translator revealed as 'Name.'

A group of teens she'd seen earlier strolled up to the boxes. A freckle-faced boy walked up to the box with 'Pyramid' on it and lifted the handle, revealing another word on a marble surface, which he scanned.

"Serpent twins," he read from his wrist-comp.

"What's that?" a brunette girl with blonde highlights asked.

The freckle-faced boy pointed back up the path into the jungle. "One statue we passed was of a pair of snakes. I bet there's a clue."

He took off, the rest of the group in tow.

Devika snorted, before raising the handle on the box with the word 'Name' adorning it. Inside the box, Devika found another marble surface with three words etched into it. She scanned it and got back:

We are the Etaem.

She frowned, showing the results on her wrist-comp to Nico. "We are the Etaem. Why did everyone refer to this alien civilization as Evanesco if their name was given here?"

"To preserve the trial," the bald man with glasses said, approaching. "We've known their name since the first visit to this temple, but we want to preserve the mystery of the trial for anyone who comes to attempt it. The name is not recorded in the Space City database, nor shared with anyone from Space City who hasn't solved it themselves. Congratulations on joining our cadre. I promise it only gets more intriguing from here."

"Thank you!" she told him, feeling the smile spread across her face. She couldn't wait to get inside and learn what came next. There would be no waiting to try later. No returning to Space City without at least exploring the pyramid and testing herself.

Granted, the first riddle hadn't been difficult. But the moving statues, giant pyramid, and number of people here taking the trial spoke to its promise.

Time to test herself.

Chapter 3

A short, narrow hallway led from the Etaem temple entrance inside to a large room covered with animated murals. On the room's left wall, figures depicted in the mural resembled the statues Devika had seen on her way in. The figures swam among sand dunes hunting giant worms. Presumably the Etaem, they possessed five legs, brown carapaces, and heads that narrowed to a point.

"They remind me of squids," Devika said to Nico. "Except with clawed feet."

"Cool tattoos," Nico said, pointing out the blue or green markings adorning much of their carapaces.

Visitors stepped through a doorway in the middle of the scene, while others studied different aspects of the murals.

Devika wrinkled her nose at the stench of sweat. "Too bad the Etaem didn't provide a place to freshen up."

On the wall to their right, the animated mural depicted tiny Etaem stacking stone blocks on what she guessed was the base of a new pyramid. Other Etaem poured mud into square molds, or carved large rocks hauled in from the jungle.

"I wonder what it took to get these back up and running?" Devika asked, marveling at the image quality.

"I heard the discoverers claimed it all functioned on its own when they found it," Nico said.

"No way. How long have the Etaem been gone?"

Nico shrugged. "Several hundred years, I believe."

Devika whistled. All this time, and yet their artifacts still functioned, showing no signs of deterioration. How long might it last?

She wished she could look behind the murals to see what the Etaem had used to make them.

In the middle of the mural of the partially built pyramid on their right was a physical door, taller than the mural itself, leading from this room to another.

The room they stood in was trapezoidal with the short wall toward the center of the temple, as if designed like a clock with each room a different hour mark. The narrow wall possessed a simple diagram of a pyramid. Lights from the ceiling illuminated the diagram.

Nico snapped a picture of the diagram. "Is this part of the trial?"

"Not sure." Devika captured an image of the pyramid in construction. "They might be scenes of early Etaem life, like their history. We may need to refer to them later."

Turning back to the main entrance, Devika found a giant image of a sun surrounding the doorway. Its rays appeared to leap off the wall.

"Which way?" Nico asked.

She shrugged. "I solved the first riddle. You pick."

He grimaced. "Picking a direction doesn't qualify as solving the next riddle."

"How do you know?" she asked. "We know nothing about the Etaem or how they laid out this trial. The direction we choose determines how this trial unfolds initially, which may help or hinder our progress."

"Maybe." He studied the two doorways before choosing left, the one in the middle of the desert scene.

Dozens of people studied new animated murals in the next room, which also had the trapezoidal shape to it, seemingly confirming her theory that the place was arranged in a giant circle. Groups formed around four pedestals, one in each corner of the room.

The wall they'd just entered through showed a city flowing across a beach and down into the ocean. Rhombus-shaped pyramids lined the beach, the bottom half shown buried underground. Larger, connected rhombus-structures created a city underwater, surrounded by an artificial atmosphere. Etaem on the beach tended to livestock of sorts, while others in the ocean navigated the city in small ships. It represented a more technologically advanced society with indoor, underwater gardens and marketplaces.

The short wall at the center of this room depicted what closely resembled a fox. To Devika, it had nothing in common with anything else in the room.

While she'd been standing there taking it all in, Nico sidled around the room capturing more images. Devika debated helping him, but found her attention drawn to the crowded pedestal in the closest corner. More than a dozen people crowded around a bronze rhombus statue, which had some sort of writing on it. Unable to get close, Devika raised her wrist-comp above her head to capture an image of the statue. It took three digitally combined images to get a clear view of the text. As she set her wrist-comp to decipher it, she caught a snippet of discussion around her.

"Are the cities a metaphor?"

"It says 'Cities without Etaem,' but there's not a single mural in this place that doesn't have Etaem in it. I've checked."

"That's why it must be a metaphor."

"For what?"

"I don't know."

Devika's wrist-comp dinged as it displayed: *I have cities without Etaem.*

She bit her bottom lip. It wasn't much to go on.

Someone asked, "What if the cities and mountains are the same thing?"

Devika checked her wrist-comp again, then the rhombus statue for additional text. There was no reference to a mountain in her translation. Had she missed something?

She decided to ask two women consulting notes off to one side.

"Have you deciphered the text on the statue?" She projected her wrist-comp screen to share. "Mine just says 'I have cities without Etaem.' Is that correct?"

"Yes, that's the first part," said the older of the two, her gray hair tied back in a bun.

"First part?"

"There's three parts to the riddle." The other woman, with a family resemblance to the first, pointed to two other corners.

"Oh! Thanks," Devika said, feeling dumb. Of course there was more to the riddle. No wonder the corners were so crowded.

She moved to the next pedestal bearing a square statue with more writing. Rather than fight through this crowd, Devika raised her wrist-comp to get pictures when someone tapped her shoulder.

"I got it." Nico showed her his wrist-comp. "It says 'I have mountains without stone.'"

Devika frowned. "That's more confusing than the first part."

"What's yours say?" Nico asked.

"I have cities without Etaem."

A puzzled expression crossed his face. "A ghost town?"

She shrugged. "No idea, but someone suggested it's a metaphor. They might both be."

"Share with me."

He held out his wrist-comp. She tapped hers against his and the two wrist-comps exchanged data, combining the two lines.

I have cities without Etaem.

I have mountains without stone.

"There's supposed to be a third part." She gestured to the woman who provided the clue.

They hurried past the beach-city mural to a pedestal with a cube statue. Nico stood on his toes to get a couple of shots of its inscription.

While they waited for the translation, Devika studied the cube. The statue also bore additional shapes resembling the outlines of continents, as if it was a globe. *Perhaps a globe of the planet?* With one vast southern continent and two medium-sized ones in the northern hemisphere.

"I have streams and rivers without fish," Nico said.

"What?" Devika was only half listening. Something just out of reach tugged at her mind.

"The third part of the riddle." He held his wrist-comp in front of her face. "I have streams and rivers without fish."

Her concentration broken, Devika tapped her wrist-comp against his, then studied the three lines of the riddle.

I have cities without Etaem.

I have mountains without stone.

I have streams and rivers without fish.

"There's the Dead Sea," Nico said.

"That's another Earth reference," she argued. "Same with a ghost town. The Etaem are unlikely to have both concepts in their world. Or to have constructed their trials for those of us from Earth."

"There must be a fourth part." He pointed to the last corner, which held another statue.

"I don't know," she said. "The lady said there were three parts."

He took the lead. "Let's check it out, anyway."

They approached the fourth bronze statue, this one of an Etaem. It leaned back on two legs while the remaining three pointed at the statues in the other three corners.

"There's no more text," Nico said.

"Brilliant observation," a young man nearby deadpanned. He was older, perhaps university age, with blond hair and blue eyes. Two other young men lurked behind him.

"Let me guess, you're here from the Space City Academy on your summer break," the blond boy said.

Devika blinked her eye contacts once, and the name Adrian appeared on the blond boy's chest.

"I bet they thought they'd just pop in, unprepared, to give the trial a go," one of his comrades sneered. Little tufts of hair lined his face, as if he was trying to grow a beard. The name Falk appeared on his chest, thanks to the contacts.

"People have been tackling this trial for twenty years," Vincent, the third boy, chimed in. "What makes you think you can solve it?"

"They must think they're child prodigies." Adrian's upper lip curled in a wicked grin.

Vincent appraised them and shook his head "Nope. Don't look like child prodigies."

Devika crossed her arms and clenched her teeth.

"Run along to mummy and daddy," Vincent added. "Ask them to figure it out and tell you."

"Come back when you're in the University." Adrian puffed out his chest.

Devika shot back, "Did your daddies pay your way in?" Anand would be proud of that one.

Adrian invaded her space, flexing his muscles as he stared her down. Nico edged closer.

Devika didn't give ground. "You don't scare me." Adrian wouldn't do anything in front of all these people.

He grinned. "I don't need to. This temple will do that all on its own."

"Feeling threatened by my presence?"

"Ha! You're no threat. What do I care if you waste your time looking at the pretty pictures?"

"Adrian, why harass my students?" Instructor Alyona Tereshkova emerged out of the crowd. Instructor Shyla Nez walked at her side, arms crossed behind his back.

"I just didn't want them to waste their summer breaks, Instructor." Adrian backed away from Devika.

Instructor Tereshkova's tone turned icy. "How they spend summer break is not your business."

Adrian shrugged. "No good deed…." He stalked off, the other two in tow.

"Don't mind them." Instructor Tereshkova focused on Devika and Nico. "They here because is cool thing with university students."

"I'm fine," Devika replied. They weren't the first boys to attempt to intimidate her. She also knew they also wouldn't be the last. However, they did serve as motivation.

"How are you enjoying trial?" Instructor Tereshkova's face brightened to a smile. It was the first time Devika recalled her smiling. Even Instructor Nez, his posture stiff as a carbon steel alloy, beamed the way her father used to after a good fishing day.

Devika smiled in return. "It's impressive."

"It is wonderful," Instructor Tereshkova agreed. "I'm glad when students take interest. I knew you are bright."

"We just wanted to have some fun," Nico demurred. "A getaway during summer break."

Instructor Tereshkova frowned. "Don't discount yourselves."

"I'm definitely here to figure this out," Devika said. At first she'd only come out of mild curiosity and to placate Anand, but now that she'd seen this place, she was hooked. There was no way she could just walk away from it.

"That's right attitude. Care to join us? Combine resources?"

Devika bristled at the offer. "We can manage. We're not helpless."

Instructor Tereshkova appeared taken aback.

Devika wished she hadn't spoken so hastily. The two were outstanding teachers.

Then Instructor Tereshkova glanced conspiratorially toward Adrian and his gang in front of the ocean-side mural. "I understand. You show them who has real brains."

Devika offered a polite smile, but said nothing, not wanting to sound arrogant.

She heard Anand's voice in her head. *Show them they never should've messed with you.*

Chapter 4

"Cities. No Etaem. Mountains. No stone. Streams. Rivers. No fish."

Devika repeated the riddle, abbreviated it, rotated the order. Nothing helped her decipher its meaning.

The murals they'd passed all depicted Etaem life. They hadn't viewed all the rooms, but if it was that simple, someone would've found the right mural by now.

What else might have cities, mountains, rivers, and streams? she wondered.

Perhaps they should learn more about the Etaem culture to understand what the riddle referenced. The rest of the temple rooms probably provided more information, but wouldn't someone have solved it by now if that was the case? What if they had to leave the temple to find answers? Did they need to visit the ruins of an Etaem city to understand? That wouldn't be easy. The pyramid was oddly remote. Still, the cities could be located. All she needed was a—

"Map!" she exclaimed.

"Yes, a map," someone deadpanned. "Great job. Now where is it?" Others in the room added similar sentiments.

Devika felt her face flush, her enthusiasm evaporating. A part of her wanted to snap that she'd figured it out on her own since no one here was going to share. If Anand were here, he would have. Loud enough for everyone in the temple to hear him.

"So, we're searching for a map, then," Nico said, getting them back on track.

Her embarrassment and annoyance subsiding, Devika nodded. "I think so."

She passed through the doorway into the next segment. The ceiling star lights formed an obvious constellation. It reminded her of a shell. On the walls, Etaem carved jewelry, painted, and crafted pots. All of it incorporated snail shells. In other scenes, Etaem received snail tattoos.

It was pretty. *Why was the snail so significant in Etaem culture?*

On the room's short, inner wall, pieces of snail shells formed a message.

"Pretty," Nico noted.

Devika scanned the message, wondering if it was a new riddle. "I don't see a map."

"Could this message hold a clue?" Nico asked.

Her wrist-comp finished translating and she read.

"Sea snails are admired for their flexibility. They carry their homes with them wherever they roam. They survive both on land and in the water. They grow a new shell when they outgrow the old or it's damaged.

"And their variety. Some are as green as a forest, allowing them to hide among bushes and trees. Near the ocean, their blue shells enable them to disappear in the water, then transform to match the white sand on the beach."

Nico bit his lip, considering. "A nice homage, but no obvious riddle or clue in there."

She re-read the text, but nothing pointed to a map. "Think we missed something?"

"Not really." Nico pointed at the message on her wrist-comp. "Just seems like more Etaem knowledge. I say we proceed on."

The ceiling star lights in the next room formed a square; a different arrangement than the shell shape in the previous room. Had the lights in the first two rooms also formed patterns?

In these animated murals, the Etaem built a city into the side of a mountain and a second, more technologically advanced one underground.

On the short inner wall, Devika found another message, this time printed in blocky lettering. Translated, it read: *The square represents our efforts to create order in a chaotic universe. Civilization depends on order both for and from every individual. Without it, we crumble to ruins and shadows.*

"Great," Nico muttered. "Etaem philosophy. How does that help?"

"It might not."

Nico spread his arms wide, sighing heavily. "What is this for, then? What is the purpose of all of this?"

"To teach us about them," Devika ventured. "Everything we've seen and learned since arriving has centered on revealing who the Etaem were."

"I thought this was supposed to be a trial, not a museum."

"It's both."

Nico threw his hands up in the air, head rocking back to stare at the ceiling. "I could do without the history lessons. I just want the challenge."

"That may be the problem." Though it was only intuition, Devika sensed that understanding the Etaem culture, and its past, would be crucial to solving this trial.

******

Bears with rhinoceros horns dominated the next room. In the animated murals, the bears battled Etaem hunters in a corralled garden surrounded by onlookers. The scene resembled a cross between a gladiatorial arena and a zoo.

The short interior wall showed a mother bear with cub and an Etaem mother with a young child, legs splayed wide as it attempted to walk. Chiseled into the wall beneath the scene, Devika found a story. An ice bear cub and Etaem child had wandered out to play and gotten lost in a surprise snowstorm. The two mothers, out searching for their children, crossed each other's tracks. After first suspecting each other and trading threats, the two mothers worked together to save their children, the start of the relationship between the Etaem and the ice bears.

"So, the ice bears were sentient?" Nico smiled broadly.

Devika shook her head. "I doubt it. If other intelligent life had shared the planet, Etaem history would have a record of it. This sounds like an ancient myth of how they tamed the ice bears."

His shoulders sagged. "This is turning into more of a class field trip than a master trial. Where are the Etaem going with this?"

The star lights on the ceiling formed a rough outline of an ice bear.

"I wonder if we're seeing the Etaem constellations?" Devika snapped a picture.

"Where?" Nico scowled.

"Each room we've been through so far has had the lights organized into a distinct shape. I wonder if each represents a different Etaem constellation."

"Could be," he admitted, "but I'm not sure how that helps us."

The next room's murals showed snakes, particularly twin serpents. Their story told of deceitful twin boys who poisoned their older brother to prevent him from becoming ruler of Metammi. The goddess Ruuminya did not want her favored kingdom destroyed; the elder son, according to prophesy, would lead that kingdom to an enlightened age. So the Goddess saved the eldest son and turned the devious twins into serpents as punishment.

On its ceiling, the star lights formed twin snakes. She got a picture of it as well, just in case.

The beach city returned on the murals in the next room, along with a rhombus constellation on the ceiling. Sharks came next.

More general marine life followed, with a constellation of a fish on the ceiling. An accompanying parable read: *Drop a fish in your neighbor's gullet and they'll rejoice for a day. Train a child to swim and hunt and they'll prosper for a lifetime.*

While this pyramid presented an interesting display of Etaem culture, Devika found her own enthusiasm waning, too. And the number of participants had noticeably decreased from outside the temple and in the first couple of rooms. Those present studied the walls while consulting their wrist-comps. *Are they all searching for a map, or are they in a more advanced stage of the Evanesco trial?*

A constellation of a fisherman adorned the ceiling in the next room. Three of the walls illustrated stories about Zethlir, the hunter/fisher god who populated Havendesh with game to support Etaem life. On the inner wall, they found another Etaem inscription.

Devika translated the text and read, "How can you stand behind Zethlir, while he is standing behind you?"

"What do you think it means?" Nico asked, without enthusiasm.

She shook her head.

"Think it's a clue to the map's location?"

They searched the room for some clue that might make sense of the riddle. They found nothing.

"Let's keep going," Devika suggested.

After the fisherman, they found a room devoted to Ruuminya, the mother goddess from the serpent twins' story. Per the Etaem religion, Ruuminya birthed Havendesh, the planet portrayed as an egg from which all life emerged. When an Etaem mother laid eggs, she both gave birth to the next generation and honored Ruuminya.

The last room's star light constellation formed a complex geometric shape.

Nico stared at it. "Is that a soccer ball?"

"Dodecahedron," Devika answered.

The animated murals showed Etaem spaceships and stations orbiting Havendesh, with most of them dodecahedron-shaped. A large number of people filled this room, studying the walls. She guessed they must think this room had a clue to the map's location. Or that the map was here in disguise.

It took her and Nico some time to take pics of the entire room and assemble them into a 3D panorama on their wrist-comps. Nothing pointed to the map's location, and this was the last room in the temple. The far doorway led them back to the main entrance with the pyramid constellation on the ceiling.

"There's no map anywhere," Nico said.

"No obvious map," Devika corrected. "Otherwise, somebody would've located it by now. Unless someone is keeping it a secret like the Etaem's identity."

"Do you think we overlooked it?"

She bit her lip, considering. "Either there's a hidden room somewhere, or the Etaem thoroughly disguised the map. What else could they use as a map?"

Nico studied a nearby mural, which showed Etaem fishing. "You know…." He shook his head.

"What?" Devika studied the mural in front of him. Had he found a clue?

Nico pointed at the scene. "A lot of Etaem life dealt with seas, oceans, and aquatic life. There's Etaem fishing. Other rooms highlight sea snails, sharks, fish, and the fisherman."

"Yes. What's that got to do with a map?"

"Back on Earth, early navigators used stars to orient them and tell time. Especially at sea."

Her eyes widened. She retrieved the pictures she'd taken of the Etaem constellations on the ceilings in each room. After isolating the constellation designs from the pics, she compared them against a picture of the night sky on her wrist-comp. On the Havendesh summer solstice, these twelve constellations created a circle overhead. A complete map of the sky!

"Check this out." She showed Nico her wrist-comp. She leaned in close, whispering. "It's our map."

"Seems we're missing something," he said, brow furrowed.

She studied the constellation map. "What?"

"There's a gap between the Zethlir and fish constellations." He pointed at an area of stars in the middle. "Like a pizza with a slice removed. Did we miss one?"

She shook her head. "I got them all. Unless they hid one. Perhaps that's our next clue."

******

"Where do we find this missing constellation?" Nico asked, studying the images on his wrist-comp.

Devika checked the Space City database. It listed more than a hundred constellations from Etaem records, but none that paired up with these twelve to complete the circle. If her theory was right, the database had incomplete records.

"Let's go back to the Zethlir and fish rooms," she suggested.

"There's no way a hidden room exists between them."

"Not between them, no," Devika agreed. "But these rooms wrap around in a circle. What if there's a hidden room at the center? Perhaps with a secret entrance."

"Novices," Adrian said, emerging out of the crowd with Falk and Vincent. "People have searched for hidden rooms for years. There's no evidence of one."

"Certainly not in the middle," Falk said, sneering at Devika. "I've calculated the size of the rooms against the temple's dimensions. There's not enough space there for a hidden room. With the structure of the temple, there must be a massive stone stud that supports the weight overhead."

"But hey, those are the simple ideas I'd expect from two Academy students." Adrian smirked. "Why don't you run along and report your findings to Instructors Tereshkova and Nez? Ask for extra credit." He swung a fist in a 'Good work!' gesture, then laughed and turned to his buddies. "Let's go do the real research, while these two discuss last decade's theories."

"Don't mind them," Nico said. "It's a good idea. Not in the center of the Temple, but perhaps there's a hidden door in the floor or ceiling."

Her jaw ached. She'd been grinding her teeth. She hated the boys' condescension, the same she'd received from so many others. Classmates who ridiculed her for taking more advanced courses at the Academy. Adults giving her 'That's nice' smiles when she told them about her work supporting Instructor Fintan with the Azymi outbreak last year, followed by knowing glances that translated into 'How naïve of this little girl.'

She hated always having to prove herself worthy just to be here.

Anand defended her every time he heard the insults, but that only made it worse. Not that he did so—he was only protecting his sister— but that he had to in the first place.

Nico tapped her on the shoulder, his expression eager. "Come on. I want to prove those jerks wrong."

They returned to Zethlir's room. They'd already searched it while trying to decipher its strange riddle and found nothing that hinted at a hidden room. So Devika checked out the fish room, re-examining it more closely, but coming up empty there as well. Nor did she see anything that made sense of the riddle from Zethlir's room.

How could you stand behind your father while he stood behind you?

Frustrated, she wondered if there was another way to get the answer. What if she could first figure out what the missing constellation must be? Thus far, they had a pyramid, a fox, a sea snail, a cube, an ice bear, the serpent twins, a rhombus, a shark, a fish, the missing constellation, Zethlir, Ruuminya, and the Dodecahedron. A mix of geometric shapes, a pair of deities, and a bunch of animals.

Could there be another deity?

She checked the Space City database, but came up empty. Once more she wondered about the possibility of having to travel to another location to learn more about the Etaem. Maybe they could find out if the Etaem had any others. Considering human history, it seemed likely.

But that wasn't information she could get today.

There were ample animals represented in the constellations. Could there be another? Possibly, but she had no way to narrow down the planet's fauna to a likely answer.

The third option was a missing geometric shape. *That* she could easily research. After all, none of those shapes were unique to the Etaem.

She ran a search of the geometric constellations on her wrist-comp, which revealed that each shape was a part of a collection known on Earth as platonic solids. The pyramid, more formally known as a tetrahedron, the cube or hexahedron, the rhombus, which was actually an octahedron, the dodecahedron, and a final one known as the icosahedron. Was that the missing constellation in the Etaem list? She checked and found an icosahedron constellation did exist in the Etaem records, and it fit perfectly into their map at the summer solstice.

There was also a historical connection between the platonic solids and the classical elements. The tetrahedron represented fire; the cube, earth; the octahedron, air; the dodecahedron, aether; and the icosahedron, water, which made sense for it to come between the Zethlir and fish constellations.

Her momentary excitement fell as she realized it still didn't help her much. The icosahedron constellation should come between the fish and Zethlir, but there was no space. There was no obvious connection between the icosahedron and the map either, or between it and the riddle in Zethlir's room.

A woman in one corner held up her wrist-comp, preparing to take a picture of a segment of a mural. As she backed up, studying her wrist-comp, she neared a group studying the opposite wall.

"Hey, watch out!" Devika called.

The woman backed into a tall man who jumped and turned around, giving the woman a startled glance.

"I'm so sorry," the woman said, blushing and holding up a hand in apology.

"That's it!" Devika rushed to Nico and clutched one of his arms in both hands. "That's the answer!"

"What is?" he asked, head swiveling from her to the woman who had backed into the other group.

"When that woman backed into the man, their backs pressed against each other. She stood behind him and he behind her."

"I think you're right," he said, smiling. "Though if that's the missing constellation, it's not very exciting. A back?"

She arched an eyebrow. "The missing constellation is an icosahedron."

"A what?"

"Icosahedron. A geometric shape with twenty faces. It's a platonic solid, same as the others in the Etaem constellation, and it's tied to water."

Nico scrunched his nose. "You lost me."

She didn't answer, instead reviewing the pieces, trying to assemble the puzzle. They needed a map, which should direct them to the next part of the trial. The Etaem constellations on the ceiling in every room mirrored a map of the Havendesh night sky, but the icosahedron was missing from where it should be between Zethlir and the fish.

She walked to the doorway between the rooms, knowing it was impossible for a hidden entrance to exist there.

"How can you stand behind your father, while he stands behind you?" she whispered.

A ridiculous notion came to her.

"Nico, come here," she said, motioning him to join her.

"This is going to sound stupid," she said as he approached, "—but stand with your back to mine."

"Right here?" he asked doubtfully, but without animosity or condescension like with Adrian and company.

She nodded. "Right here in the doorway, stand with your back against mine."

"Okay," he said.

She faced into the fish room and took a step backward, bumping against him.

"What now?" he asked.

A wall of darkness enveloped them.

Chapter 5

Devika held her breath, trying not to panic and failing as she lost her sense of Nico. Before she had time to so much as reach for him, the darkness dissipated, leaving her back pressed against him again.

Sunshine blinded her. She shielded her eyes with one hand. With the other, she reached behind her, latching onto Nico's arm.

"What was that?" she asked.

"A thorneway," he replied, his expression delighted. "The doorway between the Zethlir and fish rooms was a thorneway in disguise."

She exhaled, letting go of his arm. Her eyes slowly adjusted to the brightness of midday. They stood at the top of a ridge, with no thorneway frame in sight.

"How did we travel here?"

Nico whistled, eyes widening. "A mobile thorneway."

"There's no such thing."

"*We* don't have the ability," Nico corrected. "Seems the Etaem did."

She rechecked her surroundings for something obscure that could serve as a thorneway frame, but there was nothing but the ground beneath their feet for thirty meters in any direction. Down the right slope, the crumbling remains of an Etaem village lined a beach head. The structures, those standing, were pyramid-shaped. She recognized it as the beach city from the mural back in the temple. So those structures were actual octahedrons, with the bottom half underground.

Alarms on their wrist-comps made Devika yelp.

Warning! Warning!

Toxins detected

Distance: 5+ kilometers to the west
Levels: Undetermined
Summary: Western zone should not be explored without Level 4 safety measures
Warning! Warning!

Gloves emerged out of her sleeves, to cover her hands. Her helmet rose over her head to seal her into the suit. It was a safety feature built into the explorer suits to protect anyone who unknowingly entered a hazardous location.

Devika silenced her alarm. Down the ridge on their left, a blasted wasteland awaited where nothing grew. Dead tree stumps reached for the sky as if begging for rescue. Cracks cut through the ground in millions of places. The wrist-comp warnings exacerbated the ghastly sight.

"What was the shape of the missing constellation?" Nico grimaced at the wasteland.

"Icosahedron." She wanted to get off the ridge and away from the danger zone. But how did they reactivate the thorneway to return to the temple?

"It's tied to water, right?"

"Yes."

He took a couple of steps backward. "I vote we head to the Etaem ruins on the beach."

Since there was no obvious way to return to the temple right now, she nodded. "Agreed."

As they walked down the gentle slope toward the beach, Devika sensed the wasteland looming behind them. The warning rang in her head, not easy to dismiss even though it didn't apply to their present direction.

People appeared on the ridge behind them. Devika saw, or thought she saw, a dark black circle form for a fraction of a second, before each new person appeared. It happened so quickly, like the reverse of a flash of light, that she couldn't be sure what she observed. Perhaps sensed was a better term?

Participants flooded through the thorneway behind them. Shouts of triumph reverberated through the new arrivals.

Four Azzaro women approached Devika and Nico.

"Are you the ones who figured out the thorneway?" one asked, a hint of astonishment on her face.

"We did," Devika confirmed, bristling at the astonishment.

"She did." Nico patted her on the back. "I'd have never figured it out."

The woman's expression transformed from surprise to respect. "After years without progress, we finally have a lead! Thank you!"

The other Azzaro offered their compliments and thanks. Devika wished Adrian and his group were there. She'd love to see their faces.

Their head start had evaporated. "Come on, Nico. We've got to pick up the pace. Soon this area will be swarming with participants."

The contamination appeared confined to the wasteland, so Devika lowered her helmet, but kept her gloves in place. Broken glass from a shattered door littered the entrance of the first structure they encountered. As they stepped inside, a couple of lights turned on and a humming noise filled the room.

"This place still has electricity?" Nico arched both eyebrows.

Impressed, she nodded. She supposed she shouldn't be surprised with the temple still in working order, but these ruins were in much worse shape.

She approached a neat pile of tiny metallic blocks in the corner. Resting against the stack was a wand of similar material with a powered-on light. Nico picked up the wand, flipping it over as he studied it. The stack of blocks leapt in rhythm.

"What…?" She wished she'd grabbed the wand first.

He pointed the wand at the blocks, then at another spot in the room. The entire stack slid along the wall to the new spot where he had pointed.

"What are they?"

"I've got an idea." He grinned and flourished the wand. The stack reformed in the shape of a bench.

"How did you do that?" She wondered if he'd interacted with this Etaem tech elsewhere.

"It's thought-controlled, like our eye contacts. Or dictating messages on our wrist-comps with our thoughts," he explained. "The wand is the interface. The Etaem used these blocks to form what they needed at any one moment, then transformed it to something else as desired."

He waved the wand again, and the blocks transformed into a table. He twirled it and the table became a bed.

"That's convenient," she said in wonder, "though not necessarily super comfortable."

"Try it out." He gestured at the bed.

She backed away. "No way!"

"It's not going to hurt you. Here, I'll turn it back." He brandished the wand again, turning the stack back into a bench.

She wanted to tell him to try it out himself, but that would be a childish response. Approaching slowly, she eased onto the bench. It had a rubbery feel to it.

"So? What do you think?"

"It's okay." She placed her palms down on it. There was a little give, but the bench was sturdy.

He waved the wand again. A couple of armrests rose, and the bench narrowed around her to a chair.

She yelped in surprise and jumped to her feet. "Not while I'm sitting there!"

"Sorry." He laughed, clearly not the least bit apologetic. "I just wanted to test whether it would still respond to commands while you were sitting in it. Or if there was any sort of lock from contact."

"At least you didn't make it slip out from under me," she said. *If Anand were here, he would've done dropped me on my butt.* The thought filled her with anger and sadness at the same time.

"I wonder if it can do anything more complex?" He swept the wand like an orchestra maestro, and the chair rose into a standing table. A couple of bowls then emerged from the top of the table, along with a pair of cups.

"Wow," she said. Could it make anything she could think of? How would that work if she thought of distinctly human objects, such as the Statue of Liberty?

"Yeah, imagine the applications."

"And it's clearly very durable."

"Think I could claim this one?" he asked with a mischievous grin. "Finders keepers?"

"Not a chance," she said. "You'll never sneak it out with so many people around. Besides, it needs to go to our science labs to study how it works. Like you said, there are widespread applications for such tech.”

He wrinkled his nose. “Yeah, but it would be cool to have the first one at the Academy.”

“Just think, you’ll always have bragging rights that you found it and brought it back to Space City.”

He brightened at this, his chest puffing out. “You’re right! That’s worth something.”

“The Etaem had mobile thorneways, these simple, customizable… what would they be called? Blocks? Tools?”

“Nanocubes,” Nico offered.

“Exactly! To make whatever you need. What other tech can we find lying around here?”

In a back corner of the structure, Devika found a door in the floor. When she approached it, the door slid open. Lights illuminated a room below. Wide slabs emerged from the wall below to create a staircase.

She peeked to gauge the condition of the space below, but Nico burst past her down the staircase.

“Are you crazy?” she called after him. “You didn’t even check for trouble.”

“It’s fine,” he shouted. “There’s plenty of people on the beach now, and we can call for help on our wrist-comps. Come on.”

She sighed, shaking her head at his impetuousness, before joining him.

An array of metallic tubes, covered in dust, hung on the walls. They reminded her of organ pipes and were connected to machines— the source of the humming she’d heard upstairs.

Nico tested out buttons on some of the machines.

“Stop,” she protested, appalled at his imprudence. “These need to be investigated before you destroy this stuff or blow us up.”

He ignored her, messing with the machines for several minutes before giving up.

“Hope these aren’t part of the trial.” He shook his head, scowling. “Who knows how long it’ll take to figure out how they work. Even longer to determine if they hold anything relevant or valuable.”

“There will be tons of people looking into them, though,” she said.

He nodded and took pictures. "I could try to hack into them with my wrist-comp, but better not. They might hold some sort of virus or something for anyone tampering with them."

"That's the first sensible thing you've said since we arrived," she remarked, glad he wasn't completely reckless.

He rolled his eyes.

They returned upstairs to find several new arrivals studying the table and bowls. None of them touched the wand.

"Anything of interest down there?" a woman asked.

"Machines of some sort," Nico answered. "They appear to have power, but I can't figure out their purpose."

The woman nodded as if that was to be expected. She returned her attention to a design on the wall Devika had missed earlier. Something made from pieces of snail shells. The design could be Etaem abstract art, if they had such a thing.

Outside, people swarmed the beach, far more than had been back at the temple. Word had traveled fast.

Over the next few hours, Devika and Nico searched building after building, often crammed together with others, sometimes having to wait outside for people to leave. Many new Etaem tools and devices were discovered—Certainly things of interest to some—but nothing she thought would help them solve the Evanesco trial.

After leaving yet another building without a new riddle or clue, they found a dozen people standing at the water's edge, scanning the ocean.

"I won't say we've exhausted the options on the beach in just a few hours, but I think our best bet is to search underwater," a man said, staring wistfully out at the ocean. He looked almost as if he wanted to dive right in now. "The murals in the temple showed a lot more of the Etaem city underwater than on shore."

"Right." A second man skipped a stone out across the water, getting three bounces before it sank. "These were private residences."

"We'll need ships," a woman with glasses said.

"We can bring some droids from Space City tomorrow and put them to work harvesting materials and building ships. In a week we should have enough ships to explore the ocean."

"A week?" The man who'd skipped the stone scowled and picked up another. "After all this time, we finally get a breakthrough. I hate to be stuck here another week."

"We can get diving equipment." The woman wrote in a notebook. "Start preliminary exploration. Locate structures of interest."

"You newbs did not figure out the next clue."

Devika tensed, turning at the familiar voice. Adrian, Vincent, and Falk approached.

"There's no way you two figured out the way here on your first day." Adrian sneered. "Who helped you?"

"The instructors," Falk suggested.

"Of course." Adrian nodded as if things made sense now. "They spoon fed you."

"We studied all the clues, same as you, and figured it out," Devika snapped.

"No way. The instructors figured it out. Then, like indulgent parents, they let you take credit."

"Instructor Tereshkova indulgent?" Devika laughed. "You've got to be the first person to ever say that."

Adrian's nose wrinkled, but he didn't argue.

"I heard they just backed into each other," Vincent said. "Studying opposite rooms and bumped into each other. Boom. A thorneway lands them here."

"See? That makes more sense," Adrian chuckled. "Two bumbling newbs run into each other and stumble into the solution."

"You're just bitter we solved it," Nico spat.

"Bitter?" Adrian arched an eyebrow. "Why should I be bitter? You accidentally solved the puzzle and landed us here. Now we have a lot more to study. Thank you." He mock bowed.

Devika huffed and pivoted to leave them behind. She was not a stupid, know-nothing girl, nor a simple prankster as many of her classmates believed, though she and Anand loved a good practical joke. She was tired of always fighting others' perceptions of her. *When will they see and acknowledge my accomplishments?*

Chapter 6

"Ignore them," Nico said as he caught up with her.

Devika remained rooted in place, fists clenched, staring out at the ocean.

"They don't matter," he added. "They're jealous that you solved the riddle. And on your first visit."

"No one will care a week from now." She pointed out people combing through the Etaem ruins. "Most of these people won't be remembered for their efforts. Only the first person to complete trial will be remembered."

"That doesn't stop them from participating," he argued. "They're out here having a great time. And that's all that matters, isn't it?"

That's all Anand wanted. He always cared about making people laugh more than anything else. But now he was gone, and no one cared. She could count on one hand the number of people who had asked after him. It was as if he'd never attended the academy—or lived on Space City.

She halted, turning to face Nico. "I want to solve this. I want to be remembered."

And remember.

His nose wrinkled. For several minutes they stood in silence before he said, "We won't solve this trial standing here. If the icosahedron represents water, will we find the next clue in the ocean?"

She studied the water, sure they would find Etaem ruins down there. "Makes as much sense as any, but we won't get a ship today."

"So, we either search the beach or leave."

Something about the connection bothered her. "The Icosahedron representing water doesn't make sense. Nor the other platonic solids with the other basic elements."

"It has to be," he said. "The icosahedron was the missing constellation. Right between Zethlir the fisherman god and the fish constellation. Not to mention, solving the riddle opened the thorneway that deposited us beside water."

It didn't fit to her. "I think the thorneway depositing us by the water is a coincidence."

He shrugged, his expression doubtful. "It seems to fit."

"It does, but it shouldn't," she countered. "What are the odds that an alien civilization would make the same connection between the Platonic solids and humankind's classical elements? It's statistically improbable."

"Anything that *can* happen, *will* happen."

She rolled her eyes. "That's a lazy response."

He bristled. "I didn't make up the saying. Just acknowledging it's a possibility, no matter how unlikely."

"Sorry, I didn't mean you're lazy." She laid a hand on his shoulder. "I only mean that phrase is used to accept a possible answer, however unlikely, because the problem is too difficult to solve or it's not important enough."

"Okay." He crossed his arms.

"My point is the icosahedron connection to water is speculation. Yes, it appears between the Zethlir and fish in the Etaem constellation. But it's possible that the pictures the Etaem saw in the arrangement of stars in the sky were all unrelated.

"Second, there's the icosahedron thorneway dropping us up on that ridge. Yes, it is beside the ocean, but it's also beside that toxic wasteland our wrist-comps warned us about. To see these as proofs of the connection is confirmation bias."

"So not only am I lazy, but I only look for evidence that proves me right?"

She covered her eyes with a hand, groaning. "I'm just trying to solve this trial. We can't have false assumptions guiding our efforts.

"Think about it. First off, it's extremely unlikely that the Etaem would've perceived earth, wind, fire, water, and aether as elements the way humans once did. And it's even more unlikely they would've matched the Platonic solids to those classic elements the same way we did. However, even if we assumed they did, it would've been during their primitive history, before they advanced their understanding of the universe and how it works. Same with humanity. No one refers to those as elements anymore. That belief has been consigned to the past. Now we have the periodic table with proper elements that form the building blocks of our world and the known universe. Wouldn't a more advanced civilization such as the Etaem have done the same?"

He grinned slyly. "I'm messing with you. But the Etaem couldn't know who would find their trial. What if the connection between the platonic solids and the classic elements was intentional to make them easier to understand?"

"If they wanted to make this easier, they could've left us directions to find them."

He pursed his lips and stared at the ground.

"Any society advanced enough for interstellar travel here would have abandoned those classical elements in their past as well. If they were ever there at all."

"What if they didn't leave it behind for species from another planet? What if they intended all this for others here on Havendesh?" Nico asked.

"More speculation. We need to stop looking for anything that could've happened and focus on what likely happened."

He scrunched his nose. "Okay, then assuming that the icosahedron constellation wasn't chosen at random to be the thorneway, what is its significance?"

She ran a general search of the shape on her wrist-comp. She skimmed through the results, past the overview of the shape and its historical context for humans and some alien races.

Then she found something that fit.

"Many viruses come in the shape of an icosahedron," she read, voice rising.

He frowned. "How does that help?"

"Our wrist-comp warnings." She hurried toward the ridge, motioning him to follow.

"That's why we came to the beach," he said. "To stay away from those toxins, whatever they are."

"Yes, but it's plausible that the Etaem viewed the icosahedron as a virus symbol. Most viruses come in that shape. It could be a broader metaphor for viruses, bacteria, or what about viral weapons?"

He halted. "So, you think the next part of the trial is in the wasteland?"

She smiled. "Exactly."

He looked horrified. "But it's too dangerous."

She tapped her explorer suit. "If we raise our helmets, we'll be safe. As long as we're careful, we should be fine."

"And what if they don't protect us?"

She considered. "Okay, what if we don't go in? Just take a few ground samples at the edge and test them. Then we'll know if we need better safety equipment."

"You promise that's it?" He half turned back toward the beach.

"I don't have a death wish. I just want some idea of what we're facing. If that's where we need to go to continue the trial."

Chapter 7

When Devika reached the ridgeline, alarms on her wrist-comp sounded again. She silenced them and pulled a test strip from a slot in her wrist-comp. "Help me take a sample."

Nico removed a strip from his own device.

Devika walked a short distance down the slope into the wasteland. A strong breeze kicked up dust and, she hoped, not something more deadly.

She bent and rubbed her test strip thoroughly over a pile of grayish white stones. Then she inserted it back into the wrist-comp test slot. It was part of an Alfar technology upgrade as thanks for Space City's assistance with the outbreak on Ourania the previous year. Since she and Nico worked on Instructor Fintan's team, they received early access to the upgrade.

While the wrist-comp analyzed the test strip, she blinked to activate her contact lens's zoom function. A magnification bar appeared on the right edge of her vision. With it she could enlarge her sight up to twenty times. The contacts also made automatic diopter adjustments to account for visual differences between her right and left eye.

The contacts started off at five times magnification.

Out in the wasteland, a dissipating dust cloud revealed a pile of white… bones? Studying it more closely, she decided it must be broken branches or a narrow, shattered tree trunk.

Doubling the zoom disoriented her. She focused on one piece of bare ground, allowing her eyes to settle. Then she started a sweep of the area. A vague depression appeared at her ten o'clock. She doubled the magnification, which revealed a large crater in the ground. A perfect circle. Definitely not natural.

A chime from her wrist-comp indicated the test results were ready.

"Substance unknown," Nico groaned. "Lot of good this did us."

Devika blinked, deactivating her contacts. The suddenness made her vision swim. She rocked back on her heels, closed her eyes, and breathed. After a second, she checked her own wrist-comp. It had returned the same results—substance unidentifiable.

"It means what we tested isn't in the Space City database," she replied. "That's true for a lot of substances on the planet."

But just because they couldn't identify the substance didn't mean the test wasn't useful. It examined the properties of the substance.

"It doesn't have any corrosive properties that could damage our suits," she said after studying the analysis. "But we should keep our helmets up, anyway."

If they proceeded forward from here they couldn't come in direct contact with anyone afterwards until they'd decontaminated their suits upon their return to Space City. The prospect didn't deter her.

"I vote we go back." Nico retreated a few steps up the ridge. "We got a couple of samples. We should get those back to the lab. Plus, now that we have a specific area of interest, we can get some aerial views that will help us narrow down our search."

"Don't need an aerial. There's a hole in the ground out there," she said, pointing.

"Oh. Great. A hole in the ground." He crossed his arms. "Sounds exciting."

"We should check it out. It might be the next stage in the trial."

He yanked his wrist-comp from his arm and shoved it in her face. "The place is toxic. It's not safe to go out there. You promised we'd only get samples here."

She didn't need to look at the screen. She knew what it said. And she *had* promised him they wouldn't enter the wasteland. "That was before I saw the artificial hole in the ground. We've got the lead once more, but not for long. Others will find it soon enough. If we want to be first, we go now."

"Devika, you promised!"

"The icosahedron thorneway deposited us here for a reason," she pleaded.

His face reddened as he pointed back toward the beach. "And that reason is just as likely to be the city ruins as out here. Maybe more so."

"There's no way that's a natural hole in the ground. Look for yourself." She jabbed a finger at it. "Even from this distance I can tell it has to be Etaem made."

"For all we know it's a toxic dump," he protested. "For those chemicals our wrist-comps are warning us about."

She softened her voice, willing to give him an out. "Go back. I know you didn't sign up for this. I'll go alone."

His face reddened further. "And have Anand kill me for abandoning his sister? You're here because of me."

She slumped, her voice barely above a whisper. "You don't have to worry about Anand. He's never leaving Ourania again."

Nico winced.

They stood there in uncomfortable silence for a few seconds before he muttered, "He'd find a way to turn my scouts against me. Have *them* kill me."

She chortled. "You're right. He absolutely would."

Nico stared past her, out into the wasteland. "I don't think this is a good idea. We need more information to know if it's safe."

"Where are you two newbs going?"

They turned to find Adrian traipsing down the ridge behind them, Falk and Vincent at his shoulders. The latter two glanced nervously at their wrist-comps, which chimed warnings. Belatedly, they raised their helmets.

Devika bristled, but Nico spoke first. "We're trying to figure out how the mobile thorneways work."

"Away from the Etaem village in a barren, poisonous landscape?" Adrian arched an eyebrow.

Devika crossed her arms. "We got tired of fighting through the crowds back there. We're waiting until things calm back down. In the meantime, if we can figure out how the thorneway at the temple deposited us here where there's no frame, that would be worth a lot back home, don't you think?"

"She found something." Falk gestured out past them. "A clue."

Devika ground her teeth, doing her best to maintain her false smile. "I thought Academy kids couldn't figure out this trial."

"You got lucky once." Adrian's voice was light, but beneath it was an edge that annoyed her. He'd followed because he'd suspected she had another lead. This time he intended to tail her.

How could she get rid of them? Prevent them from stealing her discovery?

"The next clue is in the Etaem city underwater," Nico said, "but we can't get a ship out here today. And since this area is virulent, we figured we'd gather some intel. Take it back to Space City for study before someone gets hurt."

The college boys' eyes narrowed; then the trio studied the wasteland for themselves. Devika knew it wouldn't take long for them to spot the artificial hole. And once they knew, everyone would know. Even if the boys said nothing, once everyone else exhausted the beach, at least some would check out the wasteland before heading underwater.

"Be careful out here," Adrian said, a knowing smile spreading across his face. "Wouldn't want you falling down a hole."

Devika clenched her fists, raising her eyes skyward. All her hard work, and these spoiled rich boys aimed to cheat her out of it.

Adrian strolled past her, raising his helmet to secure himself inside his explorer suit. "Come on, boys. Let's get a close up."

It took all of her willpower not to trip him. She knew Anand would chastise her for a missed opportunity.

Falk and Vincent hesitated on the ridge.

"I don't think it's a good idea until we know what's out there." Vincent grimaced. "What toxin or contagion."

"I'm with you two," Nico said to Vincent and Falk. "It's crazy to go out there when we have clear warnings to stay away. Devika and I got samples. You grab some, too, and we'll take them back to get tested. We can return once we know it's safe."

"If she's willing to go, I'm guessing she knows what's out there." Adrian pointed to her. "Or at least enough to believe they're safe in their suits."

"If you say so," Falk replied, glancing down at her, then back toward the beach.

"Don't be cowards," Adrian berated. "We've never had a chance like this before. A lead on everyone else." He thumbed his chest. "I'm taking advantage of it."

Was this what she sounded like to Nico? Ignoring his hesitations?

"Are you coming?" Adrian demanded as he headed forward.

Both Vince and Falk remained where they stood a moment longer, before following.

"You don't have to go just because he is." Nico tried to catch Vincent and Falk's eyes as they passed. They ignored his pleas, so he turned to her. His eyes begged her to turn back.

She shifted her eyes to Adrian's back, unwilling to return Nico's gaze. *Was she really going to do this?*

Nico's argument made sense. It was risky to go out there right now. The trial wouldn't end if she left. Except that might not be true. Adrian might solve whatever was down that hole. Or Vincent or Falk. They'd underestimated her. She wouldn't do the same in return.

And as long as she stayed careful, her wrist-comp would warn her if her suit became compromised.

When Adrian broke into a jog, fully committed to investigating the hole, Devika couldn't turn back. She refused to be left behind on her own discovery. She could be cautious and still keep going.

When he noticed she was following, Adrian picked up the pace. The trio soon outdistanced her. She might have kept pace with them before the azymi infection she'd gotten last spring, which had substantially reduced her strength and energy. Her recovery had remained slow.

On top of that, the three boys each had a pair of oxygen tanks on their backs compared to the standard one she and Nico had with them. That meant the boys could explore out here for eight hours instead of four. Why hadn't she thought to double up before coming?

Nico caught up with her and jogged at her side. She could tell he wanted to plead with her to go back. However, he seemed resigned to pressing forward like Vincent and Falk. She didn't feel sorry for those two, but she regretted dragging him out here. At the same time, she was thankful he'd stuck with her. She couldn't do this alone.

They didn't make it far before her breathing became ragged. She slowed to a walk, hands on hips. Her frustration grew as her legs and chest screamed for her to sit and rest. While she fought exhaustion, the boys reached the hole.

What were they seeing? What was down there? She hated that they got the first look.

To make matters worse, the boys began to descend. She let out a single scream, fighting the urge not to crumple to the ground. She staggered on, placing one foot in front of the other until she reached the hole.

Thirty meters wide, the hole had been lined with some sort of dark gray-green alloy. Darkness prevented her from seeing the bottom.

They stepped onto a wide platform that could've held a tank. It attached to the wall with a roller guide system to allow it to be lowered into the hole. However, the controls looked corroded.

A ramp wrapped around the perimeter. The trio descended the ramp, already on the far side of the hole. A part of her wanted to try the movable platform to get ahead of them again. But the fact Adrian had chosen to walk down underscored her concerns about its safety.

"Yikes." Nico paled as he stepped onto the ramp, his back pressed to the wall. "Please tell me we're not going down there?"

She checked her suit oxygen levels using her wrist-comp. She had three and a half hours of air left. "I'm not letting them steal this."

"They won't figure out the next clue." Wide-eyed, Nico stared into the depths.

She wasn't afraid of heights, but she felt for him. The ramp was only a meter wide. "You don't know that. What if there's nothing left to figure out? What if this is the end? What if they get to the bottom and there's the prize just waiting to be collected?"

"If that's the case, we can't stop them."

She had no counter argument. Instead, she removed another test strip from her wrist-comp. She rubbed it over the wall and inserted it into the test slot. The wrist-comp hadn't chimed further warnings, but it would help to know if the danger levels had increased. She hoped to figure this puzzle out, but not at any cost.

While the wrist-comp analyzed her sample, she watched helplessly as the trio marched down the ramp. Their steps reverberated around the hole. She wanted to catch up, but knew that if she tried, they would pick up their pace as well.

Her wrist-comp chimed again. Concentration levels remained steady.

"I'm going." She activated her night vision function on her contacts to see on the way down, bracing for another protest from him.

He just nodded. "After you."

Chapter 8

Bright light illuminated the lower part of the hole the moment Adrian and the others reached the floor, blinding Devika. She deactivated the night vision on her contacts as closed her eyes, raising her hand to shield her face as well. When she opened her eyes, her vision swam. She grabbed the rail to steady herself. After several deep breaths, her vision cleared.

The boys entered a tunnel below, reigniting her fear that they would waltz in and claim the prize. But the moment she reached bottom, all her concerns gave way to awe. The short tunnel opened to an underground Etaem city that dwarfed what they'd seen back on the beach. Towering buildings filled the monstrous cavern. Lights shone from every window and doorway. This must be the New York City, London, or Tokyo of the Etaem world.

Once upon a time, when the Etaem still inhabited this world.

Signs flashed across giant billboard screens, accompanied by the hum of electricity. Bioluminescent trees lined sidewalks, adding to the luster. Devika blinked a few times, eyes still adjusting to the brightness.

The paved roads looked museum-quality clean. No signs of dust, fallen leaves, or spider webs. The latter might be explained by the toxins present in the city, but there must be auto-cleaning bots that tended to the place. It spoke to the Etaems' pride and skill in building things that lasted long after they'd gone.

Scientists who'd studied Havendesh and its abandoned cities believed the Etaem had left hundreds of years ago, maybe as many as a thousand. And yet neon lights flashed across billboards, and Devika couldn't spot one burned out lightbulb.

There were also no cars on the streets or other obvious modes of transportation. That would limit exploration for the remaining three and a quarter hours of oxygen she had remaining.

Her fascinated study was interrupted as she sensed someone approaching; Adrian scowled at her. Vincent and Falk lumbered on his heels.

"Don't get in our way," Adrian said through clenched teeth. "I'm warning you."

She snorted. "You don't scare anyone."

His face reddened as he got up in her face, raising his shoulders to max height like a posturing male in the wild. "You think you're so smart. Don't forget we're all alone here. We wouldn't want an *accident* to happen."

"Thanks for the heads up." Nico fished something from his pocket. "I got a picture of you three. If anything happens to Devika or me, the prime suspects are Adrian, Falk, and Vincent."

Adrian backed up a couple of steps, eyes widening. Devika barely stopped herself from laughing at his reaction.

"You can't send messages down here." Adrian's statement lacked confidence. "No signal."

"It's a good thing I have this with me then." Nico held out an upraised palm. In the middle of his hand, a tiny metallic device began vibrating four half-centimeter wings.

Before anyone could respond, he tossed the device into the air. It took off.

"When that scout reaches the surface, it'll log that message in my inbox," Nico said. "If we don't come back, that'll be the first place the authorities check."

"Just stay out of our way," Adrian snarled, before storming off into the city.

Devika exhaled. She'd have to be more careful. From the way they'd panicked when Nico had mentioned the scout, she felt confident Adrian's threats were just blowing off steam. Still, he was angry. Sometimes angry people did stupid things.

"That was quick thinking with the scout." She squeezed Nico's arm.

He scowled, staring at the trio's retreating forms. "I won't let them bully us into giving up. You worked too hard to get us to this point. I'm not running away over juvenile threats."

"So, you're with me?" she asked. "*We* finish this now?"

He raised both hands, pointing at the city. "This is amazing! We can't turn back now."

"It is," she agreed.

"So where to? Where in this city is the next clue?"

She pulled out another test strip. "I'm not sure, but let's get another sample and see if the surface contamination is down here as well."

While they waited on the analysis, she studied their immediate area, trying to decide where to look for clues. Messages scrolled across or flashed on boards from most buildings.

"We should scan some of those," she suggested, pointing to the nearest boards.

Her wrist-comp beeped, returning the latest results. *Contamination levels remain constant.*

"Gotta keep our helmets up, suits sealed."

"And here I was hoping to take in the big city smells." Nico frowned exaggeratedly as he started forward.

"*We've* done it," she called after him.

"Huh?" He halted, turning back to her.

"You said *I've* figured out everything to get us here. That isn't true. *We've* gotten here. *Together.*"

He gave her a broad smile before hurrying across the street to scan messages.

Making her own way forward, Devika found a menu-sized board with text adorning an entrance. She scanned it—a greeting to a seafood restaurant. Next came a picture of a male and female Etaem holding some sort of gear above a single line of text.

Probably nothing useful, but she scanned the text, anyway. What she got back was *Cube Escape*. Was that an ad? Movie title? Perhaps it was a movie poster. Did the Etaem have movies and cinema?

"All advertisements over here," Nico hollered.

She wondered whether her initial impression was correct. Had the Etaem disappeared suddenly? Strolling down city streets or eating at a restaurant one moment, gone the next?

As they pushed deeper into the city, Devika stopped scanning most of the signs. They didn't have the time. And she'd wager they wouldn't find the next riddle or clue displayed in flashing neon lights.

Instead, she focused on a broad study of their surroundings, examining everything they passed, searching for the one oddity. The one thing that didn't belong. A tough task, considering she didn't know what would be odd to an alien civilization.

She checked her wrist-comp. She still had two and a half hours of oxygen, so she pressed on until they reached a square filled with marble memorials.

An Etaem hologram was on display above each memorial. Every four to five seconds the image flickered to another Etaem. Her initial impression of them as squid-like creatures had been shallow. Yes, they had carapaces that ended in a point, and tentacle-like legs, which strangely ended in claws. But in each pair of eyes she caught so many familiar emotions. Many shone with love, joy, and pride. Others drooped from sadness, fear, or despair. Some burned with anger and resentment. A few shriveled with guilt.

She'd known they were an intelligent species. After all, they'd built an advanced, technological world and then left it for the stars. But it took until this moment for her to recognize them as individuals. At least a hundred hologram memorials stood in the square. And at the rate the images changed above each memorial, they represented thousands or perhaps millions of Etaem. A city's worth.

A shiver slithered up her back.

She approached the nearest memorial where digital text flowed across its surface.

"Welcome to Laquir, human," a phantom voice said. "City of the Sacrificed."

Chapter 9

Devika screamed, stumbling backward, eyes roving. Who had spoken to her?

Nico raced to her side. "What's wrong? Are you hurt?"

The Etaem hologram on the closest memorial stared down at them. Its five clawed feet gripped the edges of the memorial. Unlike the other holograms, this one didn't change every few seconds.

"I expected my first connection to be more defiant."

"Is that you?" Devika asked, staring at the hologram. "Are you speaking to us?"

"Low intellect," the hologram noted. A pale yellow color infused its pointy head. "Unexpected for a species capable of interstellar travel."

Great. Even aliens judged her.

Gathering her wits, she replied, "You just surprised me, that's all. Are you... are you a real Etaem?"

The hologram chittered, before responding. "The Etaem would not sit around some twelve hundred Havendesh revolutions to answer the questions of those attempting their trial. A more logical deduction is that I am a fabricated mind left behind to brief you on Laquir."

"Fabricated mind?" Nico cocked his head. "As in artificial intelligence?"

"Those are applicable synonyms," the fabricated mind agreed.

"The Etaem created you to answer our questions, didn't they? You're here to assist us with the trial!" Nico smiled like a kid alone in a candy store.

"To educate," the hologram corrected, its yellowish hue deepening. "About Laquir. Not the trial."

"And what is Laquir?" Devika wondered if this AI would help or hinder them.

"The city you stand in now."

"Yes, I understood that much." She decided it would be a hindrance.

"Laquir was once the Jade of the Etaem civilization," the hologram intoned. "The city shone for a thousand years."

She marveled at the longevity. "What happened to it?"

"Hate and greed. Wielding weapons we should have banished, we waged war upon our brothers and sisters and thems until our world lay in ruins, no longer hospitable to the few who remained. Survival was no blessing. We had built wonders to behold across Havendesh and even into space, yet we could not see, understand, and respect our neighbors."

The hologram paused. Standing upon its memorial, it seemed to sag in upon itself.

Devika glanced back at the city, at the tall buildings surrounding this memorial. How many millions must it have once held? "And this city—"

"The City of the Sacrificed."

"Yes. This city, Laquir, is a warning?"

"For you and those to follow. Do not let anger, pain, and suffering—self-prescribed poisons of the mind—become the means by which you touch the world."

She wanted to assure the AI they had learned these lessons. But was that true? Could she confidently say everyone aboard Space City tolerated others? Only two years ago classmates at the academy had mercilessly attacked Rois and Jaya for their relationship, and had gotten away unpunished.

"You mentioned survivors," Nico interjected. "Where did they go? Is this trial meant to show us where they've gone?"

"The survivors banded together to chart a new course for the Etaem society. They left behind their beloved home the way the sea snail leaves its shattered shell to seek another. They departed into the exile of space, intent on showing Ruuminya that we no longer hate ourselves, in the hopes she would birth a new Etaem home."

"You don't know where they've gone?" Devika asked.

"As advanced an intellect as the Etaem gave me, I cannot see the future and what became of them in exile."

Nico's shoulder's slumped. "So much for learning that at the end of the trial."

Devika shared his disappointment. While she'd enjoyed the trial, part of her enthusiasm was from the prospect of learning where the Etaem had gone. Anything less felt like a letdown.

"What about the toxins we picked up on the surface?" she asked. "Can you tell us what it was? Is that what destroyed the city's inhabitants?"

"The toxin is a combination of viral and chemical elements," the hologram replied, a dark yellow color swirling across its carapace once more. "A rot bomb."

The name made her skin crawl. "What was it made from?"

"You should not ask."

She shook her head, holding out both hands. "You misunderstand me. I don't want to know how to make one. I just want to identify the components, so we know how to clean it up. And if someone gets contaminated, our doctors will need to know how to treat it."

"A cleaning process is already in place. If you had arrived five hundred Havendesh revolutions prior, you would not have survived the trip through the wasteland. Sterilization is scheduled for completion in eight hundred forty-three Havendesh revolutions plus or minus one quarter revolution."

Her stomach churned. Had other civilizations found the trial and died in their attempt to complete it? Or had this location remained hidden until her discovery?

"As for medical care, all knowledge of the rot bomb was destroyed. After witnessing the near annihilation of their species, the Etaem wiped all records of it. Only details on the devastation it caused were preserved."

She wondered if she should destroy the samples she'd taken on the surface. Scientists could study them to develop a treatment. Would it be possible to use those samples to recreate the rot bomb?

Mainyu, leader of the Dahaka and enemy of Space City, would certainly exploit such a weapon. She wasn't sure she trusted Space City leadership, either. They might develop the weapon under the guise of self-defense. It might already be too late. Countless trial participants had reached the beach and would eventually explore the wasteland. They would surely take samples as well.

"Is there anything you can tell us to assist with the trial?" Nico asked.

"The last puzzle resides within Laquir," the AI said. "I witness. No more."

"Well, thanks. I guess," Nico scowled as he turned his attention to her. "What do you think?"

She forced down her concerns for now as she mulled their options. "Keep searching for the last clue, I guess. We might find it through here?" She gestured past the AI to the rest of the memorials.

He eyed them. "If that's how we finish this thing, then after you."

She led the way through the ever-changing images of the Etaem hovering above the memorials. As she passed one, a gray Etaem hologram with cracks in its carapace spoke. "I raised my family here, a father to three sons. As children, they were inseparable. As adults they killed each other, divided by beliefs that no longer tolerated the existence of differences."

At first she thought the Etaem was another AI, but its eyes focused ahead, not on them. Just a recording. It started to repeat its story, then fell silent when they moved on.

"I served as a doctor." A female Etaem hologram drew Devika's attention. The hologram possessed a light brown carapace, bright gray eyes, and what appeared to be a small tattoo of the Goddess Ruuminya. "I tended to everyone in need, inspired by my grandmother. As a child I learned from her that all life is sacred. The large or small, rich or poor, old or young, she did everything she could to preserve life. I took pride in her mantra, even when popular belief changed and I was branded a traitor for healing the enemy."

Each hologram they passed possessed a different tale. "I was a daughter. Grandfather. Brother. Chef. Scientist. Deep-sea diver. Teacher. Homemaker to my family."

Everyone had a story. Devika hurried past them, unable to bear the weight of the hopes, dreams, and fears wasted because they had destroyed what they couldn't understand. And what they couldn't understand, they refused to accept.

She fought back tears as they reached the far side of the memorial. It was too much, what they'd done to each other. The loss of life. Had they departed the planet, or had their civilization crumbled? Or both?

In the middle of the street stood two giant statues. Both were Etaem. The one to their right—half white, half black—had a tattoo of the sun on one shoulder and a full moon surrounded by three stars on the opposite. The statue stood straight, serene, at peace.

Ten or fifteen meters to the left, the second, blood red statue pointed one outstretched finger at the first in condemnation. Fury marred its visage. Thick chains encircled its torso and legs, securing it to the floor.

A podium on a dais stood between the statues. Devika approached it and spotted a message on the podium. *The last puzzle.*

"Lucked into the next clue in the trial, huh?" a cold voice said, as she scanned the message with her wrist-comp.

Striding down the road behind the red statue came Adrian, Falk, and Vincent. Adrian slow clapped with a mocking smile. "You two have some kind of luck."

This time Devika didn't bristle at the attack. The memorial still weighed upon her. By comparison, his insults didn't amount to much. This was probably how the war between the Etaem started. Trading insults that seemed harmless.

"What does the riddle say?" Falk asked, glancing up at the red statue as they passed it. "Man, does he look enraged."

The text had finished translating on her wrist-comp as the boys joined them on the dais. This time, rather than hide the message, she cast it into the air for everyone to see. She couldn't keep it from them. They'd just scan it themselves. Matching their abusive behavior said something about her, not them.

"Two citizens," she read. "Two paths. Two cities. One, the city of Life. The other, Death. The citizen from the city of Life always tells the truth, with all that entails: compassion, hope, and understanding. The citizen of the city of Death always lies and represents the antithesis of life in every meaning imaginable. One question asked. One question answered. Only one leads to the city of Life."

Vincent blinked, expression puzzled. "So, we ask which way to the city of Life or city of Death?"

"No. We won't know if the answer is the truth or a lie." Devika put her fist to her chin as she contemplated the message.

"We're already in the city of Death," Nico pointed out.

She shook her head as she reread the riddle.

"We want to reach the city of Life," she said. "We'll find the prize for the trial there. But first, we have to determine which citizen tells the truth and which is a liar."

"That's easy." Falk pointed at the white and black statue. "That statue is from the city of Life." Then he gestured at the angry red statue. "That's the citizen of Death."

"It won't be that simple," Devika said. "Yes, I think you're right about what the statues represent. But so far, none of the trial up to this point has been that easy."

"But if the white and black statue represents the city of Life, we can simply ask it where the city of Life is," Vincent argued.

"Forget what the statues represent," Devika said. "Assume we're asking this podium here the question. We don't know if it will tell the truth or lie. We need a question that will point us to the city of Life whether the podium lies or tells the truth."

For a few minutes they studied the message in silence.

"We should ask in which direction it would go." Adrian beamed. "If this is the citizen of Life, it'll direct us to the City of Life because it tells the truth. The citizen of death will want to go to the city of death, but since it always lies, it will also point us to the City of Life."

"That's it!" Vincent said.

"You got it," Falk added.

The pair clapped Adrian on the shoulder.

"No, that's wrong." She knew Adrian's logic didn't work.

He glowered at her. "You're just mad I thought of the correct question."

"No, listen," she protested. "We agree the citizen of death always lies. However, if we ask it where it would go, we're assuming where it wants to go. We could be wrong. Just because it's a citizen of death doesn't mean that's where it would choose to go."

"So, we ask the question and go in the opposite direction instead," Vincent reasoned.

"Then we're assuming the podium is the citizen of Death instead of the citizen of Life telling the truth. We need a question that doesn't require us to make assumptions. You know what they say when you assume."

"You make a donkey of you and me," Nico pitched in, grinning.

"Or we don't worry about who is who." Adrian's nostrils flared. "We ask directions to one city or the other and go check it out. If we end up at the city of Death, we'll know if the citizen told the truth or lied, depending on which question we go with. Then we return and flip the question to get to the city of Life. And if we guess the city of Life the first try, all the better."

Devika checked her oxygen levels. She had less than two hours' worth left in her tank. She gestured at Nico. "We only came with one oxygen tank each. We'll run out of time checking out both locations."

"Sucks for you," Adrian crowed, pointing at the pair on his back. "We came with spares. But you head back. We'll keep going. Don't worry."

She ground her teeth as she pulled up the results of her toxins tests. "I also don't think we can visit the city of Death. The toxin levels on the surface used to be considerably higher. Our suits protected us. But my gut tells me those levels in the city of Death are higher. I'd bet they're high enough to compromise our suits and kill us."

"Who's assuming now?" Adrian countered.

She hoped he could read the concern on her face, not only for herself and Nico, but for them as well. "Call it caution. I don't want to risk going to the wrong city. Based upon the parameters set by the riddle, there has to be a question that will correctly lead us to the city of Life regardless of which citizen we ask."

"Maybe we should return for help?" Nico suggested. "Someone back at the beach can figure out the right question."

Adrian crossed his arms. "No way. I'm not giving up our shot."

Devika agreed with him. She intended to solve the puzzle, not hand it over to someone else. And while she wasn't ready to admit it, she knew Adrian felt the same way. It made her think about the AI's words.

Nico consulted the pedestal text again. "We need to figure out which citizen we're talking to."

"How about we ask it?" Falk proposed. "If we ask the citizen of Life which one it is, it will answer truthfully. If it's the citizen of

Death, it has to lie and tell us it's the…" His words trailed off, as if he had realized his error.

Devika shared Falk's frustration. They all did. "If we ask a question that answers which statue is which, we can't then ask a second. We have to figure out both with the same question."

"Two birds with one stone," Adrian growled, his nose wrinkled.

Vincent threw his arms up in the air and walked off the dais.

Nico tapped an open palm onto a curled fist. "How do we learn where they are from, and which path leads there with one question?"

Devika gripped his arm with both hands. "That's it!"

"What?" Nico raised his eyebrows.

She bounced over to the podium, resting both hands on its edges. Staring down at the message, she asked. "Down which path do you live?"

******

From underground, loud gears shifted. Both massive statues rotated to face the memorial.

"No!" Nico grabbed the sides of his head. "The memorial commemorates the dead. You gotten it wrong."

Devika feared she'd overlooked some flaw in her question. "It's correct. It has to be."

"I'm with Nico." Adrian's brow darkened. "If that memorial marks one city, it's the city of Death. You got it wrong, Devika. You screwed this up for all of us." He pushed her away, taking her place. He pawed at the podium. "We have to figure out how to reset this thing. Come up with a different question."

The gears continued to churn, the sound rumbling beneath the ground.

Devika grabbed Adrian's arm to stop his efforts. "The memorial doesn't mark their death. It honors their lives. Learning from the past instead of dwelling on it leads to the future."

He shook her off. "If you say so."

"Look!" She pointed to where a spiral staircase rotated upward from within the memorial until it connected with a door far overhead. "Do you believe me now?"

Adrian leapt off the dais and sprinted into the memorial, Vincent and Falk on his heels. Devika chased after them, annoyed that they were taking advantage of her discovery once more. But as she re-entered the memorial, the Etaem holograms kicked on again, recounting their stories.

How had their destruction started? Pride? The desire to be right and get the credit they deserved that grew until it spiraled out of control?

She had solved the riddles, yes, but would she have figured it out without Nico's ideas that helped her think through it? Would she have come this far, through the toxic wasteland, if not for Adrian's challenge?

"What do you think is up there?" Nico's chest heaved as they rushed up the staircase.

"I don't know." Despite the AI's claims to the contrary, she still hoped it revealed the Etaem's whereabouts.

The door at the top of the stairs opened on a grand hall filled with hundreds of obelisk pairs—one rising from the floor while the second dropped from the ceiling. A large diamond hovered in the air between each obelisk pair. Bright white light emanated from the diamonds and filled the room, though Devika didn't think that was their purpose.

"Congratulations," the AI from the memorial said. Light pulsated from every diamond in rhythm to its voice. "You've reached the Etaem city of Life. Stored here is the sum of all Etaem knowledge. Our history, our technology, our understanding of our home and the universe. It is yours."

"Thank you," Devika said as she approached one of the obelisk pairs, staring at the diamond light.

"We bequeath it to you. In honorable hands, it provides healing for all sickness and disease. It can prolong life, show you how to access any resource you encounter, and offers methods to create wonders beyond belief. In the clutches of the corrupt, you've witnessed below the destruction it can wreak.

"We hope we've chosen wisely."

Within the diamond before her, she observed the mobile thorneways, how they operated showing like a video within the light. Then a galaxy appeared and transformed into a map with numbers along the perimeter.

"The Etaem mapped numerous galaxies down to the micrometer level," the AI told her. "They assigned precise coordinates, and with that could establish a thorneway to any spot in the galaxies they'd mapped out. They created billions of thorneway wristbands from which anyone could initiate a mobile thorneway."

She marveled at that. At present, Space City only had access to a handful of galaxies via their thorneways. With the coordinates from the Etaem database, the number of galaxies open to instantaneous travel expanded exponentially.

In a second diamond she discovered a universal vaccine. Instead of providing immunity to one specific virus or bacterium as human vaccines did, this universal one could supercharge the immune system. Given to young children, the vaccine helped the immune system identify, mobilize, and defend the body against any type of infection. The diamond also detailed how to adapt the vaccine for a wide variety of physiologies. It could work for Etaem, humans, Alfar, Malsain, Kali, Traga.

Emotion overcame her. If they'd found this place a year ago, they might've avoided the outbreak aboard Space City and among the Alfar. Anand wouldn't have needed to travel to Orestes to help with the cure when the Dahaka attacked the facility. He would've never been wounded, forcing him to go to Ourania for the healing that permanently isolated her from him.

With this technology, they could improve the quality of life for trillions throughout the universe. But it couldn't undo the healing process Anand had already undergone.

Nico whistled while starting at another diamond. "These diamonds store radiation. That's what powered the city. They can power this place for thousands of years."

Out of the corner of her eye, Devika noticed Adrian approach. He'd pursed his lips in an unreadable expression. She tensed, wondering what he wanted.

He held a thin black tube. "I'd like to give you half my spare oxygen from my extra tank."

"What?" She eyed the tube, wondering if he was trying to trick her.

"Seriously." He gestured to the tank on her back. "We might be here a while checking all this cool stuff out and I've got extra."

She stared at him. "Why?"

He grimaced. "I…" His eyes dropped to his feet, his voice hushed. "Screwed up. I assumed you were here to look cool." His thumb brushed back and forth across the oxygen tank in his hand. "This has been our passion for five years, since our first days at the Academy. And…" he sighed, "… I'm sorry I let my desperation to solve the trial lead me to unconscionable actions. I have no excuse, but my threats were empty. You were smarter than everyone who has been trying to solve this trial."

She almost snapped at him. He had been horrible to her, but her thoughts drifted to the memorial below commemorating a city's worth of dead Etaem because they couldn't get over their hatred of each other. She didn't want to perpetuate that cycle.

Adrian coughed uncomfortably, offering the tank again and drawing Devika from her thoughts.

"I wasn't smarter," she said as she accepted the oxygen tank. "I brought a fresh perspective. Though I would like to think that I earned this."

"You did one hundred percent." He smiled as he gestured to the oxygen tank. "Would you like me to help you refill your tank?"

"Thanks!" She handed it back and turned to give him access to her tank.

She felt the earnestness of his apology and thanks. She understood his feelings, even if they didn't justify his actions. But people could learn from their mistakes, couldn't they? Choose a different path that didn't perpetuate division?

He connected his spare oxygen tank to hers and transferred air until hers was refilled. Vincent did the same for Nico. They now had a little over three hours to study the Etaem tech before they needed to head back.

"Look at this!" Falk pointed at another diamond light. "They wore eye contacts like we do. Ones that let them zoom in on faraway sights, have night vision, and thermal vision. But they also had a mode that lets them see invisible gases. Like those outside."

"No way!" Nico hurried over to join him. After a couple of minutes of study, he said, "I think… I might be able to adapt the programming in our contacts to make it work for us, too." He went to work on his wrist-comp.

Devika strolled to other diamonds, wondering what other miracles they'd find in this place. Miracles that would one day be commonplace. After a couple of hours perusing this Etaem Hall of Wonders, as they'd taken to calling it, they finally decided to head back. None of them wanted to leave, their voices giddy with each new discovery. But they needed to rest, to eat, and to share their discovery, not to mention refill their oxygen tanks.

Nico uploaded some additional programming for their contacts, giving them temporary patches that allowed them to see invisible gases. Space City scientists and programmers would need to develop long-term solutions for the tech.

They hiked back through the city, marveling at the sights, and up to the surface. When they reached topside, they all halted. Devika's skin crawled as she scanned the wasteland. Bile rose in her throat.

The previously invisible gas registered as a sickly green slime that covered everything. Even knowing her suit protected her, the idea of passing through it made her shiver with disgust. Unfortunately, they hadn't discovered any wristbands that would allow them to open a mobile thorneway. She debated suggesting they go back down and search harder.

Nico's mouth wrinkled. "I shouldn't have added the new coding."

"It's okay." Adrian took one tentative step forward. "We crossed it once. We can do it again."

He was right, but Devika didn't have to like it.

He started forward. She groaned and followed. If he could do it, so would she. While she'd let the enmity between them go, she wasn't about to let him outdo her.

They pushed hard, wanting to cross the wasteland quickly. The toxic slime stuck to their shoes, and soon covered them. She wished they had some B-choppers from the Mars base to fly over it.

It didn't take long to reach the hillside that divided the wasteland from the beach. Many trial participants had departed. Someone had discovered a mobile thorneway device while they'd been underground.

An older woman spotted them and called out, "What are you five doing out there?"

Devika recognized the woman as one of the two who had helped her with the clues for the map riddle back in the temple.

"Didn't you see the warnings about the contaminations?" the woman asked.

"We did." Devika stopped short of the woman, not wanting to get too close until she'd undergone decontamination. "We also found the final stage of the trial. We completed it."

"Completed it?" The woman's eyes widened.

"Devika did," Adrian corrected, pointing to her.

Those on the ridge crowded in, barraging her with questions.

"Keep your distance. Our suits are covered in the toxins from the wasteland," Devika warned.

People backed away, but the barrage of questions continued. She answered as best she could, Nico and the others adding in their own experiences.

Finally, she sagged with exhaustion. "Could someone send me back to Space City? And alert them that I need a decontamination cleaning."

The older woman agreed and activated a mobile thorneway for her. Devika thanked her, walked up the hillside to the thorneway, and stepped through.

Her eyes widened as she beheld the flight deck of an alien ship.

It was not Space City.

Chapter 10

"Welcome, Devika, are you ready for the journey?"

She looked around for the speaker, but didn't see anyone. "Who are you? What is this?"

Why wasn't she back on Space City? Had the old woman sent her to the wrong place?

"We spoke earlier," the voice said, its tone familiar. "This is an Etaem seeker ship."

It was the voice of the AI from Laquir, the underground city, though no hologram was visible.

"Where are we?" she asked.

A series of constellations cycled across the ceiling.

She pointed at them. "What is that?"

"It's another map," the AI said.

"Map to what?"

"To the Etaem."

"What?" She backed up and bumped into a wall screen displaying ship data.

"You proved yourself worthy by passing the trial. You've been chosen as your people's ambassador to the Etaem."

Her chest tightened. She struggled to breathe, contemplating the AI's words. *I can't go find the Etaem. Where are we headed? How long will it take?*

"I sense an elevated pulse associated with fear in humans." A mechanical arm appeared with a needle. "Shall I provide sedation to calm you?"

"No!" She raised her hands and bumped into the wall screen again. "Don't. Please. I can't. We can't. I thought you didn't know the way to the Etaem?"

"I said I didn't know where the Etaem are," the AI corrected. The mechanical arm retreated. "I do have the knowledge to find them. The data you found at the end of the Evanesco trial will lead us to them."

The ship's forward viewing screen showed them in deep space, no planets in sight. She dropped into a single chair in the flight deck, her heart racing, as she struggled to catch her breath.

"I can't go." She looked around the area, wishing for a hologram of the AI to focus on. "I need to return. To go home."

"That cannot be arranged."

"What do you mean? Send me back the way I came."

"You were intercepted by a special thorneway with a booster this ship cannot replicate. We are out of range of any thorneways that can return you home. We must continue on until we reach the Etaem."

"Out of range? Are you saying I can't ever go back?" She gasped for breath, heart thudding in her chest.

"Not until we reach the Etaem. They can send you back."

That was a relief. "How long will it take?"

"Exact data cannot be calculated. Perhaps it is best if I sedate you. You need rest." The arm with the needle reappeared.

"No." She gripped the seat arms until her hands hurt. "Do not sedate me or inject me with anything."

"Understood."

"What can you tell me about where we're going?"

"Only that I have coordinates to a location. There we should learn more about where the Etaem have gone."

"Great. How long will it take to reach that location?"

"Approximately one point three five Havendesh revolutions."

She did a quick calculation. It equaled eighteen earth months. She moaned.

"A sedative so you can rest would be good for your health."

"Absolutely not!" If that arm got too close, she would break the needle off.

"Very well. Then, to use a human term, 'Buckle up.' We are in for a long ride."

Sacrifices

Chapter 1

Arielle Delven's wrist-comp chimed seventeen hundred hours. Her free weekend had arrived! She'd taken an extra day off to travel with Dirk to Sundara.

Standing from the mini desk crammed into her closet-sized office, Arielle dressed in her waterproof coveralls that ran from her feet up to her waist. The coveralls stank from wading through filthy water wherever she went. Krozitch rested in the middle of a swamp, the same as all the other Malsain cities she'd encountered in her limited travel time. Perhaps all of Gleeson was a swamp.

At the door, she grabbed her jacket from the wall hook and flipped off the light. No sooner had she stepped out of her office than Berren Sadik, her supervisor, called out to her.

"Have you finished Holgersen and Petrescu's expense reports to Paalou?"

"Just finished," Arielle answered, approaching his corner office. "It's awaiting your approval."

"What about Holgersen's briefing before the Malsain committee on Foreign Affiliations?" Berren's gray eyes narrowed, accentuating his wrinkles.

"I've gotten Holgersen's revisions. I'll update the package on Tuesday."

In addition to the Holgersen briefing, mounds of digital paperwork filled Arielle's wrist-comp. As a Consular officer, she assisted all Space City travelers to Gleeson with their approvals to visit, oversaw their itineraries, and ensured they attended a security briefing Berren gave here at the Space City Embassy in Krozitch upon arrival.

On top of that, Berren had her handling the expense reports for the two diplomats stationed at the Embassy. He transferred all the diplomats' receipts to her, along with any brief summaries, although the diplomats rarely bothered with those. Instead, she had access to their calendars so she could write a mini summary of their activities based on the meetings.

None of it was the kind of work she'd imagined during her diplomat training programs.

"Why don't you work on it this weekend?" Berren suggested. "I'd like it for review by lunch on Monday."

Arielle smiled, taking care not to show her annoyance. "This is my travel weekend to Sundara."

He frowned. "Travel weekend? I didn't approve any travel off Gleeson."

"I completed the travel authorization form and got your signature a month ago." She kept her voice neutral, as if reminding him, not accusing. "I also put it on your calendar."

He pulled up his calendar on his wrist-comp and studied it a moment. "Very well. But I want that briefing ready first thing Tuesday morning."

She started to remind him she had Monday off as well—final review with Holgersen was the end of the day on Wednesday—but she decided not to press it. She'd work it Monday evening when she returned.

"I'll have it ready." Arielle fled before he could add to her duties.

Emerging from the embassy, she stepped down into knee-high swamp water. The one-story embassy, rather small and unassuming compared to most government buildings she'd seen, still dwarfed most other Malsain buildings here in Krozitch. It rested on massive concrete pillars that raised it just out of the water, although during heavy rains the floors flooded several centimeters.

The rotten stench of swamp water pervaded everything out here. Thick-trunked Glabrous Hag trees covered with Home Shade—what she thought of as Spanish moss—comprised most of the city. The Malsain built their homes and offices up among the branches, open to the elements except for the Home Shade covering.

Arielle waded past gray Drowning Nectar plants, which ate any insects foolish enough to sample their sticky sap. It was no wonder the Malsain stank. Tepid water filled their cities. But even with the coveralls and jacket to protect her from getting soaked, her regular clothes stank, too. She sweated profusely from bundling up in such a humid environment.

Whenever she left this assignment, she planned to throw away her entire wardrobe and buy a new one.

The Malsain she waded past gave her amused smiles, their long tongues licking the air.

"What'ss your russhess?" a Malsain asked.

"Don't you want to sssmell the nectar?" another taunted.

While she hurried from place to place, they luxuriated in the swamp water. Many swam, scaly tails propelling them through the waters.

"Catchess."

A flick of a tail splashed the water, sending a blood-banded serpent flying at her head. She screamed and ducked. The serpent hissed as it soared past her left ear.

Did every Malsain in Krozitch consider it their personal mission to make her daily excursions miserable?

The diplomats had their own private thorneway inside the embassy, allowing them to minimize outdoor excursions. Berren got exceptions to use the private thorneways, too. But not her. Not even for travel off world.

When she arrived at the Krozitch public thorneways, Arielle presented her ID to the guards. Tomorrow she'd see Dirk for the first time in over two months.

Unlike her, he'd been lucky. He had landed his first job at the Embassy on Niveum. During the spring he'd applied for several jobs, while she had only applied for the Space City Embassy in Tanarille on Sundara. Despite knowing it was one of the more coveted Space City Embassies, she'd relied on Tiru's backing to get her a job. As a retired Azzaro diplomat, Tiru maintained many contacts at the Space City Embassy. Arielle had assumed that would be enough. When that had fallen through, she'd received an assignment to Krozitch, underscoring the importance of not putting all one's toads in the same pot, as the Malsain put it.

"Travel from Krozitch to Tanarille ready for access," a guard announced.

A thorneway activated, and Arielle stepped through it.

First on her agenda: head to Tiru's house to clean up and change. Thankfully, Dirk wouldn't see her before then. Tonight, she would have dinner with Tiru and her husband, Instructor Zelo. Tomorrow they'd travel out to the Otoch monuments to meet Dirk before the Triplet Geysers erupted.

Arielle shifted through the crowd filling the Otoch monuments—the ruins of an ancient Azzaro city. Enormous, flat-topped pyramids comprised most of the buildings still standing. She angled toward the blue stone bridge where she and Dirk had watched the eruption last year.

After dinner with Tiru and Instructor Zelo the previous night, she'd wandered the streets of Tanarille, reminiscing. She'd loved living in the Azzaro capital, and the diplomat training program had been incredible. Even after the craziness of Nochil Rassa, an ambitious local official in the town of Kaahrim, holding her and Dirk hostage, she wouldn't trade the experience. Though now she triple-checked for her Azzaro ID before she went anywhere and had Tiru's direct contact information on her wrist-comp.

Landing a job at the Space City Embassy in Tanarille remained her goal. But instead of a consular officer as she was now on Gleeson, she intended to one day become Space City's diplomat to Sundara.

She strolled onto the bridge, the walls etched with early Azzaro pictograms. They told the story of K'inn and T'amm, the Sun twins. From Azzaro mythology, the brother and sister raced each other around Sundara, carrying the twin suns on their shoulders. To motivate the twins to keep racing, every year at the summer solstice the Azzaro held a festival to cheer them on. If everyone on Sundara participated in the festival, the twins would bless them for another year.

Arielle scanned the crowd for Dirk. A blue-eyed, blonde-haired German should stand out among the blue-skinned Azzaro. Either he was hiding or he hadn't arrived. If the latter, he was cutting it close. One hour remained until the Triplet Geysers erupted.

Her last message from him that morning indicated he was finishing some paperwork, but it would in no way stop him from coming. He'd assured her of that. Had he misjudged how long it would take him to travel here from the Macab home planet, Niveum? She'd asked him to join her in Tanarille, but he'd said he had a surprise for her and would meet her here.

Her eyes halted on a figure dressed in dark orange robes staring straight at her. Hard eyes peered out from a bright orange mask shaped in the classic depiction of K'inn. The costume was common during the festival. Still, the hair on the back of her neck rose. She glanced away, unsettled. When she turned back, the figure had evaporated into the crowd.

Unable to shake her discomfort, and with no sign of Dirk, she pulled up her wrist-comp. He still hadn't responded.

"Where are you?" she asked, dictating the message to her wrist-comp. "I hope you're not going to be late for the one-year anniversary of our first date." She added a winking emoji to the end of her message and sent it.

What was taking him so long? And what was he planning?

Still unsettled, Arielle wandered for a bit. Azzaros milled about, some chatting, others buying food from vendors; but everyone kept one eye on the wisps of steam rising from the beautiful turquoise water that shimmered in the pools where the Triplet Geysers would soon erupt.

The Triplet Geysers eruption marked the summer solstice and the start of the festival. Tonight, many more Azzaros would wear the sibling costumes, with red representing T'amm. They'd release thousands of orange and red sky lanterns in celebration.

With thirty minutes until the eruption, she drifted back to the bridge. Her discomfort returned, this time for Dirk instead of herself. At the fifteen-minute mark, she sent a follow-up message.

"When I said I hope you're not gonna be late I was joking, but now I'm starting to wonder. Where are you?"

Nervous energy bubbled in her gut. Had something happened to him? What would prevent him from coming, or at least messaging her? Could it be part of his surprise?

Water shot more than seven meters into the air from all three geysers. Arielle jumped, a small gasp escaping her. Everyone cheered. The summer festival had started. She couldn't remember why the eruptions marked the start, but Dirk knew. She remembered him remarking on it. Why hadn't he shown?

Then she remembered he'd given her his GPS locator information for his wrist-comp. She could check his exact location at this moment.

She activated the locator. After a few seconds, she frowned and scanned the crowds. His wrist-comp had pinged in the area, but she couldn't spot him. Why hadn't he come to the bridge? They'd agreed to meet here.

She checked the locator again. It pinpointed him inside a pyramid nearby. She frowned. Why would he be there? He couldn't have gotten lost.

She pushed through the dispersing crowd toward the pyramid, her agitation growing. Unlike the splendid palace at the heart of the ruins, it was not large. Two carved stelae, carved to depict K'inn and T'amm, guarded the entrance. Hieroglyphics and depictions of strange, winged creatures covered the walls of a narrow hallway leading inside. Her instinct said to retreat, but the place would interest Dirk, so she pressed forward.

The hallway ended at a corbel arch, which served as an entrance for a chamber with vaulted ceilings. A dozen stone fire pits filled the chamber, over which large vats bubbled with some dark liquid. The orange-robed figure from earlier entered the far side of the room.

"Hello, Arielle." The figure lifted his mask to reveal Nochil Rassa.

Shee backed up, turning to run.

"Don't!" he warned. "Don't run or Dirk will die."

Chapter 3

Arielle's heart raced. "What have you done with Dirk?"

"What do you know about the festival of the twins?" Nochil Rassa asked.

"What's that got to do with Dirk?"

"It marks the summer solstice—"

"I know what it means," she snapped.

Nochil Rassa held up a finger. "Yes, but did you know there's another ritual to K'inn held from the time his sun sets until it rises the next morning?" He waited for a response. She had no intention of indulging him, so he continued, "After millennia carrying his sun across the sky in his race with T'amm, K'inn had grown old and tired."

Nochil Rassa spoke like an orator who had delivered this story countless times before. No. Not Nochil. Just Rassa. He'd lost his title after what he'd done to her and Dirk last summer.

"During one festival of the twins long ago, K'inn visited Akanna Caarus's court."

Her tradutor translated "Akanna" as "King."

"K'inn appeared old and wrinkled, but revealed himself by holding his sun in one hand. K'inn told the akanna and his court that he could no longer race T'amm. He required a younger body with greater strength. K'inn gave Akanna Caarus until one hour before the dawning of his sun to choose a sacrifice from his court as K'inn's new body. He warned Caarus against choosing any male who was weak, sickly, or near death. To race T'amm, he required a powerful body. Without it, his sun would never rise again."

Sweat broke out across Arielle's body, the room hot from the steam rising off the giant bubbling vats over the fires.

"That night the king and his court deliberated for hours. The wealthy among them blocked their sons, not wanting to lose their heirs. They argued that those carrying bricks for the temples or working the fields were the strongest, making them most suitable.

"The King refused to ask the least among them to make the greatest sacrifice. With the dawn drawing nigh, the king's eldest son rose. 'I will do it. I will be the sacrifice.'

"The king protested, not wanting to lose his heir either, but his son insisted. 'As you yourself said, you've no right to ask others to make the sacrifice. I volunteer. And my brother can succeed you in my stead.' The King grieved, but agreed to his son's decision.

"Before dawn they sacrificed the prince. K'inn's sun rose again to race T'amm once more. For the entire year K'inn raced daily across the sky, first pursuing, then leading T'amm. Then the following year during the summer solstice K'inn returned, and every year thereafter."

Despite the heat, chills rippled along Arielle's arms like icy rain on a pond. Was this why Rassa had captured Dirk? She activated her wrist-comp and prepared to send a warning to Tiru.

"Stop." Rassa took a couple of steps toward her. His eyes flashed anger. "If you call for help, I'll be gone before they arrive. You'll ensure Dirk's death."

She swallowed a scream, struggling to control the dread flooding through her at his confirmation of her suspicions.

He turned and gestured behind him, deeper into the temple. "If you come with me, you'll have a chance to save him."

"You're lying." She backed away. "You're trying to capture me, too, so you can finish what you failed last year."

He laughed. "I don't need you." He shrugged as though she didn't matter at all. "I've got Dirk. He's the only one that matters. But in honor of custom, I'm giving you a chance to save him."

"Doing what?" she asked.

He pointed at her wrist. "First, hand over the armband; then come with me. I'll tell you on the way."

"What?" She took a step back, covering her wrist-comp with her free hand. She'd heard him, but she asked anyway to stall.

He pointed at her wrist-comp again. "Give it to me. I won't have you alerting anyone to where we're going."

This was a trap. She knew it. But she was also sure he wasn't lying to her. If she left now, she'd never see Dirk again. She couldn't let him die like that, a sacrifice to a mythical god.

"Okay, I'll go with you." She did her best to look defiant. "But if you've hurt Dirk and lied to me—"

"Save the empty threat," Rassa said. "Hand it over."

As she removed the wrist-comp, she activated it before holding it out. He crossed the room, snatched the device away, and threw it into a boiling vat.

Chapter 4

Without the wrist-comp, no one could track her. Arielle's mouth went dry as she stared at the vat, feeling truly vulnerable for the first time since last summer. She forced down tears.

Rassa lowered the orange mask over his face once more. Then he pulled another mask and a spare robe from within his own and thrust them at her. They were bright red for T'amm.

"Put these on."

Shee donned the mask and robe. The mask's narrow eye slits hindered her vision.

Without waiting for her to get adjusted, Rassa grabbed her wrist, yanking her deeper into the temple. The next chamber held altars where holographic Azzaros cleaned animal sacrifices, mostly birds and snakes. From there they entered a dark tunnel sloping downward. Arielle barely detected Rassa's outline ahead of her. It took every ounce of self-control not to retreat. She should escape and come back with help. But if she ran now, she'd lose Dirk forever. She believed Rassa on that account.

After an interminable hike underground, the tunnel inclined toward sunlight. They emerged in the middle of a forest, the pyramids nowhere in sight. Nor any other distinguishing landmark.

Again, she resisted the urge to run, to save herself. Rassa had her with an invisible leash. So, she tried to recall the landscape around the Triplet Geysers from her arrival. There were mountains to the southwest, but the tunnel hadn't led in that direction. Hadn't there been a forest to the northeast?

A short walk led them to a meadow with a stream running through it. Beside the water waited a private aircraft. Rassa hurried to it and opened the door.

Arielle halted. "Where are we going? And what do I have to do to save Dirk?"

"Once we're in the air."

"No." She crossed her arms. "Tell me first."

He growled and motioned her to get in. "I told you I don't need you. I have Dirk. If you want to keep playing games, I'll leave you here and your chance to save him will end."

If she clubbed him with a branch and stole the aircraft, could she use it to track Dirk down and free him? She indulged in the fantasy as she approached the aircraft, which gave way to revulsion as she passed Rass to climb inside.

He jumped in behind her and forced her to the back seat.

"Where are we going?" she demanded, fists clenched.

For answer he locked the doors.

He lifted off, clearing the forest, then turned southeast. Ten minutes later, they flew over the pyramids and Triplet Geysers. Other aircraft took off nearby as those in attendance began the trek home.

She studied the other aircraft, hoping to spot Instructor Zelo and Tiru, but they'd be on the ground searching for her and Dirk by now. Would they be able to track her at this point?

But that didn't matter right now. Rassa had her. And if she was to escape with Dirk, she needed to figure out what he had planned. "Tell me about this ritual."

The Azzaro smirked as he focused on the landscape. "After the setting of K'inn's sun we hold a Lusus, a competition between two teams."

Within minutes, they were alone once more. No one else traveled a similar flight path.

"Unlike Akanna Caarus' son, no one volunteered for sacrifice the following year. The akanna, not wishing to order anyone's death, instead devised the Lusus to determine the chosen. Two male potentials are chosen, and teams composed of their friends and family members fight for them. At the Lusus' conclusion, the losing team's potential is sacrificed.

"I'm giving you the chance to compete. Win and Dirk will be spared."

She gaped at him. She had to play in a game with Dirk's life as the prize. And if she somehow emerged victorious, that meant someone else died in his stead.

"It won't be easy to win," Rassa said as though he was her coach trying to prepare her. "But I'm granting you the chance."

They descended toward an old airport, with one enormous building surrounded by a half dozen smaller ones, all in various states of deterioration. Arielle couldn't imagine the place saw regular traffic, yet a variety of aircraft sat in and around the hangars.

Rassa landed on a cracked runway that was narrowed by encroaching greenery. He guided the aircraft toward a hangar, parking out front. Three armed Azzaros emerged from the largest building. After Rassa climbed out, the one with a long nose climbed in and yanked her from it.

"What? Afraid I'll take the aircraft and run you lot over with it?" she snapped, rubbing her sore elbow.

"Silence." Long Nose glared at her.

Rassa split off from them without a word. Arielle opened her mouth to demand to see Dirk, but Long Nose prodded her with his gun toward the main building. The other two surrounded her and led her inside.

A huge pen area filled with prisoners took up most of the interior. Many of the prisoners were Azzaros, but she saw other species as well. A Macab, a few Malsain, and a Traga in his own confined area.

What was this place? The prison-like atmosphere was strange considering Azzaros abhorred imprisonment. If someone committed a crime, the Azzaros used rehabilitation and other punishments.

So, what was Rassa doing with these prisoners?

Toward the rear of the cells, Dirk sat on a cot staring at the floor. There were no obvious bruises on him, but he was too far away for her to be sure. She took a step toward him, but Long Nose blocked her path, motioning with a glare for her to follow. She hesitated, eyeing Dirk a moment longer before following the front guard.

How and where had Rassa captured Dirk?

The armed Azzaros led her out a side door, not passing anywhere near Dirk, and into one of the smaller buildings. A private corridor with minimal lighting led to secluded cells. The guards forced her into an unoccupied cell with a cot and a stone basin holding a little water.

"When is the Lusus?" she asked.

The guards departed without a word.

"Hey!" she shouted after them, smacking her hand on the bars. "Rassa promised I'm involved."

Was there even a Lusus? Was it all a trap to punish her for escaping last summer?

Chapter 5

"Get up." An Azzaro guard kicked the bars of her cell.

Arielle's eyes popped open, blinking back sleep. She held up a hand to shield her eyes from the flashlight pointed at her. Despite her fears, the stillness and limited visibility had lulled her into a restless semi-consciousness.

The cell door squealed open. She rose from the cot, taking tentative steps forward.

"How is Dirk?" she asked, trying to make out the Azzaro guard through the bright light in her face.

"This way." The guard headed back toward the front entrance.

She stumbled after him. Her vision swam after the light shining in her eyes, causing her to stumble and reach out to the wall for support. When they emerged back in the open pen area, K'inn's sun had set. It was the point in the day when, according to their myths, K'inn demanded his sacrifice.

Funny how only the god demanded sacrifices. The goddess never asked for anything, not even the festival tribute.

They passed the pen that had held Dirk, but he was no longer inside. Her heart quivered. Had Rassa lied to her? Had he already sacrificed Dirk?

She squeezed her shaking hands into fists, but she could no more banish her fears than fix her present situation. Or save Dirk.

They exited the rear of the facility. The Azzaro guard led her between a series of nondescript buildings. They emerged onto a wide hill. Torches taller than the guard stood scattered across the hill, which sloped down to a stadium built into the ground. Thousands of figures clad in the orange or red twins costumes packed the stands. Their raucous shouts filled the air.

She followed the guard into a torchlit tunnel beneath the stands where he retrieved a jersey from a crate along one wall and tossed it at her. She caught the dark green jersey.

"Put that on," he ordered.

The jersey was a little large, but she slipped it on over her regular shirt. Then she followed him out onto an enormous, grassy field. They stood inside a stadium.

Murals depicting a violent sporting event covered walls surrounding the field. Many of the figures punched, kicked, or knocked their opponents down while advancing a ball up the field. Along the walls' base, markers at regular intervals denoted one hundred meters from end to end and forty across.

From center field, the number of fans present up in the stands was overwhelming. It surprised her how many Azzaros took part in this barbaric tradition.

At the top of the high wall closest to her stood an Azzaro male chained to a pillar. Tall and strong, he gazed out at the crowd, his chest puffed out despite the chain. Was he daring them to sacrifice him, or proud that they might?

Beneath him, about halfway up the wall, a metal bar was mounted perpendicular to the wall's surface. From the bar hung a rusty metallic ring whose inner diameter looked to be half a meter.

In a panic, Arielle turned to face the far end of the field where Dirk, head bowed and shoulders slumped, stood chained atop the wall. She ran across the field, conscious of all the eyes on her, but not caring.

"Dirk, are you all right?"

His head shot up at her words, his eyes widening. He bore no visible signs of abuse. "Arielle? What are you doing here?"

"Getting you out of this," she replied, fighting back tears she didn't want to show.

"No!" His eyes pleaded with her. "Don't risk yourself. Get out of here."

"I…" Her voice choked with emotion. "… don't think I have a choice."

Another ring hung suspended from the wall beneath him. She wanted to grab it, climb the wall, unchain him and check for injuries, then escape.

But if Rassa had told the truth, the only way to protect Dirk was to compete here on the field. Yet, if she somehow won, she condemned the Azzaro at the opposite end of the field to death. It was a lose-lose proposition. But despite the guilt that filled her at the thought, she would ensure Dirk wasn't the sacrifice tonight. Somehow.

"I'm going to save you," she said, hoping her fear, guilt, and self-doubt didn't show in her voice or on her face.

"Forget about me. Protect yourself," he said.

Four Azzaros approached her on the field, staring at her with mouths agape. They all wore the same dark green jerseys.

"You're on our team?" one female asked. She was shorter than Arielle and almost sickly thin, with a maze haircut. She didn't seem the type to compete in a physical competition.

Arielle blinked once, activating her eye contacts' name recall function. The name Bayru appeared on the Azzaro's chest in glowing neon letters as Arielle had customized it. The names of her other teammates also appeared on their chests. Thanks to the treaty with the Azzaros, the Space City database could identify all citizens.

Besides Bayru, Arielle had one other female Azzaro teammate, who was the tallest of the group. Her left arm ended just short of her wrist.

Arielle also had two male teammates—one thin-as-a-rubberband with the name Zume and the second a large, lumbering Azzaro named Gavie. None of them looked athletic. If she had to guess, all four were competing for the first time in such an event. They all wore pads on their wrists, elbows, knees, and shoulders, but their gear didn't fit.

"I am," Arielle replied. "Dirk is my...." Her words trailed off.

Velly pointed at Dirk and asked in a sympathetic tone. "He's yours?"

"Yes," Arielle stammered, again blinking back tears. "Please. We have to save him."

None of them responded, their eyes shifting in other directions.

She just stopped herself from lashing out at them in frustration. "Don't give up on him. Don't consign Dirk to death."

Bayru handed her forearm and shin pads for a response.

The crowd roared as the opposing Azzaro team entered the field. Three males and two females wore bright yellow jerseys. All five Yellows were strong and fit, like their chained counterpart. They also wore pads, though theirs fit as if custom made for them. Rassa had stacked the deck against her.

This wasn't fair. No wonder the chosen Azzaro didn't mind his chains. What did he have to fear? His team wasn't likely to lose.

An Azzaro official in an orange mask and robe stepped out onto the middle of the field. He carried a large red ball in one hand. The Yellows jogged toward him.

His voice amplified, the official said, "It's time to get this Lusus started!"

The crowd cheered.

Chapter 6

"How does this game work?" Arielle asked Bayru as she donned her pads.

"You don't know how to play?" Bayru's eyes bulged.

"I never even heard of this game before Rassa made me play to save Dirk." Arielle felt a surge of guilt, like she should've known all about a Lusus and how to play.

Bayru made a circle around her head with one finger, an Azzaro gesture that meant K'inn or T'amm help us. Arielle hoped Bayru meant T'amm.

"Get the ball through the ring at the opponents' end," Bayru replied. "And never touch the ball with your hands."

The Yellows spread out in a rough semi-circle surrounding the masked official with the ball. Arielle's team did as well.

"Tonight, we honor the twins and their race," the official said. "In accordance with tradition, we begin the annual Lusus to choose a new host for K'inn. This sacrifice keeps him strong, that he may continue to race every day."

The crowd cheered louder. Arielle shook her head in disbelief. How could this many people cheer on a sacrificial ceremony to a mythical god? Most Azzaros had progressed past such backward thinking. At least she'd thought so. But she supposed it was akin to flat-Earthers who refused to accept a round world despite clear evidence.

The official tossed the ball high in the air and sprinted off the field. The Yellows moved as one toward the ball, but stayed evenly spaced. Bayru and Zume moved toward the ball as well.

But as he neared a Yellow, Zume hesitated. The Yellow was much larger and stronger than Zume. The ball bounced off the Yellow's extended arms as if he were playing volleyball. It angled right toward a waiting teammate. The Yellow stepped forward and rammed Zume with his shoulder, sending him flopping to the ground.

Arielle looked for a foul call, but the official was nowhere to be seen. Her gaze shifted to the murals adorning the walls, to the violence in them.

We're on our own out here.

The Yellows pressed forward, passing the ball between them. Despite its size, the ball clearly weighed little. The Yellows struck the ball with forearms, legs, and hips, passing it to each other as they advanced it up the field.

Bayru and Zume hovered around the ball, but neither engaged the Yellows. They seemed to hope someone would drop it.

Arielle knew they couldn't afford to hope for mistakes. She darted in and attempted to steal the ball. A forearm slammed into her chest. She stumbled backward.

The ball bounced off the ground, and the Yellow used her hip to knock it toward a teammate.

The Yellows closed in on Gavie, who had taken up a defensive position in front of the ring on the wall beneath Dirk. A Yellow hit the ball toward the ring. Gavie blocked the ball with both forearms, sending it rocketing back past everyone.

Arielle whooped, elated that the Yellows hadn't scored. They stared wide-eyed at Gavie, shocked for a moment at how hard he'd hit the ball. Arielle hoped Rassa wore the same shocked expression.

Bayru took advantage of the moment to race after the ball.

"Go," Arielle cheered, as she rushed after her teammate.

The Yellows regrouped and caught up with Bayru before she reached their goal. Arielle tried to help, but they blocked her out. One Yellow slide tackled Bayru, sending her crashing to the turf. Then the Yellows pushed the ball back up the field. This time, as they approached Gavie, a Yellow faked a shot. Gavie jumped to block it, but the ball bounced instead to another Yellow whose shot ricocheted off the goal.

Arielle smiled in relief. Her enthusiasm evaporated as the ball bounced to another Yellow. This one didn't miss, sending the ball straight through the ring.

Fans in the stands erupted in cheers. Bright orange numbers glowed in the air above the field: 2-0.

Grimacing, Arielle glanced up at Dirk. He looked crestfallen. She gritted her teeth, determined not to give up for him.

As the teams lined up at midfield once more, the official rushed back out to the field. A Yellow had retrieved the ball after the score and she handed it to the official, who tossed it in the air to resume play.

Once more the Yellows took control of the ball and this time guided it in Velly's direction. She backpedaled out of the way, avoiding the abuse the Yellows had been dishing out. While Arielle might normally have sympathized with Velly, Dirk couldn't afford such timid play. As a Yellow bent to jump for the ball, Arielle swiped his legs out from under him, dropping him onto his back. Then she passed the ball to Zume before glaring at Velly, letting the Azzaro know she needed to step up and help. Velly returned a weak smile before averting her eyes and running up the field, still giving the Yellows a wide berth.

Meanwhile Bayru had run ahead of everyone. Zume passed the ball to her. Then the two of them raced to the ring, passing the ball back and forth. Their fluid movements and smooth passing surprised Arielle. The Yellows too, it seemed, because they gave chase too late this time. Zume made one last pass to Bayru, who knocked it through the ring to tie the score.

Arielle shouted for joy again, but her joy soured when she looked up at the chained Azzaro on the wall above the ring. He remained standing tall, chest puffed out, staring down like an akanna surveying his subjects. But his arrogance didn't lessen her guilt at wanting to save Dirk's life instead of his. No one deserved to die tonight in sacrifice to a false god, whether they welcomed it or not.

With the score tied once more, both sides increased their aggression. Bayru and Zume seemed to gain confidence from their score—Arielle had—and the trio harassed the Yellows. Not underestimating them anymore, the Yellows increased their physical attacks. Before long, Arielle's ribs ached, and she had tweaked her left ankle during a fall. She did her best to play through it.

Two Yellows crisscrossed, with Bayru and Zume giving chase. Bayru's full attention was on the Yellow she pursued. Taking advantage of the moment, the Yellow with the ball kicked it straight into Bayru's face. Many in the crowd cheered as Bayru dropped hard, covering her face with her hands. For a second Arielle stared in shock before sprinting forward.

"Bayru, are you okay?" she asked, bending over the writhing girl on the ground. "Let me see it."

Bayru withdrew her hands. Her right eye had already started to swell, the skin split at her cheekbone. Blood trickled from the cut, as well as from her nose.

Arielle groaned. "You need to get that looked at." They couldn't afford to play without Bayru, but she also couldn't ask the Azzaro to risk significant blood loss on Dirk's behalf.

"I'll be fine in a moment." Bayru wiped away blood from her upper lip and rolled onto her knees.

"Fine? That cut won't stop bleeding on its own."

"It'll be fine." Bayru pushed herself to her feet and glared at Arielle.

To Arielle's surprise, the cut had already closed, leaving some blood on her cheek.

"How?"

"I took a shot of nanobots before the game," Bayru responded. "Injuries happen in a Lusus. The nanobots are stitching up the wound. They can also help with breaks or fractures, though healing still takes a while. Let's get back to it before they score again."

The guard had mentioned nothing to Arielle about a nanobot shot. She guessed Rassa had ordered him not to mention it. *Another way he's rigged the deck against me.*

Despite the Yellows' best efforts, Gavie knocked away quite a few shots, and diverted others wide. One Yellow, heavily muscled himself, passed the ball to a teammate before bull rushing Gavie, who braced for the collision. At the last second, Gavie lunged forward and thumped the Yellow hard in the chest, sending him flying backward.

The Yellow lay in the grass, eyes wide, gasping for air. Gavie glared at him, then the others. Arielle wagered none of them would attempt to attack him again.

The crowd erupted in cheers. Surprised at the delayed reaction, Arielle looked around. While Gavie had defended himself, another Yellow had scored. Even when something good happened for them, it seemed to go bad.

And worse.

A shot from a Yellow brushed the top of Gavie's outstretched hands. Bright orange letters appeared again, the score five to two. The Yellows had received an extra point.

Arielle gaped. *How? Oh no, I forgot we can't touch the ball with our hands.*

A couple of drives later, she intercepted an errant pass and kicked it back the other way. She landed on a Yellow and pitched over, hitting the ground hard. Pain erupted through her ribcage. She struggled to her feet, gasping. Pain lanced through her core as if someone stabbed her repeatedly. She guessed she'd fractured a rib, if not a couple.

Tears welled up in her eyes, but she refused to seek medical treatment and leave her team shorthanded. That would spell the end for Dirk for sure.

At least Bayru had scored off the play, cutting their deficit to one point. Despite the nanobots, her right eye had swollen shut. The Azzaro grinned anyway.

After that, Arielle struggled to remain aggressive. Every time a Yellow lunged at her, she shielded her ribs. She growled at herself for it, yet she couldn't stop it either.

It was largely thanks to Gavie that they remained in the game at all. An immovable force, he kept the Yellows off balance and unable to score further. The most the rest of them seemed to accomplish was to annoy the Yellows, to keep them a little off balance. Although with the lead, the Yellows seemed content to control the ball and defend violently.

A half dozen Azzaros carrying horntets appeared on top of the wall on one side. Arielle turned to Bayru and pointed up at the instrument-carrying Azzaros.

"What are they doing?"

Around gasps for breath, Bayru answered. "They're preparing to signal the end of the match. We've got somewhere around five minutes left."

They had to act.

After Gavie blocked the ball, it bounced toward a Yellow. Before the ball reached him, Arielle rammed him from behind, sending him face first into the ground.

Desperate, she charged up the field, searching for Bayru or Zume—both guarded. A heavily muscled Yellow charged hard toward her. But Velly was open up the field.

Arielle passed the ball as the Yellow lowered his shoulder. Her battered ribs took the full force of the blow. She struck the ground. Flickering lights popped in her vision. She curled into a fetal position. She wished to pass out, die, anything to end the pain. Tears spilled down her cheeks.

A blare of horns rang out.

"Arielle, are you okay?" A hand touched her shoulder, and she flinched away.

"No," she cried, afraid she'd get hit again.

"Arielle, it's me. Bayru." The Azzaro's words brought her back to the present beyond her own pain.

"Did Velly get the ball? Did she score?"

She rolled onto her right side, shielding her broken left ribs, and opened her eyes. Bayru stood over her, expression concerned. Zume ran up to join them.

"We won!" he shouted, elated.

Arielle sighed and closed her eyes. Dirk would live!

Chapter 7

They'd done it! They'd saved Dirk!

Arielle's relief was supplanted by the pain in her side. She took slow, shallow breaths, avoiding movement. She longed to get up, to see Dirk freed from his chains, but the beatings had taken their toll on her.

"Arielle, are you okay?" Gavie appeared behind her, his large hands gripping her shoulders and lifting.

She cried out.

He let go. "What's wrong?"

"My… ribs," she gasped. "Pretty sure… they're broken... uhhh."

"Zume, get the doctor," Bayru ordered.

The crowd's celebration quieted.

"What's going on?" Arielle raised her head; even that little movement sent a shot of pain through her chest.

High on the wall near Dirk, Rassa gazed over the crowd. "The judges have ruled the last score occurred after the sounding of the horntets. It does not count."

"What? No!" Arielle couldn't believe it.

"That's a lie," Bayru protested.

"Velly scored." Gavie pointed at the ring at the far end of the field, as if he could see a replay.

"Now that K'inn's new vessel is chosen, we will proceed with the sacrifice," Rassa announced. Cheers erupted, but also plenty of boos. Perhaps not everyone in the crowd agreed with the sacrifice or Rassa cheating?

Arielle rolled onto her side, ignoring the pain. Guards led Dirk to an altar, where they forced him to his knees and chained his hands to posts on either side. Rassa sneered.

"We scored!" Arielle yelled. "We won. We saved him." The crowd drowned out her words, not that Rassa cared. He had broken his word, and Dirk would pay the price.

A new pain filled her chest, one more distressing than the broken ribs.

She focused on Gavie. "Help me up!"

He wrapped an arm around her, ducked a head under one of her arms and lifted. She cried out, vision blurring as she gasped through the pain. She leaned against him for support to remain upright.

"We have to save Dirk." She took a step forward, but Gavie pulled her back.

Bayru, her expression a mixture of pain and pity, also moved to block her. "There's nothing we can do. We can't fight the guards alone."

Arielle yanked free of Gavie's grip. A new flare of pain dropped her to her knees. Moaning, she struggled to her feet. After everything, she'd still failed.

Dirk raised his head, and his eyes found hers. He smiled faintly, as if to let her know this wasn't her fault.

"No! I won't let Rassa kill him!" She shoved past her teammates, staggering toward Rassa.

"Hear us K'inn, mover of suns," Rassa shouted, voice amplified. "We offer thanks for another year of light."

"Will K'inn honor lies and deception?" Arielle pointed an accusatory finger at Rassa. Some in the crowd watched her, but most remained focused on Rassa, unable to hear her challenge.

An Azzaro woman, dressed in red for T'amm, streaked across the field toward Arielle. At first Arielle feared the Azzaro would attack her for protesting, but the woman held out a bluish metallic orb in one hand.

"Speak," the Azzaro prompted.

Arielle stared at the orb, confused.

"Expose Rassa's lies. They will hear you." The Azzaro raised the orb toward Arielle's mouth.

"Will you let this deceiver make a mockery of your ritual?" Her voice boomed, making her wince. She held firm, not wanting to show weakness. "All of you witnessed the Lusus. We won, and yet Rassa subverts it. Is K'inn the god of deceit and treachery?"

"Seize the heretic!" Rassa shrieked. "She would have us fail K'inn and lose his sun."

A few guards headed for her, but more than a dozen Azzaros in red costumes raced onto the field and formed a circle around her. They braced for a fight.

The support emboldened Arielle. "What value is the Lusus if they rig the outcome?" She pointed at Rassa. "Does he not dishonor K'inn?"

Boos filled the stadium. A larger contingent of guards closed in on Arielle and her defenders, but her teammates and even the opposing team joined the circle surrounding her. The male who had rammed her earlier approached.

"She speaks the truth." He flexed thick muscles. "And anyone who wishes to silence her must face us first."

Rassa snarled at her, eyes gleaming with fury. Then he seemed to regain control of himself. He turned and motioned to someone behind him. A guard wielding a scythe strode forward.

"Hear us K'inn, we offer this new body to keep you hale and strong for another year." Rassa raised his hands to the sky.

A few more cheers erupted, but mores boos drowned them out.

"Don't let him desecrate your ceremony!" Arielle cried, afraid Rassa would carry out the sacrifice before any stopped it.

The executioner hesitated. Other Azzaros, most dressed in red but some in orange as well, leapt from the stands to the wall and rushed to stop the executioner. Guards struggled to block them, but the crowd-turned-mob overwhelmed them, tossing them from the walls. The mob surrounded the executioner, wrestling the scythe from him and tossing him from the wall as well.

Rassa shouted that everything he'd done was in service of K'inn, that he had kept tradition going, but the mob shoved him away. One Azzaro freed Dirk from his chains, leading him from the altar.

Before Arielle could exult in her victory, the mob led the opposing team's sacrifice candidate to the altar and chained him on his knees in Dirk's place.

"The right sacrifice will be made," an Azzaro shouted, hefting the scythe in the air. "K'inn will be honored."

Bile rose in Arielle's throat. What had she done? She hadn't stopped the sacrifice, only changed the victim. These Azzaro were insane. All of them.

A rumble built up as a half dozen military aircraft flew in, circling overhead. The crowd in the stands scattered like cockroaches spooked by light.

Arielle and her teammates retreated as three aircraft, massive propellers rotating from a vertical to horizontal position, descended onto the field. Out poured armed Azzaro officers, followed by Instructor Zelo and Tiru.

Several dozen officers jumped out of the remaining aircraft in the sky, descending on cables. They all prepared for a fight, but the mob and guards fled. Relief washed through Arielle as the soldiers took Rassa into custody. He raged at them, but they ignored him.

Arielle pushed through her defenders, gritting her teeth against the pain, and pressed toward the steps to climb the wall to Dirk.

"Stop," an officer warned, aiming his weapon at her before she got halfway.

"It's okay." Instructor Zelo crossed over to Arielle, shielding her. "She's under my protection."

The officer nodded and turned away.

"We got your warning," Instructor Zelo said. "Though your device stopped working right after, which slowed us down for a while."

"I thought-dictated the message right before Rassa forced me to hand over my wrist-comp. Then he threw it in a boiling vat."

"When we couldn't locate you, we determined where Dirk had arrived. From there, we discovered Rassa had taken him. Tiru guessed why Rassa wanted Dirk, but figuring out where he'd brought you was a struggle." He grinned ruefully.

She threw her arms around him, sucking in air as her ribs protested. "It doesn't matter. You found us."

"Are you okay?" he asked, pulling back with a concerned expression.

"Broken ribs I think, but I want to see Dirk."

"Of course." He took her elbow and led her to the steps.

One captured Azzaro in orange met her eyes and tapped three fingers against the underside of his jaw, an offensive gesture in their culture. Was he angry she'd won? Or because there would be no sacrifice? Anyone who welcomed a death like that, or prized it, would never make sense to her.

She climbed the narrow stone steps, gritting her teeth against the stabs of pain each movement caused. Instructor Zelo hovered behind her. At the top of the wall, he walked beside her, hands outstretched to catch her if she fell.

They passed by Rassa, arms chained behind his back, and two soldiers gripping him. They'd removed his mask.

"You've flouted K'inn's will," he snarled at them as they passed. "May darkness follow you everywhere you go."

Instructor Zelo's whole body went rigid, hands curling into fists. "The sun will rise same as every day before. K'inn never was. Your sacrifices are a waste of innocent life."

Rassa lunged at them, face contorted into fury, but the guards hauled him back. "Others will save us," Rassa growled. "You've stopped nothing."

Instructor Zelo didn't respond this time. Neither did Arielle. She was angry with him. Hated him even. Shouting at him would give her satisfaction. But he was beyond reason. Nothing she said would change his beliefs.

"I will kill you! Both of you!" Rassa screamed.

It made her skin crawl. All she'd done was fight to survive—to protect Dirk.

A hand on her arm made her jump.

"Ignore him," Instructor Zelo said, pulling her forward. "He won't bother you again. He'll never get another chance."

Arielle wondered if that was true. Then she spotted Dirk watching her, waiting, surrounded by officers. He looked haggard, his eyes bloodshot, his wrists bruised. She wanted to run to him.

"Dirk!"

An officer moved to stop her, but Instructor Zelo waved him off and the others let her through.

"Arielle…" Dirk pulled her into a hug. Her ribs complained at the contact, but she ignored it. To touch him again, alive and well, was worth any pain.

"Thank you. I thought I was dead," he said, voice choking up. "I was so afraid that… that I'd never get the chance to—"

She grabbed his face and pulled his mouth to hers. Her pain evaporated, as did the world around them. She needed the reassurance that this ordeal was over. That they'd survived and would be okay.

When she let go, he grinned.

"Maybe I should get captured more often."

She slapped his arm, her own smile fading. "Never joke about that. I almost lost you."

The pain in her ribs flared again. She groaned, falling into him. He caught and held her.

"Are you okay?"

"Yes. I'll be fine." She leaned her head on his shoulder, enjoying the strength in his arms. Strength she had come so close to losing forever.

From the field her teammates waved to her, and she waved back. Then she pulled free from Dirk and grabbed his hand. "Come on. I've got some new friends you need to meet."

Chapter 8

After taking Arielle to the hospital in Tanarille to receive treatment for her injuries—x-ray and CT scans confirmed two rib fractures and a sprained wrist—Instructor Zelo and Tiru flew them back home for dinner.

The castle reminded Arielle of a fairytale. Spires soared up from crenelated, blue-green stone walls overlooking the large estate on the outskirts of Tanarille. Flowers filled an enormous garden along the left side of the grounds. Icelet bushes formed a perimeter around most of the garden. Star blossoms rested on the surface of a small pond at its center. Beside the pond, flowering Mooncup vines covered a gazebo. At the back of the estate grew an orchard of purple melon trees imported from Niveum.

Instructor Zelo landed the aircraft on the private runway and pulled it into a mini hangar alongside the house.

"Wow, this is your place?" Dirk asked.

Arielle wanted to give him a tour of the grounds, but wasn't sure she had the energy for it right now.

Tiru chose for them, whisking everyone into the castle. Lavish paintings of natural Sundara settings hung from the walls. Potted pink Janthems and light purple Purgias rested on tables throughout. The pleasant, earthy scent relaxed Arielle. Or it could be the medications the Azzaro doctor had given her.

They passed by Instructor Zelo's study, with wall-to-wall bookshelves filled from the floor to the ten-foot ceilings. Little critters peaked out from between books on various shelves.

"Are those rea—" Arielle cut herself off as she realized they were little statues.

Instructor Zelo's grin indicated she wasn't the first to make that mistake. "They are so life-like that even I do a double-take now and again. Tiru and I are far too busy to take care of animals, so these are my substitutes."

Arielle's stomach grumbled, and she covered it, embarrassed. "Sorry."

Tiru steered them on to the dining room. "No apologies. When did you last eat?"

Arielle considered it for a moment. "Not since breakfast before we left for the Triplet Geysers eruption."

"Well, have a seat." Tiru gestured to a large blackwood table surrounded by sixteen chairs. "We'll retrieve lunch." She looped an arm through Instructor Zelo's and pulled him into the kitchen.

Dirk pulled out a chair and motioned for her to sit. "After you."

"Thank you." She slid down onto the chair. Thanks to the meds, the pain from her fractured ribs no longer overpowered her. Still, she winced as Dirk pushed the chair and her closer to the table. Then he took a seat beside her.

Instructor Zelo returned first, with a large platter filled with sliced cheeses and a couple of loaves of dark bread that smelled wonderfully of yeast. Tiru followed with a tray of crackers surrounding a large bowl of a dark green dip. On their second trip, they brought out vegetable skewers, purple melon slices, and two bottles of wine.

Arielle passed on the wine, not wanting to mix it with her medications.

"I'd planned something more extravagant for dinner last night." Tiru set plates before them. "With our mad search and rescue, I didn't have time to prepare anything fresh today."

"This is wonderful," Arielle assured her as Instructor Zelo filled up Tiru's glass with a bubbling white wine.

"I'm just thrilled to be here to enjoy a meal," Dirk said, raising his glass. "Thank you. Thank you both for rescuing us. For saving my life." With his free hand he reached out and clasped Arielle's hand, squeezing it. "And thank you for fighting so hard for me. I wouldn't be here right now if it wasn't for all you did to save me."

Unshed tears filled his eyes. Arielle blinked back her own tears. She was too overcome to trust herself to reply, so she nodded and squeezed his hand back. It was a relief to touch him again.

"I can promise Rassa will trouble neither of you further," Instructor Zelo said as he sliced the dark brown bread.

Arielle's mouth watered. If not for her ribs, she might've lunged across the table for a slice.

"How can you be sure?" she asked, not wanting to put a damper on the mood, but it worried her. "This was the second time he captured us."

"Not after this time." Instructor Zelo shook his head. "We have ample evidence against him. After his judgment he will be exiled to Joorm, our moon. He'll never return to Sundara."

Arielle had her doubts, but kept them to herself. For the next several minutes they ate in silence.

It was Tiru who broke it. "Will you two stay the night? We have guest rooms prepared."

"I'll need to leave in a couple hours." Dirk gave her an apologetic grimace.

Arielle hated that he'd have to leave so soon. They'd spent so little time together. Then she remembered she had the briefing to finish for Berren to review by lunch tomorrow.

"I can stay, but I've got to write a briefing this evening." The thought of working on it underscored her exhaustion. She wanted nothing more than to sleep. And she needed another day off to recover from the Lusus. Would she ever see Bayru, Gavie, and the others again?

"Well, you may not have to finish that briefing if you don't want to," Tiru said, smiling.

"Why is that?" Arielle wondered if Tiru had informed Berren about everything that had happened. But while he might give her an extra day to work on it, she doubted he'd let her off the hook.

"Our public diplomacy officer was recently promoted to a new position on Araxia."

Arielle stared at Tiru, her food forgotten. Did she dare hope?

"I've spoken to Ambassador Zaman," Tiru said. "The position is yours if you want it."

"Yes. Yes, course!" Arielle exclaimed, barely stopping herself from squealing like a little girl. "I'd love it. Thank you."

Tiru nodded. "The transfer will be initiated tomorrow, though it might take a couple of weeks before you start."

Now Arielle wished she wasn't on medication so that she could have a drink to celebrate.

Dirk squeezed her hand again. "That's wonderful! I'm so proud of you."

"Thank you," she said, not quite believing her good luck after the last twenty-four hours. She half expected to wake up in the cell where Rassa's men had imprisoned her. Then she moved a little too much in her excitement, and the pain in her ribs made her gasp for breath. This was real and not a dream.

"Careful." Dirk leaned closer, eyes and mouth drooping with worry and obvious exhaustion.

"I'm okay," she assured him when the pain had eased a little.

"You'll also be happy to know the role comes with regular travel," Tiru continued. "You'll need to visit all Sundara's major cities and some rural towns."

"That sounds great." After the travel restrictions on Gleeson, the opportunities would be nice. And she would not let her encounters with Rassa cause her to hide away and fear others. She got into diplomacy to meet and work with other people and species. Learn about new cultures. She was more determined than ever to do just that.

"You'll also have more freedom to go off planet on your own time as well."

This time Arielle squeezed Dirk's hand as she turned to him. "I'll be able to visit you more."

"I'd love it." He wore a mischievous smile that made her blush and turn her attention to her food.

She looked forward to many more moments with him. Their time together had been limited over the summer. But after this weekend, with how close she'd come to losing him, she intended to make up the time. Hopefully there would be more dinners here at this table, with the four of them.

"Thank you," she repeated to Tiru and Instructor Zelo. "Thank you both for everything you've done for me."

Tiru raised her glass in salute. "You have a great future ahead of you, Arielle. I'm glad to help you along."

Antimatter

Chapter 1

Bright white light shone through a gaping hole in the roof of the closest AED research and development facility, like a stage light illuminating the star of the show. The jagged hole the result of an explosion six weeks earlier.

A warning popped up on the dashboard of Cade's ship.

Space City quarantine zone. Do not cross.
This AED research facility is closed and quarantined by the Space City Council. No admittance is permitted per the Zlondin Treaty of 2015.

Cade switched off the warning and proceeded toward the facility, one in a swarm of hundreds of solar-powered satellites, laboratories, and space habitats orbiting Equuleus, the white dwarf star. It was Equuleus's light that spotlighted the fissure in the closest orbiting facility.

Aileen McKensie had been right. AED was covering something up, and it had cost her father his life.

Mr. McKensie had worked as an engineer on the AED antimatter engine development program to power Space City's next-gen spaceships. Cade's research indicated these future spacecraft would capture dark matter as they flew through space. With scientific estimates projecting five times as much dark matter in the universe as regular matter, future space cities could travel into interstellar space instead of remaining within a solar system to collect solar energy. AED promotional material also indicated the antimatter engine would exhaust zero harmful emissions.

The engine sounded like a gold mine for AED. What had caused the explosion and shutdown of the facility?

In addition to telling Aileen's family that Mr. McKensie's body wasn't recoverable, they'd also paid her mother a seven-figure sum. As their CEO had put it when he made the offer, "we take care of our own." Of course, the payment had come with an agreement that the family would not pursue legal action against AED. To Aileen's horror, her mother had accepted. That was when Cade had discovered her crying in the garden beside the spaceport back home.

A second warning popped up on his ship's dashboard.

High levels of radiation within the facility. 6.8 roentgens per second.

He flinched, his blond hair falling across his face and covering his eyes. He tucked it back behind his right ear and raised his wrist-comp to his mouth.

"What were the radiation levels of the worst nuclear disaster on Earth?" he asked.

"The ionizing radiation levels within the Chernobyl reactor meltdown were estimated at 5.6 roentgens per second," a feminine AI voice with a British accent answered.

He fought off the panicked desire to abandon his investigation. "What are the effects of exposure to that much radiation?"

"If exposed, a human being would suffer a fatal dose of radiation poisoning in less than one minute," the AI replied. "I would not advise landing."

"Thanks for the wisdom," he muttered.

The ship had ample shielding and he wore a rad-hard explorer suit. But one untimely breach in the ship's hull, or unnoticed nick in his suit, would likely spell his end. He wanted to know what was going on and help Aileen get some closure over her father. They were friends. But he didn't want to die at seventeen discovering the truth.

As the main docking port for the facility with the hole in its roof drifted onto his forward viewing screen, a surprised shout escaped him.

A Malsain ship was docked there.

He stuck out his right hand and a hologram of his ship's controls wrapped around it like a glove. With it he maneuvered his ship behind a nearby facility. Had anyone on the Malsain ship noticed him? Why was a Malsain ship here?

For several minutes, he debated what to do. He couldn't land and confront the Malsain alone. He doubted whoever it was had come alone, unlike him. Nor could he alert Space City authorities to their trespass without revealing his own.

He should return home now. This whole thing was crazy. He never should've come. But if he slunk away now, what would he tell Aileen McKensie? *Sorry about your dad, but you're on your own?*

A concussive blast rocked his ship, slamming him forward into his restraints. Alarm bells rang.

Cursing, he activated full throttle. Nothing happened.

"Please, don't let there be a hull breach." Not with all this radiation. He raised his helmet and pulled up a damage report.

A second blast pounded the ship, eliciting more curses from his lips. Three engines offline and the fourth at minimal efficiency. His ship drifted.

He couldn't escape. The best he could manage was an emergency landing at the main docking port, which extended from the facility about two hundred meters into space.

A third shot shook the ship so hard he bit his tongue. His eyes watered. The hologram controls around his hand disappeared. The ship angled into a collision course with the Malsain ship.

Who was shooting at him?

He frantically typed on the hologram computer screen to reboot the system and get the steering back online. In the time it took the system to restart, the Malsain ship loomed large ahead.

He raised his hand, but the hologram controls didn't re-engage. Screaming in frustration, he braced for collision.

At the last second, the Malsain ship vanished. He crash-landed on the dock. The rough landing threw him back in the captain's chair. A rending screech from his hull scraping over the dock made him cringe.

The ship came to a stop at the edge of the dock. He didn't dare breathe for fear that any little movement might cause the ship to fall off into space. He was already within Equuleus' orbit. The ship seemed settled. He heaved a sigh of relief and slumped back against his chair.

He was alive.

Chapter 2

Cade's short-lived relief gave way to panic as he checked the ship's _damage reports_ monitor for hull breaches. He might have only seconds to activate foam sealant before lethal levels of radiation penetrated the ship. But according to the reports, only the engines had sustained damage. Someone had shot him down, but hadn't tried to kill him.

The attack hadn't come from the Malsain ship. How had it disappeared like that?

Was it ever there at all?

With that, he realized it had been a hologram. Someone had placed it on the dock as a distraction. And he'd been too mesmerized by the gaping hole in the facility to do a detailed scan upon arrival.

He punched his open palm, angry with himself for getting tricked. He activated his comms. "Emergency! This is Cade Martin in an Eagle IV. I've been shot down at the closed AED facility orbiting Equuleus. My ship's immobilized. Please send immediate aid."

He hated exposing his trespass, but better that than die or become a prisoner of whomever had attacked him.

Almost immediately, a notification popped up: _Transmission failed._

Frowning, he re-sent the distress call, but again it failed.

"Oh great," he groaned.

He had seen nothing about damage to the comms system. He double-checked, confirming the comms system remained online. It alerted him to an incoming message from another ship. He played it.

"Attention unidentified vehicle," an angry feminine voice said. "You're trespassing at a private research facility. Prepare to surrender yourselves to AED personnel."

He dropped his head in his hands. Instead of exposing whatever AED had done here, they now had him for trespassing. And without proof, no one would believe anything he said. This day couldn't get any worse.

Until he realized he recognized the feminine voice from the incoming comm.

"Ansa?" he asked. His brother's ex-girlfriend had shot him down and now jammed his comm.

"Evacuate your ship," Ansa said. "Surrender and you'll be taken to Space City for prosecution."

He snorted. She couldn't return to Space City. She faced greater criminal charges than trespassing. But her bluff didn't mean she posed no threat.

He needed to get away from her, but with his ship engines blown, his only chance was inside the facility. Retreating to the back of the ship, he found an extendable arm holding an oxygen tank. The arm secured the tank to the back of his suit. Then, he attached a backup tank, covering him for eight hours. He had to assume the radiation filled the facility, too, rendering its air system unusable. As a precaution, he also grabbed a vial of sealing bots—a nanobot solution that worked like glue. If his suit incurred damage, he could spread the solution over the hole to seal it up within five seconds.

Protective gear in place, he reattached his wrist-comp over his left arm.

When his ship's airlock cycled open, Cade discovered how close he'd come to sliding off the dock. The ship's nose extended out past the edge. He only had a couple of meters of room to walk alongside the ship.

It was the second time he'd nearly died in the last few months. After the explosion at the Alfar base on Orestes, he, Maellyn, and Anand had been rushed to Ourania for medical attention. However, at the last minute the Alfar had determined his injuries weren't as severe as Maellyn's and Anand's, so he'd undergone a simpler medical procedure. After he'd been stabilized, he'd returned home to Space

City, unlike Maellyn and Anand, who would spend the rest of their lives on Ourania due to their treatment.

He had no wish to tempt fate a third time, so he needed to get inside the facility before Ansa landed her ship. Find somewhere to hide.

The moment his feet slapped down on the dock, the magnetism function in his boots auto-fired. The facility's gravity, if it was still online, didn't extend onto the dock. But as long as he didn't do anything stupid, like dive off the side, he'd get to the facility fine.

Despite being thin and form fitting, his explorer suit had great insulation, blocking out the cold of space. In fact, he felt a little warm.

Before he limped more than a dozen steps, cursing his bad leg for slowing him down, another Malsain ship landed, cutting him off from the facility. He continued forward, hoping this was another hologram illusion.

Seconds later, three figures emerged from the ship. The one in the middle wore a knockoff of the Space City explorer suits. It was dark gray, but with the same red line running along the outside of each arm and leg. The two on either side wore bulky, dark green suits. All three held large guns—S-360s—that could blast huge holes through him.

He froze, debating whether to flee back into his ship. Was Ansa one of the three figures approaching him? He couldn't see faces inside their darkened helmets.

The figure in gray activated a flashlight on top of their gun, then pointed it at him. He blinked against the glare but didn't raise his hand to shield his face, afraid the three figures might misconstrue the action.

A second later, his wrist-comp buzzed. He accepted and his suit comms system connected with one of the three figures in front of him.

"Cade? What are you doing here?" It was Ansa's voice. The front figure clicked on a light in their helmet, which illuminated her face. Her upper lip rose in a cunning smile. She had control of the moment and knew it.

An idea came to him. "I'm out here on assignment, finding out why this research facility was shut down. My supervisor sent me."

She laughed. "I doubt that. You work for the Academy paper. Your supervisor would never agree to your traveling here. He thinks you're on a summer trip, am I right?"

Annoyed, he went on the offensive. "What did you come here to steal?"

"Steal?" She feigned hurt. "AED hired me."

"Right." He rolled his eyes. "To do what?"

"Better question is why are you here?" She pointed her gun at him.

His breath caught in his throat. The muzzle pointed at his chest made him keenly aware how quickly his life could end.

"You're trespassing at a private facility," she added. "I'm not."

He grimaced and crossed his arms. Whether she worked for the AED or had lied, any response from him wouldn't improve his situation. And he had no illusions about appealing to her better nature.

"Kill him," one of the other figures hissed. It seemed their comm systems were tied in with Ansa's, and since he'd accepted the connection request from her, it worked for all of them.

The figure moved close enough for him to see into their helmet. A Malsain with a large bolt piercing her dark green scales right below her mouth. She stood larger than Ansa or himself, reminding him of an upright Komodo dragon.

The second figure on Ansa's other side, also a Malsain, possessed pale yellow-green scales. It was the smallest of the group. Instead of watching him, its eyes roved his ship. Was it looking for others or assessing the ship's value? Or both?

Fortunately, his suit protected him from smelling them. He didn't relish puking in his suit and enduring that for however long they kept him hostage.

"Anyone else with you?" Ansa asked, looking past him.

He opened his mouth to say yes, but that lie wouldn't stand much scrutiny. Only so many people could fit on an Eagle IV. Plus, if he'd had anyone else with him, why would they send him limping out alone?

So again, he remained silent.

She approached him, clucking her tongue. "Being difficult won't make your situation any easier."

"Trusting you didn't work out so well for me last summer," he replied.

"Oh, come now," she said, bristling. "I freed you and Aiden from Laza. If not for me, you'd both be slaves on Araxia."

"You're the reason I was one to begin with. Planning to repeat history?" he asked.

She shrugged. "Not to the Murgin, no. You and Space City ensured there's no market on Araxia." Then her lip curled in a sly smile. "There are other options. Guess we'll see how cooperative you are while we complete our mission."

"We should kill him," the dark-green Malsain repeated, her gun aimed at him.

Not his best day.

Ansa threw an arm around his shoulders and pulled him in close. "Now where's the fun in that?"

When the Malsain started to respond, Ansa overrode it as she squeezed his shoulders. "Don't worry. Cade's no threat."

Chapter 3

Ansa dropped her arm from around Cade's shoulder and grabbed his wrist-comp with her free gloved hand, her gun dipping toward his feet. He tried to pull away.

"Unh Unh." Ansa raised the muzzle into his side. "You're not keeping that. I'm not taking chances."

He stopped resisting and let her take it. The device was his last hope of contacting Space City, but it wasn't worth getting shot over.

She threw his wrist-comp on the ground several meters away and put a few rounds in it. He stared with remorse at the debris until she nudged him with her gun.

"Double time, princess," she ordered, motioning toward the facility.

He strode toward the entrance, keeping a wary eye on the Malsain as he passed them. Neither had lowered their weapons. He was half-afraid they'd shoot him from behind.

"Why are we not killing him?" the dark green Malsain asked. "He's a liability."

"Epnis, we don't need to kill everyone we encounter on a job," Ansa said.

"It's warranted here," Epnis replied. "He's a cripple. He's got nothing to offer. Keeping him alive is an unnecessary risk."

Cade bristled at the name, and also that she'd spotted his limp so easily.

"Epnis, Zethys, lower your weapons," Ansa demanded. "We're taking him with us. I won't tolerate any further insubordination."

The shorter, pale yellow-green Malsain licked the air with its forked tongue but didn't touch the glass face of its helmet. Were the two debating whether to take him and Ansa both out right now?

Several seconds passed before they lowered their weapons. Cade breathed a sigh of relief. He had a feeling that the wrong word or move from him might end with one of them *accidentally* shooting him.

"Let's go," Ansa growled as she prodded him in the back with the muzzle of her gun.

Only their flashlights, which Ansa and the Malsain attached to the tops of their guns, lit up the facility as they entered. Aluminum trunks, equipment, and other debris littered a long, dark hallway, as if people had abandoned stuff as they fled. As he considered it, Cade supposed they probably had.

He gave everything they passed a wide berth, afraid of tearing his suit on an unseen jagged edge and exposing himself to radiation.

The lighter-scaled Malsain pulled out a square device similar in shape to a wrist-comp, but larger. Its screen glowed, lighting the Malsain's face—a female he believed—through the faceplate. A half-dozen yellowish scars marred her right eye, left cheek, and her neck.

"The engine is one floor up," she said, taking the lead.

"Are you here to steal the AED antimatter engine?" Cade asked. Why hadn't he guessed that earlier? Even a prototype would sell for a high profit.

"Salvage it," Ansa corrected. "The AED hired us to retrieve it and anything else of value not ruined in the explosion."

"Why hire you?" he asked. "Why not send their own employees?"

"They wanted people who could get what they needed and not ask *stupid* questions."

He got the hint. It also confirmed the AED were conducting illegal activities.

They marched up a flight of stairs, soon coming across gaping holes in the walls. The ruptured remains of equipment littered the floors all around them. Several blockages forced them to detour through the holes into offices and labs strewn with debris.

As they waded through the wreckage, Cade searched for weapons, or comm equipment he might use to send out a distress signal, or places that might serve as hiding spots if he escaped. He wished Ansa hadn't destroyed his wrist-comp so he could check the radiation levels inside the facility.

Before long they reached a bright lab with most of the roof blown away and a good size chunk of the floor gone, too. The light from Equuleus shining through the hole in the floor illuminated everything. The telltale signs of an artificial magnetic barrier sealed off the hole in the floor. Another secured the hole in the ceiling. *That's how the facility's artificial gravity is still operational.*

Blackened scorch marks and soot covered everything in the lab. Most of the equipment appeared ruined beyond repair, either destroyed in the initial explosion or burned up in a subsequent fire.

"This is it," the scarred Malsain called to them, standing over a twisted machine along one side.

"Good work, Zethys," Ansa said, hurrying over to the Malsain.

The antimatter engine was smaller than Cade expected, no more than a four-by-four black box with one side blown out. It must've been a prototype engine. It couldn't fly any spacecraft with passengers. Perhaps it could power rovers or smallsats.

"The magnetic containment for the engine core cracked," Zethys said, inspecting the engine. "That likely caused the explosion."

"Meaning?" Ansa asked.

"It's not reusable."

Ansa clucked her tongue in disappointment. "Let's take it, anyway."

"We won't be able to carry it. Too heavy."

"I've found help for that," Epnis said from across the lab. She returned with a large AED robot on wheels. It had thick metallic rods for arms and legs and resembled a mechanical power lifter.

Zethys pressed her device against the side of the robot for a moment, then studied the screen. "It's an AED hauling droid, model: FG746W29Z. It should be able to handle the antimatter engine based upon its specs."

She ordered it to do so, and the droid's arms reached out and grabbed the engine, hoisting it easily.

"That thing could be worth some money, too," Epnis said, studying the droid.

"Forget selling it," Ansa said. "Think what we could carry with that thing on future missions. Let's see what else of value we can find in here."

I thought you weren't stealing, Cade thought. Then another thought occurred to him. "Why didn't AED take the engine with them when they cleared out all personnel? Why send you later to pick it up?"

Epnis pointed her gun at him again. "I'm telling you, we should kill him."

"I'll handle it." Ansa marched over, raising her gun and holding it before his faceplate. His eyes locked onto the hole in the gun's barrel, and chills rippled through him.

"Keep talking and I'm going to throw you out the hole in the floor," she warned. "Leave you as part of the wreckage orbiting this star."

"O… Okay," he gulped.

She kept the gun in his face a few seconds longer, perhaps to underscore the threat, before resuming her search of the lab. The Malsain joined her, ignoring him.

Why did she snap at his questions about AED hiring her? What was she hiding?

Whatever the answer, staying in their hands was dangerous for him. He searched for anything that might assist his escape. As he passed a desk along one wall, he spotted a wrist-comp strap sticking out from beneath an overturned drawer. He retrieved it. The wrist-comp seemed in good shape.

Would it work? He slipped it into a pocket in his explorer suit for later.

Chapter 4

A half dozen other droids, in various states of destruction from the explosion and fire, lay scattered around the lab.

"If we get them back to the ship, I could fix them," Zethys said.

"We'll return for them later," Ansa said as she motioned for them to follow her out.

They pushed past charred debris, taking care not to puncture their suits. At a couple of points, Cade thought they'd have to retreat. Instead, one of them directed him, at gunpoint, to crawl over or under debris, his heart thudding in his chest until he reached the other side.

Along the way, Ansa peeked into other labs, but didn't bother searching them.

"What are you looking for?" he asked.

She shook her head.

"If AED hired you to retrieve tech from the facility, didn't they give you a list of what they wanted and where to locate them?"

"There might be other valuable items not on the list." She pushed open a door to what turned out to be a utility closet.

"So, you *are* here to steal." The world made sense to him again. She had conned AED into sending her here.

"It's an abandoned facility," she said, letting the door close with a bang. "Are deep-sea divers stealing when they salvage wrecks in the ocean?"

"Nice justification." In any situation, she seemed to discern every way to exploit it to her advantage, and she had no qualms doing so.

Up another flight of stairs, they stumbled upon another lab. As they entered, Ansa's eyes widened and her lips curled into a greedy smile. "This is what we're looking for."

A silver coronal mass ejector, mostly assembled, rested in a firing chamber in the floor pointed toward Equuleus. No. The CME was complete, but modified—the barrel shorter and curved outward a bit at the end.

Ansa ignored the CME, instead slinging her rifle over her shoulder as she approached a crate filled with what looked like mobile rocket launchers. A nuclear symbol marked the side of the crate. Dozens of similar crates filled the room.

Were those mobile nuclear launchers? He hadn't read anything about AED manufacturing weapons, especially not nuclear ones, in the research he'd done on the company. That must be the reason AED was trying to cover up what had happened here. He doubted they were doing so legally.

Ansa picked up a launcher and cradled it in both arms. She carried it to a long, clear tube in the wall no more than a few meters in diameter. Without warning, she pulled the trigger.

"Are you crazy?" He tensed to run, but a cap inside the hole sealed it off. The rocket soared downward and crashed into Equuleus. An explosion rippled across its surface.

Ansa whistled. "These babies will be worth a fortune."

He couldn't disagree, but the question was, to whom? Would she let AED know she had recovered more of their tech and charge them an increased payday? Or would she try to sneak it to some other buyer?

Zethys and Epnis lifted other heavy-duty weapons and grenades from other crates. Antimatter engine R&D formed only a piece of the work AED had conducted at the facility. And at least a dozen more facilities like this one were part of the AED swarm surrounding Equuleus. With that size operation, who all were they selling to?

"How did the AED expect you to bring all this back to them?" Cade asked. "In one small ship."

"They didn't," Ansa replied, returning the nuclear launcher to its crate. "They wanted the antimatter engine prototype only. The rest they wanted covered up, so they paid us to blow up the facility and crash into the sun. We've already wired up explosives at strategic points."

His skin crawled at the mention of explosives. He hoped none of them had made a mistake setting them up.

"If we can get more of those droids working, they can haul these crates back to the ship," Ansa said to Zethys.

The Malsain left the lab.

Between retrieving the antimatter engine, the droids, and all these weapons, Ansa's ship would overflow. Even then, they'd have to leave plenty of valuable tech behind or have no room for themselves. Or an extra passenger. Especially one who knew what they'd stolen.

It was time to find an escape.

While Ansa and Epnis searched crates, Cade eased back toward the open door, peeking out into the hallway for any sign of Zethys.

Hoping she'd been gone a while, he ducked out into the dark hallway and activated his night vision on his contacts. Striding quickly but taking care to remain silent, he moved deeper into the facility and away from where Zethys likely went to retrieve the droids. He debated returning to his ship, but didn't know how long it would take him to repair it, if he could. He needed another way to escape.

Before long he found an elevator. He tapped the call button, not expecting anything since the facility lacked power, but he tried anyway.

Shouts from behind alerted him that Ansa and Epnis had noticed his disappearance. Thudding boots swept closer. This time he knew they'd shoot first.

Across the hall, a ladder well ran up through the ceiling and down through the floor. He abandoned the elevator, crossed to the ladder, and descended. At the next floor he debated getting off but decided to put more floors between him and Ansa. As he neared the third-floor landing, a cry of rage from above preceded gunfire. He fell out of the well to the floor, clapping his hands over his ears.

They had shot at him!

He checked himself, but didn't see any wounds. Not even a nick to his suit.

They'd actually shot at him!

It was one thing to expect it, quite another to experience bullets flying past him.

He scrambled to his feet, knowing they'd be down the ladder in seconds. He had to find somewhere to hide.

Chapter 5

Cade dove through the first doorway he found. A server farm. He hurried through row after row, searching for a hiding spot. Quite a few servers lay on their sides, broken into pieces. Nothing provided good cover. He panicked as he neared the far wall. Ansa would be here any minute. He didn't have time to backtrack and find a new room.

On the last row, he found an exposed air vent at ground level between two servers. Its blackened cover lay on the floor near the opposite row of servers. The vent was narrow, but he could crawl inside. He retrieved the cover and dropped to his hands and knees to back in.

Something sharp scraped his right side. He hissed, arching away from it, before freezing. Had his suit ripped?

He slid forward and checked his side. A tear one dozen centimeters long marred his suit just below his ribs. He swore. How quickly could radiation penetrate his suit? From his pocket he yanked the vial of sealing bots. He smeared some of the glue-like substance onto his suit around the tear and pinched it shut for a count of five. When he let go, the tear had sealed. The sealing bots had done their job.

He was okay. He'd fixed the cut too fast for much radiation to get in. He would be fine. Right?

He capped the vial and thrust it into his pocket, reassuring himself that the sick feeling in his stomach was just anxiety.

"Find him!" Ansa shouted from the hallway. "He's got to be in one of these rooms."

He dropped to his belly. He grabbed the vent cover and slid inside, this time avoiding the sharp edge on his right.

The vent groaned under his weight. He tensed. Would it break? Had Ansa heard it?

Holding the cover with his fingertips, he sealed himself inside. He took a deep breath to calm himself. The tight space was uncomfortable, but better than them catching him.

To distract himself, he fished the wrist-comp he'd found from his pocket. It still had 10% battery power. A little luck his way.

He dimmed the screen to five percent brightness in case the vent cover didn't block the light. *Don't give yourself away doing something stupid*!

Anything else with the wrist-comp required a password, and the owner had chosen an old fashioned 'numbers one through nine' option.

Maybe the wrist-comp's owner was lazy? He started to enter 12345, before a memory surfaced. During a class studying common field tech the previous year, Instructor Aldrin had spent a week teaching them about unusual or not-commonly known uses of everyday technology. During one class, he'd discussed the use of their eye contacts in fingerprinting. He'd shown them how fingerprints left behind salts from sweat on surfaces they touched. Using x-ray optics, a feature within the eye contacts, law enforcement could see the salts and take a high-res pic.

Blinking once, he activated the x-ray feature in his eye contacts. Fingerprints covered the wrist-comp screen. However, the largest number overlapped the numbers two, four, seven, and eight. He entered the numbers in order. The password failed. He entered another. Fail.

After the third failed attempt, he wondered if there was a lock out feature for too many failed passcodes, but what choice did he have? After the tenth failed attempt, he realized there were a lot more combinations of four digits than he'd anticipated. And the wrist-comps owner didn't seem that concerned with security. How many attempts would he get? On the twentieth try, he got lucky.

He was in!

Typing out an emergency distress signal, he sent it to Space City. Within seconds, he received a message failure notice, identical to the one he'd received on his ship.

Awesome. Ansa had kept her signal jam active. *How many ways can she screw me over?*

His left knee ached from cramps. Ignoring them because he had no other option, he searched the wrist-comp for an escape. The device belonged to Pali Dibra, the manager of the antimatter engines project. It held numerous reports on development status and progress. The reports used a lot of technical language, but Pali was excited, sure they'd have a completed engine by year's end. He made no mention of weapons development or production. There were also no references to what had gone wrong. But perhaps he hadn't taken the time to write up reports yet.

Cade swapped over to Pali's messages. There wasn't much of interest in his inbox, which was strange considering his role. Wouldn't he have been communicating a good bit with corporate leadership after the explosion?

Checking Pali's sent messages yielded answers in a series of urgent messages with the subject "Handling the engine explosion."

June 14th
Ally dear,
Tam is dead. Engine explosion in the facility. What will I tell his wife? His daughter? I've known Tam and his wife since the Academy.

We planned to conduct environmental testing today. Suddenly, the antimatter engine started accelerating on its own. Tam hadn't even activated it yet. Then the engine pushed beyond its maximum design limits, running like it was possessed. Tam tried to stop it, but the engine exploded, ripping a hole clear through the floor and ceiling. He died on the spot.

June 15th
Ally,
Someone sabotaged our work! Drilled a hole in the core. Would've gotten away with it, too. The surrounding area was destroyed in the explosion. But Tam always insisted on taking pics of the engine before all tests. He wanted visuals of its pre-test state that we could analyze in case of an accident or anomaly. If only he'd seen the hole before we got started, he'd still be alive. I don't blame him

*though. The hole was perhaps a centimeter in diameter. Not easy to
spot.*

June 16th
Ally,
*AED is developing nuclear weapons. I can't believe it! Those
bastards!*
*A core, maybe more than one, was damaged from the antimatter
engine explosion.*
*This one saturated the facility in radiation and those of us still
here. Ally, I've received a fatal dose. I'm sorry dear.*

June 16th
Ally,
*Besides the hole in the core, someone inserted a flaw in the test
software, which caused the engine to go into overdrive, leading to the
quick explosion. Who could do so? And when?*
*I raised up what I've discovered to leadership, but I'm getting no
answers back. They don't trust anyone, even me. Me! I've been with
AED for thirty-three years!*

June 17th
Ally,
*I'm sorry. Sorry I didn't retire last year like you asked so that we
could travel. I should've listened to you, and now I'll never get to tell
you. And my guess is you'll never see these messages. I know AED is
blocking all external communications from the facility, while they try
to figure out who did this.*
*If you do see these, tell Keti and Aileen what happened to Tam.
They deserve to know.*
I love you!

Cade's skin crawled as he realized it had been six weeks since the
last email. Pali had died a while ago. He held a dead man's wrist-
comp. How many had died from the radiation?

"Any signs of him?" Ansa asked.

"Negative," Epnis said. Lights swept the floor in front of him.

"None," Zethys added.

"He's got to be here somewhere," Ansa growled from close by.

"Why? Because you need him to be?" Zethys retorted. A shadow passed the air vent cover slits.

Cade held his breath.

"What's that supposed to mean?" Ansa asked.

"You failed to kill that boy when he arrived. Now he's become a significant liability. You believe he's nearby because you have to correct your failures."

"It doesn't matter what he knows because he can't communicate with anyone," Ansa said. "There's only one way off this facility and that's on our ship. Once we leave and blow it up, he won't be an issue anymore. He presents no liability to any of us. No one will ever know we were here."

"But you are a liability," Epnis said.

"Excuse me?" Ansa asked.

"Your failures with the boy are a pattern," Epnis said. "They may not cost us on this job, but your poor decisions will cost us down the line."

"It was me who found this opportunity," Ansa said, her tone icy. "Me who found out how to disable the AED protections that would alert them to intruders stealing from them."

Cade ground his teeth. Ansa had lied to him. He knew AED hadn't hired her to retrieve the tech. But why hadn't they removed all of it? Why leave it here to be stolen?

"Opportunities are worthless if you're caught or dead," Epnis growled.

"Fine. If you feel that way, we'll finish the job and part ways."

"It's best if we part now," Epnis said. "Hand over your weapon."

"I will not!"

Ansa cursed. Bodies slammed into the servers around Cade's vent.

"You traitorous b—"

A loud smack was followed by a groan from Ansa.

The growing cramps in Cade's left leg and knee made him desperate to stretch it out. He covered his mouth with a hand and turned off the wrist-comp with the other.

"Good luck finding a buyer without me," Ansa spat.

"Oh, we've got a buyer lined up," Epnis said, tone smug.

"You planned this from the beginning."

"Of course. How do you think the facility explosion happened? Mainyu wanted the weapons."

Mainyu? Of course the Dahaka leader wanted an antimatter engine. He'd only been behind every major attack against Space City over the last couple of years. And with antimatter engines, the Dahaka would become the most advanced spacefaring species outside of the Alfar. Cade couldn't let the Malsain deliver the engine or any weapons to Mainyu.

But he couldn't escape alone either. He needed help. And with the Malsain turning on Ansa, maybe she'd welcome an ally. He couldn't trust her, but at the moment neither of them had a better choice.

Easing the air vent cover down, he peeked out. A Malsain stood a little to his left, back to him, gun raised. The other Malsain stood a few feet away, also with a gun aimed, presumably at Ansa who was out of sight.

"You'll make more if you let me find other buyers to compete," Ansa said.

He crawled forward, left leg protesting.

"We have a deal with Mainyu," Epnis answered.

Slowly rising behind Zethys, Cade hit her hard with the air vent cover. She crumpled at his feet. Epnis spun his way, gun swinging toward him. He ducked.

Ansa sprang forward, tackling Epnis, who cursed. They rolled on the ground a moment, trading punches, before Ansa leapt to her feet and charged him, a flashlight in hand.

He backpedaled, panicking, but she grabbed his shoulders, spinning him around and shoving him forward. They ran. The cramp in his leg made every step painful.

She pulled him down another row of servers right before gunfire erupted behind them. They rushed toward the door, her shouts and the ricochet of bullets propelling him forward.

"This way." She directed him toward an elevator, its door pried open. "Inside."

The top half of the elevator stuck up above the floor. He dropped to his knees and lowered himself into the elevator, but lost his grip and flipped over, landing on his back. A pole flew through the door and struck the back wall before banging to the ground. He rolled away to avoid getting hit. Then Ansa slid in and slammed the doors shut.

Chapter 6

Chest heaving, Cade stared at the door. The sound of gunfire had ceased. Did the Malsain see them duck inside?

He stretched his left leg, easing the cramp. When it seemed like the Malsain didn't know they were here, he stood and whispered, "What do we do now?"

Ansa glared at him and sliced a hand across her throat.

There was an escape hatch in the elevator ceiling. That was a popular escape method in movies, but he'd never succeed in climbing out and ascending the shaft to safety. Ansa might pull it off, but that would just mean abandoning him.

Why did he have to be stuck with her?

After several agonizing minutes, she stood and approached the door, pressing her ear against it. Then she pulled the door back open, grunting with exertion. The elevator hung suspended between floors, with room to crawl out either way.

He half expected the Malsain to appear above, guns in hand. They didn't and Ansa gracefully slithered out the bottom to the floor below, pole in hand. Meanwhile he had to lie awkwardly on his belly and stick his legs out of the elevator, then push backwards until he almost lost control, before dropping free. This time he landed in a crouch instead of falling on his butt, but his left leg seized up on impact. He cut off an audible gasp, and it took him a moment to straighten.

Ansa already marched along the corridor, pole in hand, as though she intended to hunt down the Malsain. She leapt over and dodged around debris littering the hallway, not bothering to check any rooms they passed.

He couldn't catch up, especially while remaining quiet so the Malsain wouldn't hear him. Squeezing past overturned bed frames, dressers, and tables—with bedrooms, bathrooms, and a couple of mess halls on either side—he struggled to keep her in sight.

"Facility explosives activated," a warning announced up ahead. "Five minutes to detonation."

Ansa raised her wrist-comp to check the screen. Even from a distance, Cade spotted flashing red lights.

She cursed and bolted forward. He gave chase, abandoning his efforts to keep quiet. The Malsain must have returned to the ship to set off the explosives. They hadn't bothered looking for the two of them. They'd retrieved the antimatter engine with a working droid, possibly a few other weapons if they'd found other working droids, then hightailed it back to let the explosives take care of them.

"Stop!" he shouted. "We won't make it." It would take them longer than five minutes to reach the dock. And even if they somehow got there in time, the Malsain would've lifted off. There was no reason to stay behind.

With his ship destroyed, he and Ansa needed another means of escape.

He pulled out Pali Dibra's wrist-comp and searched for a facility map. There had to be secondary docks or emergency escape thorneways. But the facility was too large, with too many segments. Multiple thorneways spread across it, but none were close enough to reach in the next five minutes.

Was this it? Would he die here chasing a conspiracy?

His eyes hit on a lab one floor below. The label read Etaem technology R&D. A couple of weeks back, Nico had filled him in on Devika solving the Evanesco trial on Havendesh. An ancient species that had fled their home planet centuries ago, the Etaem had left behind the Evanesco trial as a test for any spacefaring species that visited Havendesh. Most participants in the trial had believed that completing it would provide answers to where the Etaem had gone. However, when Devika solved it she'd only discovered a large trove of Etaem technology. But on her way back to Space City, Devika had vanished, and no one had seen her since, leading many to believe she'd found the means to locate the Etaem after all.

"What have you found?" Ansa asked.

He jumped, not having noticed her return.

"Some of the new Etaem tech is here," he said, pointing out the lab on the map. For a half second he wished she hadn't seen Dibra's wrist-comp. He'd wanted to keep it hidden. But what did it matter? They would live or die together.

"Who are the Etaem?" she asked, steering him toward a stairwell.

"An advanced civilization. They had some sort of mobile thorneway."

Her head swiveled toward him, eyes wide. "Seriously?"

"Yes."

She tossed aside the pole, gripped the side bars of the ladder, and slid down to the next floor.

How much time did they have left? He wished he'd set a timer.

He hurried down the ladder, but when he reached the floor, Ansa had already ducked into the Etaem lab. With every breath he expected to hear an explosion. Or would it be so big he died without knowing it?

Equipment filled the Etaem lab. It was the first place in the facility that didn't appear damaged. Ansa strode along one wall, grabbing items, inspecting them, then tossing them aside.

"What are we looking for?" she asked.

He stared, unsure where to begin. They could sift through this stuff for hours, maybe days, without finding the right device.

Had Nico described the tech? Pacing along the wall opposite Ansa, his gaze roving over the tech, he wanted to try everything yet was afraid to touch any of it.

He recalled that Maellyn's father used digital tags for all equipment in the science labs on Space City. The digital tags were viewable with his eye contacts. Might AED use the same method?

Show me any digital tags, he thought, *or labels.*

Digital tags appeared in the air next to all the equipment.

Cade skimmed the labels as he walked along the shelves lining the room's perimeter. How much time remained? Two minutes? One?

He picked up the pace as he passed Ansa, who bit her lip as she studied the tech. No hint of her usual cockiness or greed.

Scanning ahead, he spotted the mobile thorneway device back by the door where Ansa had started.

"It's there." He pointed, hurried around to it, and scooped it up. Made from a light gray alloy, almost white, the portable thorneway was quite small, shaped like a wristband.

"That's it?" she asked, looking over his shoulder.

A series of six square buttons lined the device. Which one did what?

"How does the Etaem thorneway work?" he shouted at Dibra's wrist-comp.

Nothing popped up through his eye contacts. He guessed Dibra wasn't involved in studying the Etaem tech.

Where to begin? Which button activated the thorneway? How would he set their coordinates?

An explosion rocked the facility. In a panic, he hit the first button. A yellow light filled the circle inside the band, but nothing else happened.

A second, then a third explosion shook the facility.

"Give it to me," Ansa demanded, reaching for the device.

He pulled away, not about to hand over their sole means of escape. He'd have to hope the last coordinates for the device were still good. Guessing which button activated the thorneway, he pushed the last one. Darkness covered his vision. A hand latched onto his wrist, squeezing. The familiar pull of the thorneway launched them forward. Then they stood in the middle of a jungle. Where he didn't know, but they were alive. And free.

The sun shone overhead. Birds squawked. Insects buzzed. Thick humidity saturated the air, causing sweat to bead his forehead.

Ansa yanked the thorneway device from his hands.

"Really?" He reached to take it back, but she dropped it down the front of her shirt. He pulled his hand back. "I saved your life and you're going to steal from me?"

"I'll also take that wrist-comp," she said, gesturing at the device.

"No way." He backed away. "I'm not giving you anything!"

She removed a small gun from her pocket. "The wrist-comp. Now."

He ground his teeth, but handed it over.

"So, what now? Still planning to kill me after all this?"

"I don't need to kill you." She snapped the wrist-comp on her left wrist, then retrieved the mobile thorneway.

"Without knowing how to set the coordinates, I wouldn't use that thing," He warned. "It might send you straight back to the AED facility. What's left of it."

"I stole a little more access behind the AED firewall than you had." She held a button on the thorneway, and a moment later, the wrist-comp had paired with the device.

"You couldn't have said that a few minutes ago when I was trying to figure out how to use it to get us out of the facility?"

With a satisfied grin, she slipped the mobile thorneway device onto her arm, sliding it into place next to the wrist-comp. "I tried, but you wanted to play with buttons. Figure it out for yourself like most men." She clapped him on the shoulder, squeezing. "But congratulations, you helped us escape. Now, if you'll excuse me, I've got to catch up with Zethys and Epnis. Their betrayal won't go unavenged. Good luck."

"You're going to abandon me here in the middle of the jungle? That's not much better than killing me." He debated grabbing her arm like she'd done to him.

"Where's the nearest city, town, village, or anywhere with a thorneway?" she asked.

“The Evanesco trial starting point is five kilometers due East,” the wrist-comp announced.

“There you go.” She pointed over his right shoulder. “I’d wager there’s still people there.”

Before he could respond, she shouted in triumph, then pressed a button on the mobile thorneway device and disappeared.

“Stupid, backstabbing…” his words trailed off.

He screamed once, furious that she’d gotten the better of him again. Then he set off in search of the temple that served as the starting point to the Evanesco trial. He’d let Space City authorities know about the thefts as soon as he got back, but how would they find her?

She’d gotten away again.

About the Author

Jared Austin is a young adult science fiction author who lives in the Rocket City—Huntsville, Alabama. With Space City and the books in the series to follow, he hopes to show and inspire his daughter and son, as well as all of his readers, that science and technology are not dull subjects, but gateways to a brighter, exciting future.

If you would like to learn more about the series and future novels, visit: https://jareddanielaustin.com

Facebook Author Page: www.facebook.com/jareddanielaustin

Instagram: jared_austin1981

Twitter: @JaredAustin1981

Thank you for reading my book! If you enjoyed it, please consider leaving a review. Even just a few words would help others decide if the book is right for them.

Best regards and thank you in advance!